Praise for

THE FORGOTTEN AFFAIRS OF YOUTH

and Alexander McCall Smith

"McCall Smith's latest novel featuring the wise but impish Edinburgh philosopher Isabel Dalhousie. . . . [And] countless small adventures and gentle observations."
—*The Toronto Star*

"Totally absorbing. . . . Isabel is everything you'd want in a philosopher, but she is also quirky and witty."
—*Booklist* (starred review)

"You needn't be a series-long admirer of Isabel Dalhousie to be beguiled by this curious philosopher and casual sleuth. . . . A heroine worth following."   —*Publishers Weekly*

"McCall Smith's talent for dialogue is matched only by his gift for characterization. It's hard to believe that he could make up a character as complex and unique as Isabel. She is by turns fearless, vulnerable, headstrong, and insecure, but always delightful."   —*Chicago Tribune*

"Isabel is a force to be reckoned with."   —*USA Today*

Alexander McCall Smith

THE FORGOTTEN AFFAIRS OF YOUTH

Alexander McCall Smith is also the author of the No. 1 Ladies' Detective Agency series, the Portuguese Irregular Verbs series, the 44 Scotland Street series, and the Corduroy Mansions series. He is professor emeritus of medical law at the University of Edinburgh and has served with many national and international organizations concerned with bioethics. He lives in Scotland.

www.alexandermccallsmith.com.

BOOKS BY ALEXANDER McCALL SMITH

THE FORGOTTEN AFFAIRS OF YOUTH

THE FORGOTTEN AFFAIRS OF YOUTH

Alexander McCall Smith

Vintage Canada

VINTAGE CANADA EDITION, 2012

Published in Canada by Vintage Canada, a division of Random House of Canada
Limited, Toronto, in 2012, and simultaneously in the United States of America by
Anchor, a division of Random House, Inc., New York. Originally published in
hardcover in Canada by Alfred A. Knopf Canada, a division of Random House of
Canada Limited, in 2011, and simultaneously in the United States of America by
Pantheon Books, a division of Random House, Inc.. Distributed by Random
House of Canada Limited.

Vintage Canada with colophon is a registered trademark.

www.randomhouse.ca

Excerpts from poems by W. H. Auden appear courtesy of Edward Mendelson,
Executor of the Estate of W. H. Auden, and Random House, Inc.

Library and Archives Canada Cataloguing in Publication

McCall Smith, Alexander, 1948–
The forgotten affairs of youth / Alexander McCall Smith.

(Isabel Dalhousie series)

ISBN 978-0-307-39960-1

I. Title. II. Series: McCall Smith, Alexander, 1948– . Isabel Dalhousie series.

PR6063.C326F66 2012   823'.914   C2011-902241-9

Cover design by Linda Huang and Brian Barth
Image credits © Bill Sanderson

Printed and bound in the United States of America

2 4 6 8 9 7 5 3 1

This book is for Diane Martin, editor and friend.

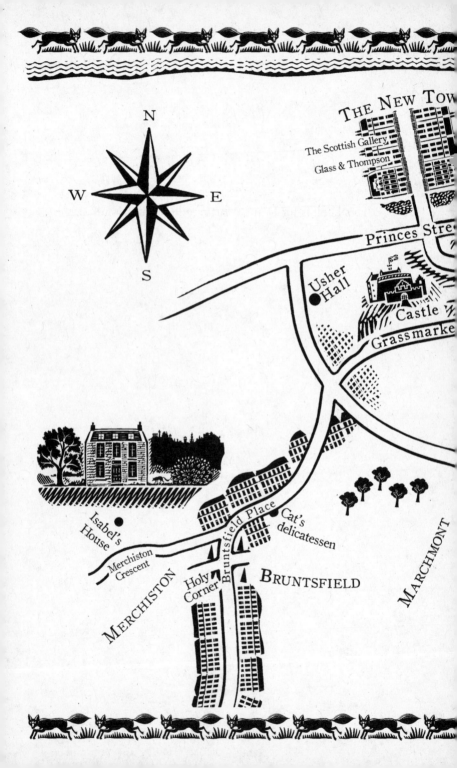

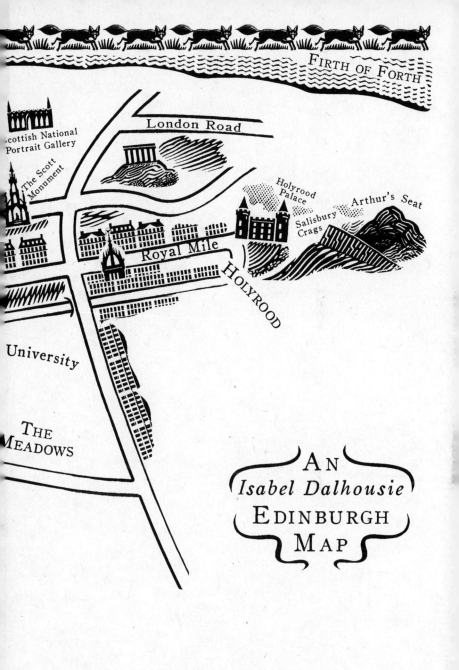

FIRTH OF FORTH

Scottish National Portrait Gallery

The Scott Monument

London Road

Holyrood Palace

Arthur's Seat

Salisbury Crags

Royal Mile

HOLYROOD

University

THE MEADOWS

AN
Isabel Dalhousie
EDINBURGH
MAP

THE FORGOTTEN AFFAIRS OF YOUTH

CHAPTER ONE

ISABEL DALHOUSIE, a philosopher, lowered her copy of the *Scotsman* newspaper and smiled. On the other side of the breakfast table, buttering a slice of bread for their young son, Charlie, who was now two and a half, and hungry, was her lover and fiancé, Jamie. She loved them both so much, so much. They were her world—a tousle-headed little boy and a bassoonist; more important to her than anything else—more than the complete works of Kant and Aristotle, more than the city she lived in, more than Scotland itself.

"Something amusing?" Jamie asked.

There was normally little to laugh at in the papers. Political scandals, economic disaster, suffering in all its familiar forms—these were the daily staple of a disaster-prone, uneasy planet. Add to that the seeming inability of the Scottish rugby team to defend itself against the predations of a group of hefty New Zealanders on a summer tour, and the newspaper's offering for that day was bleak.

Isabel had read out to Jamie the opening paragraph of the rugby report, in which the Scottish side's performance had been described in less than glowing terms. Jamie, however, had listened with only half an ear; he liked tennis and golf, and found that games involving a ball any larger than those used in these two games held little attraction for him. For her part, although she did not follow sport at all closely, Isabel enjoyed reading about rugby, a game that struck her as being one of the few remaining tribal rituals on offer to males in modern societies. An anthropologist might have a field-day in pursuing this interpretation; might note with some interest the famous rugby haka of the New Zealanders, as their players lined up and challenged the other team with thumbed noses and intimidating grunts; might listen to the Scottish supporters singing "Flower of Scotland," with its fourteenth-century military references (*fourteenth* century!); might remark upon the wailing bagpipes at the beginning of the game and the painted faces and . . .

And there was another, more personal reason for her interest: as a schoolgirl she had been in love, at a safe distance, with a boy who had seemed impossibly handsome, even when covered in mud and in a heaving scrummage. Some men were like that, she mused: they were much improved by mud.

But it was not the rugby news that made her laugh; it was a small item in the paper's political diary.

"Very amusing," she said to Jamie. "There's a story here about a Glasgow politician who held a surgery. You know those consultation sessions they hold—they call them surgeries; constituents can drop in and tackle them about local problems."

Jamie nodded. "I went to see my local Member of Parliament once. He was actually very helpful."

"Yes. That's what an MP's surgery is for. But this one apparently had a constituent coming in to complain about a sore nose. Can you believe it? A sore nose."

Jamie smiled. "Well, I suppose if you call it a surgery . . ."

"Yes," said Isabel. "But surely people understand that it's a politician they're seeing—not a doctor." She paused. "Or are there people who really think that their Member of Parliament should be able to do something about their aches and pains?"

She thought there were; once the state in its benignity embraced us, then the routes by which it dispensed its succour could easily be confused.

She picked up the newspaper. "People are pretty strange, aren't they? They can be so . . . well, I suppose there's no other word for it but *misinformed*."

"Yes," said Jamie. "They can. I was reading somewhere or other about a woman who wrote to an advice column asking whether a baby adopted from Korea would speak Korean when he grew up, even if raised elsewhere."

"She's not alone," said Isabel. "Natural language. Scottish kings have believed in that—James IV, I think, even conducted an experiment. He had a couple of children taken off to Inchkeith Island and looked after by a nurse who was dumb. He wanted to find out what language children would speak naturally if they weren't exposed to English—or, rather, to Scots. He thought it would be Hebrew."

"And it turned out to be Korean?"

Isabel smiled. "It was nothing, I imagine. Just sounds. Or, as Walter Scott suggested, they might have sounded like birds. There are lots of birds on Inchkeith Island."

Jamie wondered whether the children might have invented a language.

"Not from scratch," said Isabel. "Or only a rudimentary one."

Jamie passed a piece of buttered bread to Charlie, who seized it, examining it intently before putting it into his mouth.

"Rudimentary? So they'd have no grammar—just nouns for the various objects? Not that they'd need many. The sea. Birds' eggs. Food. Fish."

"Yes," said Isabel. "And a word for Scotland too, perhaps. They'd look across the firth and see the mainland, and they might give it a name."

He shook his head. "I find that story rather sad," he said.

Isabel put the newspaper down on the table. She thought about the children on the island, imagining them huddled together in the winter, with no words to describe their misery. A familiar question occurred to her: if you had no language, then what form did your thoughts take—if you thought at all? Of course you thought—she had never had any difficulty with accepting that—but how limited would your thoughts be in the absence of any words to express them?

She looked at Charlie and smiled. He returned the smile. He had no words for what had just passed between them, she told herself; they had engaged with one another, and affection and amusement, tinged with a note of conspiracy, had been in the mind of each. These were feelings, though; not articulated intentions or thoughts as such. Or had Charlie thought, *She's smiling at me*, even if he as yet had no word for smile? It was, she decided, rather like looking at an unfamiliar stretch of landscape; one might not know its name but one could still be said to know *it*, and knowledge of the geographical name would make no difference to how one thought about what one saw. And people still felt hungry, even if they had no name for hunger.

Jamie reached for the newspaper, found the diary item and read it. Then he looked up. "But he's a doctor," he said.

"Who?"

He pointed to the column in the newspaper. "Him. The Member of Parliament who was asked about the sore nose. He's a doctor. I've seen him on television. He's the health spokesman for his party."

"Oh."

"So that constituent who asked about his nose wasn't so stupid after all."

Isabel made an apologetic gesture. "I suppose I jumped to a conclusion," she said. "But so did the newspaper. *Mea culpa,* or rather, *nostra culpa.*"

Jamie looked at her with mock disapproval. "Maybe we shouldn't judge others too quickly." He tried to make it sound as if he was joking, but the comment came across as censorious.

"All right," she said. "It's very easy to get things wrong when we aren't in possession of all the facts."

"And I suspect that we hardly ever know everything we should," said Jamie.

He might as well admit to a serious point: he wanted her to think about it; he wanted Isabel to be less *certain*; he wanted her to know that there were times when she might not be right.

But she was not thinking chastening thoughts: Isabel was a philosopher and she could not help but follow a challenging train of thought once it had been mooted. Jamie had suggested that we had to make do with imperfect knowledge, and he was right, she thought. Yet not knowing everything might be preferable to having all the facts set out before one. For example, did any of us really want to know the exact day, the hour even, when we were to die? She considered not. Nor did we necessarily want to know what would happen after we were gone.

That, of course, raised a whole range of issues about confidence and belief. Civilisations arose because people believed in them and in the values they represented. People built cathedrals and palaces, painted masterpieces—or paid other people to paint them—because they felt that what they were doing would last. If they thought that everything was just for next year, then they would hardly bother. It would be rather like living in a campsite, or like being a passing tenant of a patch of earth. So when a lover said, "I want to be with you always," he had to mean it, even if he knew that it could not be true.

Charlie had finished with the piece of bread Jamie had fed him and was now waving his arms in the air—his signal for more.

"I adore the way he does that," said Isabel. "Imagine if one could go through life waving one's arms in the air whenever one wanted something."

"Some do," said Jamie. "Conductors, in particular. They wave their arms at you if they want you to play with more expression."

He remembered something that made him smile. "And sometimes they forget that they're not in the concert hall. I saw Giorgio—remember the conductor I introduced you to last year? Well, I once saw him buying pistachio nuts at a delicatessen in Glasgow. The assistant was measuring them out and he urged her to put in more by waving his arms in just the same way as he gets us to play *fortissimo*. I imagine he had no idea he was doing it."

Isabel took over the feeding of Charlie, glancing at her watch as she did so.

"Time," she said.

It could have been a comment on the matters she had been pondering—on permanence and our sense of the future—but it was more prosaic than that.

"Yes," sighed Jamie. "I know. I must go."

He had a rehearsal that morning in Glasgow and would have to catch the train from Haymarket Station in an hour or so. The journey was so familiar, a meandering ride across the waist-belt of Scotland, the hills of Stirlingshire off to the right, gentle, soft; past small towns in which nothing happened; past the grey barracks of Glasgow's outskirts, and culminating in the echoing halls of Queen Street Station: a trip that lasted not much more than forty-five minutes, but which took one out of one culture and into another; from a clear Eastern light to a diffuse Western glow; from cold to warmth, some might say.

He now rose from the table, planted a kiss on Charlie's forehead and went off to get ready.

Isabel prepared another piece of buttered bread for Charlie, this time spreading it with a thin layer of Marmite. Charlie was an unusual child, at least in his taste for savoury foods. His first word had been "olive," and this had presaged a taste for anchovy paste and horseradish sauce, even for mild curries. His contemporaries from the playgroup he now attended each morning would not have understood; they had eyes only for brightly iced cupcakes and they would have spat out the pickled gherkins to be found neatly packed in Charlie's plastic lunch box. Isabel called the lunch box a tiffin box, a word she had picked up from her paternal grandfather, who had been in India. She had been five when he died, and her memory of him was hazy. In fact, all that she remembered was his moustache, which was an elaborate salt-and-pepper affair, and the ancient brass-bound tiffin box that sat on a table in his hall.

"Tiffin," Charlie suddenly announced. "Charlie want tiffin now."

Isabel gave him the piece of bread, which he examined briefly before throwing on the floor.

"Tiffin," he said.

Isabel picked up the bread. "Don't throw food, Charlie. That's not nice."

Moral philosophy for two-year-olds, she thought. *Don't throw food*. It was as good a starting point as any to begin the teaching of responsibility towards the world around us. And it was helpful to back it up with some justification too: *That's not nice*. Again, a simple expression said it all. Philosophers might tie themselves in knots over the question of conduct that was morally wrong—that debate, after all, was what Isabel's job was about—but perhaps the ultimate answer was so much simpler: *that's not nice*. Did one have to go further than that? She sighed. Of course one did; morality was not about what you liked or disliked; it had to be justified, to have some reasoning behind it.

"Tiffin is for later," she said. "You can have tiffin at playgroup."

"Tiffin now," said Charlie.

"No," she said. "Tiffin comes later—at tiffin-time, darling. Eleven-thirty."

She reflected on this short exchange. Charlie had given voice to a desire: he wanted tiffin now. She had refused him— tiffin came with conditions: it could be enjoyed only at a certain time. Charlie might well think: why? If one can eat tiffin at eleven-thirty, one can surely eat it now. It was an arbitrary rule perhaps, but it offered a more general lesson besides: that we cannot always have what we want. The age of two and a half, Isabel thought, was as good a time as any to learn this most difficult and disappointing of lessons about life.

But there could at least be an explanation, although she doubted whether an explanation was what a child would want.

"Tiffin is for later, you see, darling. Tiffin is for when you're hungry. See?"

"Hungry now," said Charlie.

WITH CHARLIE DROPPED OFF at his playgroup, and his tiffin box entrusted to the supervisor for safe keeping, Isabel walked along Merchiston Crescent to Bruntsfield. Conscience dictated that she should have returned to her desk and tackled the pile of unedited manuscripts awaiting inclusion in the next issue of the *Review of Applied Ethics*, but one of the few faults from which Isabel suffered was a slight tendency to prevarication, which became more evident in good weather. And the day was a fine one, luminescent and warm, with the wind, such as it was, coming from the south-west, from Dumfries and Galloway, and from the Atlantic before that. Scotland's weather was rarely second-hand, blowing in, as it did, from the west and south-west. So while cities on the continent had to contend with hand-me-down winds from elsewhere, from Italy and North Africa—if they were lucky—or from the Steppes and Siberia if they were not, Scotland's weather was usually entirely its own, freshly minted above the wide plains of empty ocean. Isabel had always thought of it as *white* weather: the white of clouds, of shifting veils of rain, of air that was attenuated to fine mist, of pale light from a hazy sun.

She took a deep breath. There were times when life's problems were convincingly outweighed by its possibilities, and this, she felt, was one. Here she was, in her forties, with a child at a time when many might have felt it was too late for children; blessed, too, with a fiancé whom she would shortly marry; solvent—though she was discreet about that, and generous beyond measure; working for herself—the list of good things, on any view, was a long one. She stopped herself: the making of such an inventory could attract the attention of a Nemesis always sensitive to hubristic thoughts, whose concern it had always been to cut down to size those who got above themselves. But I am not proud of any of this, Isabel said to herself; I am grateful, and that is something quite different. Nemesis, she hoped, had no axe to grind with those who were simply thankful for good fortune; her objection was to those who thought that they *deserved* what they had and boasted about it.

She had no real reason to go to Bruntsfield: the store cupboard at home was copiously stocked with everything they needed for the coming week; she had nothing to put in the post, or nothing that could not wait until tomorrow; and she did not need to go to a cash machine. But she was in the mood for a walk and for a cup of coffee in Cat's delicatessen. Cat, her niece, had run her food business for several years now and had recently expanded into a small adjoining shop that she had been able to buy at a tempting price. Isabel had offered to lend her the money to make the purchase, but Cat had declined.

"Don't think I'm being ungrateful," she said. "But I really want to do this by myself."

Isabel had explained that there would be no strings attached to the loan and that it would be interest-free; in fact, how about an outright gift? Cat, though, had been adamant.

"It's pride, I suppose," said Cat. "I want to prove that I can do this on my own. I hope you don't mind."

Isabel did not mind at all. Her relationship with her niece was far from simple, and she did not wish to imperil the delicate understanding that they had recently reached. The awkwardness between them had two causes.

First, Isabel was Cat's aunt—even if only fifteen years separated them. Cat's father, Isabel's brother, had distanced himself from the family and had little contact with his own daughter; not for reasons of antipathy, but from a curious, almost absentminded indifference. Isabel had always felt that Cat blamed her for this; that insofar as she wanted to punish her father, but could not, Isabel would have to do as the focus of her anger.

The second reason for awkwardness was even more understandable. Jamie had been Cat's boyfriend and had eventually been rejected by her. But then Isabel had taken up with him. She had not planned this turn of events; she had merely continued what had started as a friendship and this had blossomed, very much to her surprise—and delight, it must be said—into something more. Isabel understood why Cat should have been taken aback by this, but had not anticipated that she would be quite so resentful. She had not *stolen* Jamie, and there was, she felt, something of the dog in the manger about Cat's attitude. She might not have wanted Jamie, but did that mean that nobody else could have him? The answer, from Cat's point of view, was probably yes.

The situation had been made worse by Cat's abysmal taste in men. Jamie had been the exception in a rather too long line of flawed boyfriends, ranging from Toby, with his crushed-strawberry cords and his irritating manner, to Bruno, a boastful tightrope-walker who had been revealed to be a wearer of elevator shoes. There was a great deal wrong with Bruno, but the elevator shoes had seemed to point to the presence of something deeply untrustworthy. Isabel had wrestled with herself over this: she was quite prepared to accept that elevator shoes need not say anything negative about the wearer—there were, presumably, entirely meritorious people who resorted to them to gain a few extra inches—and so one could not condemn such shoes out of hand. But there would also be those whose elevator shoes were symptomatic of a chip on the shoulder, an aggressive personality—and Bruno, she felt, was one such.

Bruno had effectively dismissed himself as a boyfriend when he publicly upbraided Cat for causing him to fall off his tightrope—not exactly a high wire, as it had been only three or four feet off the ground at the time. But that was enough to end the relationship, much to Isabel's carefully concealed relief. He had then been followed by a teacher, who had seemed suitable enough, but who had, perhaps for that very reason, also been dismissed.

Now there was nobody—as far as Isabel knew—and that, she hoped, was how it might be, for a while at least. She did not think of Cat as promiscuous, but at what point, Isabel wondered, might eyebrows be raised as to the frequency of boyfriends? Was a new one each year too many? If one carried on in that way from the age of twenty, by the time one was forty-five one would have had twenty-five boyfriends, which surely was rather too many.

So what was a respectable number of boyfriends over a lifetime? Five? Isabel herself had had . . . For a moment she stopped in her tracks, halfway along Merchiston Crescent, and thought. There had been the rugby player, but he did not count as they had spoken only two or three times and he never knew that she had fallen for him. The first real boyfriend had come a little bit later, just before she left school; a shy boy with that—for her—fatal combination of dark hair and blue eyes, who had kissed her in the darkness of the Dominion Cinema one Saturday afternoon, and had written her the most extraordinary love letter that she still kept, tucked away with her birth certificate. Then there had been John Liamor, her former husband, who had been disastrous, who had broken her heart again and again, and of whom it was still uncomfortable to think, even if she had come to terms with what had happened. Then Jamie. And that was all. Was that typical, she wondered, or might it be considered thin rations?

The important thing, she told herself, was to try to see it from Cat's point of view—and she could certainly do that. Like all of us, she thought, Cat was searching for the company of one who would make her happy. Some of us did not have to look long for that person, some of us found him or her with little difficulty; others had longer to look, and had less luck. They deserved our sympathy rather than our disapproval.

Passersby, of whom there were one or two, paid no attention to the sight of a rather handsome-looking woman suddenly stopping and appearing to be lost in thought. Had they done so, they might have concluded that Isabel was trying to remember what she had failed to put on her shopping list; they would not have guessed that she was thinking about the problem of boyfriends. And these passersby, anyway, were students, making their way to lectures at Napier University nearby. And there was never any doubt as to what students—at least the male ones, as these happened to be—thought about on their way to lectures. Sex.

She continued her walk, and five minutes later was standing in front of the delicatessen. Looking inside, through the large display window, she saw that Cat was pointing out something to a customer, while Eddie, her young assistant, was standing behind the counter. He caught Isabel's eye and waved enthusiastically, beckoning her in, in the manner of one who had important news to convey. Eddie was normally shy, but not now; now he had something to tell her.

CHAPTER TWO

EDDIE SAID TO HER, "You sit down, Isabel. I'll make you a cappuccino. And I've got something to tell you."

"I sensed that," said Isabel. "Good news, obviously."

She smiled at Eddie encouragingly, pleased that he was so manifestly happy. There had been little happiness in his life, she suspected, not that she knew too much about him. She knew that he was in his early twenties; that he lived with his parents, who had moved a few months ago to a new flat in Sighthill; that his father had something to do with the railways; and that something traumatic, something dark and unspoken, had happened to Eddie when he was seventeen or eighteen. Cat knew what that was, but Isabel had never asked her and did not want to know—not from indifference, but out of respect for Eddie. If he wanted her to know, he would have told her, and he had not.

Eddie was making progress. There had been one or two girl-friends, and this had helped his confidence, and over the last year or so he had shown greater readiness to accept responsibil-ity. Cat could now leave him in charge of the shop for an entire day, even if he was still unable to look after it for much longer than that. Of course, he knew what to do and did it competently, but if he felt that he was on his own he panicked. This had something to do with what had happened—Isabel was sure of that—and only the passage of time would help with that.

Eddie ushered her across to one of the tables at which coffee was served. "We haven't got that Italian newspaper you like," he said. "But here's the *Scotsman*."

"I've already done the *Scotsman*," said Isabel. "And I don't really need anything to read. You go and make my coffee. Then give me this news of yours."

Eddie left her, and Isabel glanced at Cat, who was still with her customer. Her niece noticed and nodded. Something in Cat's expression indicated to Isabel that this customer was taking a long time to make up her mind over which tea to buy.

Eddie produced the cappuccino with a flourish. He had recently taken to signing the frothy milk-top with a thistle, a trick he had learned from an Irish barman who served Guinness with the outline of a four-leaved clover traced on the foam. He sat down and smiled broadly at Isabel.

"Guess," he challenged. "Go ahead and guess."

She made a show of thinking. "Let me see. You've won the Spanish lottery. *El Gordo*—the fat one. A million euros, tax-free."

"Nope."

"All right. You went in for a screen test and they've just phoned to say could you come back, and bring your agent?"

Eddie shook his head. "No, I'd never be an actor. I don't like having my photograph taken."

She made a gesture of defeat. "I'm not going to get it, am I? You tell me, Eddie."

The young man leaned forward in his chair. "All right. Listen to this, Isabel. You know I've got this uncle?"

She did not.

"Well, I have. He's called Donald and he's my mother's older brother. He used to have a wife, who was my aunt, and then she went off with this guy from Glasgow. It was her fault—my dad said that. So Uncle Donald was left by himself."

Isabel nodded. "Yes. These things are . . . well, they're not very pleasant."

"He was really cut up over it for a long time. But he's better now and he's got a girlfriend—you should see her, Isabel—she's amazing. Much better than his wife. So there's Uncle Donald and he gets a letter one morning from a firm of lawyers in Dundee and they say that his cousin, who never married, has died and left him her house in Montrose. And her car. The car's useless—Uncle Donald went to look at it and said that the gearbox was shot: it was the way she used to change gear, like stirring porridge, he said. But the house is quite nice. He doesn't need it because he's got his own place in Dalkeith, and he doesn't even have a mortgage."

"So he's going to sell it?"

Eddie beamed with pleasure. "Yes. And he wants to treat me to a trip. He's always said that he wanted to go to the United States and Canada. He's never been, you see, but now he can afford to take a couple of months off and go all the way from Miami up to Alaska, with a bit of Canada in between. The Rockies and Vancouver. Him and me, in a car he's going to rent. His girlfriend can't get that much time off, but she'll come for the first three weeks."

Isabel thought of driving across the Midwest and the experience of its sheer vastness. It would be like being at sea, she imagined.

"That's wonderful, Eddie," she said. "All that way . . ."

"Yes," he said. "Places like Nebraska. Imagine going there. And the Grand Canyon. And Las Vegas."

Isabel thought. "Las Vegas . . ."

"Yes," said Eddie. "And Cat's said that it's fine. I've got a friend, you see, who can do my job here for me. He's worked in a deli before. Cat has spoken to him and says that it's all right."

Eddie finished and sat back in his chair, waiting for Isabel's reaction to his news. She leaned across the table and patted him lightly on the forearm. She did not mean the gesture to look condescending, but she realised it did. He did not notice.

She spoke warmly. "That's marvellous, Eddie," she said. "I think that's just wonderful."

She did not, but that was not the point. It was wonderful for him, as it would be for any young man who had never been any-where, other than a trip to London once and five precious, heady days in Spain as a teenager.

He smiled at her. "America!"

She nodded. "Yes. You know that I'm half American?"

He expressed surprise, and she explained to him about her sainted American mother.

"She was a saint? Really?"

Eddie could take things literally—maybe a slight hint of Asperger's, she wondered—but no, he was too sensitive in other ways for that diagnosis.

"Of course not. Not in the real sense. I call her that be-cause, well, because I thought she was a very good woman. She was kind, you see."

"Like you," said Eddie.

The compliment was not contrived; it came naturally, and Isabel felt its effect, like a shaft of warming sun.

"That's nice of you, Eddie. But I don't think I'm particularly kind—or not any kinder than anybody else."

He said she was, and then Cat finished with her customer and returned to the counter to ring up the sale.

Eddie sighed. "I'm almost too excited to work, but I have to, I suppose. Sinclair starts the day after tomorrow. I'm taking a week off before we go. We're flying from Glasgow."

"Sinclair?"

"My friend. You'll like him, Isabel . . ." His voice trailed off, and Isabel realised that she would not like Sinclair.

"I'm sure I will."

She thought: we have just expressed to each other the exact opposite of what we truly feel. And yet, in doing so, we have made our meaning perfectly clear. Isabel glanced at Cat, who was looking in her direction. If I don't like Sinclair, she thought, then I can be absolutely sure that Cat will.

On impulse, Isabel whispered to Eddie as he rose to leave the table, "This Sinclair . . . It's a silly question, but tell me: is he good-looking?"

Eddie seemed bemused. "Well . . ."

Isabel saw that Eddie was unwilling to discuss Cat's love life and she could understand that.

Eddie grinned. "Yes," he said. "Of course. He's been a model in his spare time, you know. I saw a picture of him in an ad once—an ad for jeans. I think he'd like to do it full time."

Isabel said nothing; Cat was coming over to the table as Eddie returned to work. The information that Eddie had just imparted was not at all welcome. Cat did not *need* a young man who posed as a model for jeans; not in the slightest.

"Jeans," she muttered under her breath.

Arriving at the table, Cat looked puzzled. "Jeans?"

"Just thinking," said Isabel.

Cat sat down. "Eddie's told you his news? He's as high as a kite about it."

"Yes," said Isabel. "He's pretty excited. And who wouldn't be?"

"Not me," said Cat. "That uncle of his—I met him, you know. He came in here once, and . . ."

Isabel waited for Cat to finish. Her niece could be uncharitable.

Cat lowered her voice. "Seriously dull. Terminally boring. And . . . well, there's no way round it: he's got these most dreadful teeth—all crooked, and half of them look rotten. I couldn't be in a car for five thousand miles, or whatever it is, with teeth like that sitting next to me. The Americans are going to freak out—you know what they're like about teeth. They'll probably cart him off to an emergency dentist the moment he opens his mouth. Or they won't let his teeth into the country. They might say, 'Look, you can come in, but teeth like that stay out.'"

Isabel did not want to smile, but could not help herself. "He'll be all right. I don't think Eddie notices teeth."

Cat shrugged. There was not much more to be said about the uncle, and her conversation now went off in another direction. "I gave your telephone number to somebody," she said. "I hope you don't mind."

"Oh?"

Cat went on to explain, "There's a woman who's been dropping in here for coffee over the last week or so. She's staying in a flat in Forbes Road. She's one of you."

"Of me?"

"A philosopher. I got speaking to her and she told me she's over here on sabbatical. Four months, or six months, or whatever it is. She's working on something or other—she told me what it was, but I forget. She's Australian. She's called Jane—I don't know her other name. She told me, but it went in one ear and out the other." Cat paused. "I thought that she seemed a bit lonely and so I asked her whether she'd like to meet you, since you were a philosopher. She said she's heard of you—she reads that journal of yours."

"One of the two thousand four hundred and eighty-seven," said Isabel. That, she explained, was the number of readers that each issue of the *Review of Applied Ethics* was calculated to have.

Cat listened to the explanation. "That's tiny. You could probably invite all the readers to tea."

"Very funny," said Isabel. "And, actually, it's not a bad figure at all—at least as far as academic journals go."

She did not have to say this to Cat; she did not have to justify herself, but she continued, as one who is made fun of will make fun of another to distract attention, "I have a friend who edits a journal that has a circulation of fifty-eight. And he wrote a book—on the nature of existence—that sold thirty-two copies."

Immediately she felt ashamed and disloyal. *I should defend him against people like Cat. And if books on existence did not exist, then . . .*

Cat glanced out of the window. "Do you ever wonder whether what you do is worthwhile? I'm not saying it isn't—I'm just asking."

Isabel gave an answer that Cat had not expected. "All the time," she said. "Don't you?"

Cat frowned. "Me? Ask myself whether what I do is worthwhile?"

"That's the question," said Isabel.

"Of course not."

"Well, maybe you should," said Isabel. "Maybe everybody should—even you."

"I sell cheese and Italian sausages," Cat retorted. "I don't have time to think. Most people don't. They do what they have to do because they need to eat."

So life was reduced to cheese and sausages, thought Isabel; that was what really counted. Such reductionism was hardly attractive, but Isabel felt that Cat was probably right about people not having the time or energy for philosophy. Self-doubt was a luxury, as, perhaps, was the examined life. And yet the examined life, as the adage had it, was the only life worth living.

She looked at Cat. Ontology, self-doubt, cheese, sausages—it would be best to leave these for the time being.

"This Australian woman," she said. "She'll get in touch, will she? I could ask her round. It can't be much fun being in a strange place by yourself."

"She said she'll phone you," said Cat. "And now, I'd better go."

Isabel nodded. "You'll miss having Eddie to help you. But I gather you've got somebody lined up. I was hearing about Sinclair . . . You've met him?"

Isabel tried to make the question sound innocent, but it was not, and Cat's manner revealed that she knew this. Her reply was guarded. "Yes. Once. He'll do."

Isabel held Cat's gaze. Something had passed between them; an unspoken mutual understanding that came from having known one another for so long. There's something there, thought Isabel. And then she said to herself: *Here we go—again*.

BY THE TIME she got back to the house, having been interrupted on the way back by bumping into a garrulous neighbour, the morning was already almost over. For Isabel, the watershed was always eleven-thirty; that was the point at which if nothing was achieved, then nothing would be, the point at which one had to think about lunch, now just an hour away.

Since Charlie had started going to his playgroup, the mornings had become even shorter, as he had to be fetched shortly after noon, and it took ten minutes to get him back and another ten minutes to get him changed out of his morning clothes; by this time, he would be covered in finger paint, crumbs, pieces of a curious modelling substance much approved of by the playgroup authorities, grains of sand from the sandpit and, very occasionally, what looked like specks of blood. Boys, it seemed to Isabel, were magnets for dirt and detritus, and the only solution, if one were wanted, was frequent changes of clothing. Or one could throw up one's hands and allow them to get dirtier through the day and then hose them down—metaphorically, of course—in the early evening.

Isabel opted to change Charlie, and so his morning clothes, once abandoned, were replaced with afternoon clothes. She decided that she rather liked the idea of having afternoon clothes, even if one were not a two-year-old. Changing into one's afternoon clothes could become something of a ritual, rather like changing for dinner—which so few people did any more. And the afternoon clothes themselves could be the subject of deliberation and chosen with care; they would be more loose-fitting than one's morning clothes, more autumnal in shade, perhaps—clothes that would reflect the lengthening of shadows and sit well with the subtle change in light that comes after three; russet clothes, comfortable linen, loose-fitting collars and sleeves.

"You thinking?"

It was Isabel's housekeeper, Grace. She had worked in the house when Isabel's father was still alive, and had been kept on by Isabel. It would have been impossible to ask Grace to leave—even if Isabel had wanted to do so; she came with the house and had naturally assumed that the house could not be run without her. Isabel had felt vaguely apologetic about having a housekeeper—it seemed such an extravagant, *privileged* thing to do, but a discussion with her friend, Peter Stevenson, had helped.

"What good would it do if you were to stop that particular item of expenditure?" Peter said. "All it would mean was that Grace would be out of a job. What would it achieve?"

"But I feel embarrassed," said Isabel. "Somebody of my age doesn't need a housekeeper. People will think I'm lazy."

Peter was too perceptive to swallow that. "That's not it, is it? What's worrying you is that people will think that you're well-off, which you are. So why not just accept it? You use your money generously—I know that. Carry on like that and forget what you imagine people think about you. It's not an actual *sin* to have money. The sin exists in using it selfishly, which you don't."

"Oh well," said Isabel.

"Exactly."

Now Grace stood in the doorway of Isabel's workroom, a bucket in hand, on her way to performing the daily chore of washing down the Victorian encaustic-tile floor in the entrance hall. Isabel was not sure that this floor had to be washed every day, but Grace had always done it and would have resisted any suggestion that she change her routine.

Now Grace's question hung in the air. She often asked Isabel whether she was thinking; it was almost an accusation.

"I suppose I am thinking. But not about work, I must admit." Isabel, who was seated at her desk, gave a despairing glance at the piles of paper before her. "I'm afraid that I've accomplished very little this morning."

"Me too," said Grace. "I've done none of the ironing yet, I'm afraid. All those shirts of Jamie's."

"Leave them," said Isabel. "Jamie can iron them himself. It's very therapeutic for men to iron. Therapeutic for women, that is."

Grace shook her head. "I'll do them later this afternoon." She put down the bucket. "Where does the time go? Do you ever ask yourself that?"

"Constantly," said Isabel. "As most people do." She smiled. "Mind you, how much of our time, do you think, is spent asking ourselves where the time goes?"

Isabel remembered that it was a Friday, which meant that Grace would have spent the previous evening at one of her spiritualist meetings. She enjoyed hearing about these, as Grace was always prepared to give a candid assessment of the visiting medium. The previous week the visiting medium had been from Glasgow and had made contact with spirits who voiced an interesting, if somewhat unusual, complaint.

"He said that there were a number of spirits trying to get through. He said that that they were all from Glasgow."

Isabel had raised an eyebrow. "Do spirits live in particular places? I thought that the whole point about being disembodied is that you rose above constraints of place. Have I got it wrong?"

Grace shook her head. "Spirits often hang about the places that were special to them before they crossed over," she said. "He said that these spirits wanted to get back to Glasgow because they weren't happy in Edinburgh."

"A likely story!" snorted Isabel.

"My feelings too," Grace had replied.

Now, Isabel asked about the previous evening. Was the medium any good, or at least better than the man who contacted the unhappy Glaswegian spirits?

"Much better," said Grace. "He was one of our regulars. We had him about four months ago and he was really good. He saw somebody's husband—clear as day, he said. I was sitting next to the woman and I comforted her. It was very moving."

Isabel said nothing. The fundamental premises of Grace's spiritualist meetings might not have withstood rigorous, rational examination, but there was little doubt in her mind about the solace that they gave. And what was wrong with anything that gave comfort to lives bereft of it?

"Yes," Grace continued. "This medium—he's called Mr. Barr; I don't know his first name, I'm afraid—he works in a bank. In the back room, I think; he's not a teller or anything like that. Anyway, he has a real talent for getting through to the other side. You can see it in his eyes; he just has that look to him—you know what I mean?"

Isabel did. "The light—"

"Exactly," said Grace. "It's the light that shines from the eyes. There's no mistaking it and he had it. It was like . . ." She searched for an analogy, and then decided, "Like a lighthouse."

Isabel struggled with the image. Lighthouse eyes would presumably send forth beams at intervals, which would create a rather odd impression, she felt, especially at night, and if such people lived by the sea . . .

"He said something very interesting," Grace continued. "He said that he was getting a strong message from somebody who had been a stockbroker in Edinburgh in his lifetime. He was now on the other shore and wanted us to know that everything would be all right."

"That's reassuring," said Isabel.

"I think he was talking about the country's economy. He said that we shouldn't worry—it was going to be all right."

Isabel raised an eyebrow. "I wonder how he knows?"

Grace assumed a rather superior expression. "They know," she said. "We may not understand how they know, but the important thing is that they know. It's to do with time. Time has a different meaning in the spirit world."

Isabel did not contradict this; she knew there was little point. If asked to justify her claims about the world beyond, Grace tended to shelter behind the idea that there were some forms of knowledge that somebody like Isabel simply could not grasp.

"Scepticism closes the mind," she would say. "Like a trap."

Grace continued with her report. "He became quite specific, you know. He mentioned a particular company that he said would do well. He said that all the conditions were right for this to happen."

Isabel expressed her surprise. "A tip? An investment tip?"

"No," said Grace. "It was not like that at all. The spirit was just sharing something with us. He was obviously happy that this company would do well and he wanted us to share his happiness."

Isabel hesitated for a moment. Grace's meeting must have been rich in comic possibilities, with the medium issuing what amounted to a stock-market prediction, and some of those attending, perhaps, discreetly writing down the details.

"What company?" she asked on impulse.

"West of Scotland Turbines," said Grace. "You'll see their shares in the paper. Look at the stock-market page."

"So they exist?"

"Yes, of course they exist. I looked them up. They make turbines for hydroelectric schemes."

Grace appeared to feel that they had spent long enough on turbines and went on to say something about needing new scouring liquid for the upstairs shower, which was becoming mildewed. She looked at Isabel slightly reproachfully, as if she were responsible for the mildew. Isabel thought: It's not my fault, but Grace will always blame me.

Then Grace said, "Oh, somebody phoned while you were out. I asked for her name, but she just left a number for you to call back. It's in the basket. Some people don't give their names, which is odd, I think. It's as if they've got something to hide . . ." She examined Isabel as if she were conniving in, or at least condoning, a whole series of anonymous calls. Then she continued, "She sounded Australian."

It was the woman whom Cat had met. Isabel glanced at her watch: there was time to return the call before she went off to collect Charlie. That would mean, of course, that she would have done no work at all that morning, and would probably do very little that afternoon. Did it matter? Would the world be changed if the next edition of the *Review of Applied Ethics* did not come out on time? The answer, of course, was that it would make very little difference—a humbling thought.

Isabel rose from her desk and made her way into the kitchen. If Grace wanted to leave her a note, there was a small basket on top of the fridge in which notes were placed. There was one now, with a number scribbled on it in pencil. Underneath the number, Grace had written: *woman*. Isabel smiled; she was reminded of her father, who had once said to her, "Don't write—or say—any more than you have to. Just don't."

Or think, perhaps?

Isabel took the note back to her study. There she wrote on it *West of Scotland Turbines*, and then picked up the telephone.

CHAPTER THREE

ISABEL HAD SUGGESTED meeting Jane Cooper the following day at Glass & Thompson. This suited both of them: Jane had somewhere to go in Princes Street, and Dundas Street was no more than ten minutes' walk from there—and Isabel had to return a catalogue to Guy Peploe at the Scottish Gallery, a few doors down.

Her visit to Guy was brief, as the gallery staff were hanging paintings for the next show and she knew that this was not a time when they needed distraction. The invitation to the private view was on her mantelpiece: *A History of Scotland in Landscape.*

"Landscapes," said Guy, pointing to a number of paintings stacked against the wall. "Solid and reliable landscapes. People love them."

"Which is just as well for galleries," said Isabel, peering at the vaguely familiar view depicted in one of the paintings. It was somewhere in East Lothian, she thought; looking back along the coast towards Edinburgh. But there was something not quite right.

"When was this done?" she asked, trying to make out the signature at the bottom.

Guy glanced at the painting. "Last year. You've probably heard of him. We showed him a couple of years ago."

"This is the view from somewhere near Tranent, isn't it?" asked Isabel.

Guy nodded. "Yes, in the direction of Edinburgh. That's Arthur's Seat over there, isn't it? He's got the haziness of it rather well, don't you think?"

Isabel agreed. The artist had captured the misty, blue light that seemed to play around Arthur's Seat when one looked at it from some distance. Blue remembered hills, she thought; Housman's phrase about the hills of Shropshire, made so striking because the *remembered* was in the wrong, or at least an unusual, place. *Remembered blue hills* would have sounded so different and would have been quickly forgotten; *blue remembered hills* had an entirely different effect.

Then she realised what was wrong. "Where's Cockenzie Power Station?" she asked. *Remembered power stations.*

Guy crouched down to examine the painting more closely. "Well," he began. "Now that you mention it . . ."

Isabel laughed. "It's possible, of course, that this is just a sketch and that the artist intended to put the details in later on." She paused. "And then forgot. It's so easy to forget about power stations, I find."

Guy straightened up. "It's a particularly ugly power station, isn't it?"

"Aren't all power stations ugly?"

He thought for a moment. "Battersea?"

Isabel thought of the extraordinary four-chimney art deco building on the Thames. Guy was right: Battersea was beautiful and richly deserved its iconic status. But there was nothing art deco about Cockenzie Power Station, which was a large, late-sixties box, a windowless block that marred that lovely stretch of Scotland's coastline.

"Of course there are some conditions," she said, "that prevent one from seeing unpleasant things. It may be that there are those who simply do not *see* power stations. Perhaps a special form of agnosia that cuts out power stations."

Guy smiled. "It's more likely a case of a landscape painter doing what landscape painters have been doing for a long time—editing nature." Guy pointed to another painting that had already been hung. "That's a Nasmyth. Scottish painters did a lot of editing in the nineteenth century. There's a famous example—his painting of Glencoe, which makes the hills much craggier than they really are. Really soups them up."

"Because that's what people wanted? The romantic Highlands?"

"Exactly. They lapped it up in the nineteenth century—positively lapped it up. Scotland was the most romantic country in Europe at the time. All that Walter Scott and so on."

Isabel looked down at the painting. "Power stations don't really fit with that, do they?"

"Unfortunately not. And now we have wind turbines. They'll have to be edited out, now that we're covering our hills with those great behemoths."

Isabel thought for a moment. Dutch windmills were so much more pleasing to the eye than the spiky things of our own times; those old windmills had great sails, comfortable and creaking, not blades of steel slicing into the sky.

"The Dutch left them in, didn't they? The Dutch masters painted the windmills."

"In some cases. But who can tell? Perhaps there were many

more windmills than Dutch landscape art lets on. Dutch portrait painters were just as capable of improving nature as any
others—so their landscape artists no doubt did much the same
thing."

Isabel reflected on this as she walked the short distance up
the street to Glass & Thompson. Beauty—whether in nature, in
art, or in music—was always ready to do its work; all we had to
do was to open our hearts to it. Mozart, Puccini, Titian, or even
a mathematical proof, spoke to the heart; they gave us completeness, peace, a glimpse of the divine. We wanted beauty; we
wanted to take it into ourselves, to possess it, to absorb it, so
that it became part of us. That was why we appreciated a wel-
coming landscape just as we appreciated a handsome face or
body, and that was why a painter might feel tempted to beautify
that which he saw before him, making virginal that which had
been sullied, improving on that which was not quite magnificent enough. Smaller and smaller corners of unsullied nature
were left to painters, now that we had covered so much of our
world with concrete, with highways and wires and streams of
cars—such ugliness.

Art might still remind us of beauty, might still rescue us
from the wasteland we were creating; but there were those in
the arts who rejected the view that art should edify and uplift,
who thought that it should aspire to be nothing more than a lens
trained on an increasingly sordid reality. To create anything
harmonious was seen by such people as superficial; the dark,
the discordant, the unresolved—this, they believed, was the
province of art, of film, of literature.

She considered all that, and then, as she crossed the thresh-
old of the café, she considered the opposite—or at least she

...ned the possibility that the opposite was true. Perhaps it really was the role of art to confront and disturb, to jolt us out of our comfort zones, to dispel our protective assumptions, to horrify us, to make our teeth rattle. Perhaps that was what she should really think, even if she were tempted to persist in a belief in beauty and all its works. That was the problem with being a philosopher: it was not easy. As a philosopher one could not believe just one thing; one had to explore the possibility that what one thought was true might be false; that what one *wanted* to believe might not be what one really *should* hold to be true. So much for the examined life: how uncomfortable it could be.

But at least she knew what she wanted for lunch.

SHE WAS THERE before Jane.

"It's a small place," Isabel had said over the telephone. "You'll know it's me, and I'll know it's you, even if we haven't met before."

"I've seen your photograph," Jane had interjected. "I looked you up online. There's a photograph of you on the *Review*'s website, as you probably know."

Isabel hesitated, and then decided to come clean.

"Well, I looked you up too," she said.

She had always felt that one could not refrain from confessing to an equal fault if somebody else confessed first; not to do so was to leave the other at a disadvantage. Of course it was not necessarily a fault to research another person if you were about to meet; indeed, it could be taken as rude not to do so—implying, perhaps, that the other was unworthy of your curiosity.

Jane laughed. "There's a *very* unflattering picture of me online," she said. "It must have been put there by one of my enemies." She paused. "Not that I have many enemies—I hope."

"We all have enemies," Isabel had said, trying to think of who hers were—or had been. Minty Auchterlonie, that scheming, ambitious woman with whom Isabel had crossed swords more than once? Hard-faced . . . No, she should not be uncharitable. Christopher Dove, the plausible, ruthless philosophical sidekick of Professor Lettuce? She wondered whether Jane had come across Christopher Dove, or even Professor Lettuce, great slug, great— Charity. Charity.

Now Jane came in, and Isabel, waving, rose to greet her.

Jane took off the lightweight mac she had been wearing; there had been a few drops of rain—not much—and she brushed these off the fabric of the coat before she sat down opposite Isabel.

Isabel pointed to the menu on the board behind the counter. "You choose from that," she said. "I always have the same thing. Mozzarella and tomatoes. Caprese. And if you ask, you might get olive oil from the Zyw estate in Tuscany. Aleksander Zyw was a Polish painter who settled in Edinburgh after the war. His son makes olive oil in Italy. And his grandson, Tommy, works with Guy Peploe in the Scottish Gallery."

Jane smiled. "What a nice thing that even the olive oil in your life has its associations. That's what I like about Edinburgh. Everything is . . . connected somehow. It still has a sense of itself, of what it is."

Isabel said, "But Melbourne must be like that too."

Jane shook her head. "A bit, but only a bit. Our identity's changing—as everybody's is." She looked at Isabel. "I'm not at all sure what it is to be an Australian. Do you know what it is to be Scottish?"

"I think so," said Isabel. "I'm half American, though—on my mother's side. So I suppose I know what it is to be a half-Scottish, half-American woman who's a working philosopher and a mother and . . . well, that's the whole point about identity today: it's much freer, much looser. Which is a good thing, don't you think?"

Jane inclined her head slightly; she agreed.

"It used to be very hard to be British," Isabel continued. "The strain on the upper lip was pretty intense. Or American. All those short haircuts for the men and Betty Crocker cakes for the women. Identity was a straitjacket. Not any more."

They were both silent for a moment. Their conversation had started in the deep end, unlike most conversations, which launched themselves into the shallowest of shallows.

Isabel had not finished. "Identity's difficult. I suppose it brings about social cohesion, but it's not much fun if you don't quite fit. Being gay, for example, used to be pretty miserable. Or being a Protestant in a place like Ireland when the Catholic Church ruled the roost. Or being a woman in Ireland under the thumb of all those priests. Those big, dominant identities have been weakened, I suppose, but I think that might be a good thing, on balance. It's allowed other identities to flourish."

Jane did not look convinced. "Yes, but if you weaken identity, people end up not knowing who they are. They end up living bland lives with no real content to them. No customs, no traditions, no sense of their past. And I think one needs to know who one is." She hesitated. "I guess we've spent so much time feeling ashamed of ourselves, it's made us rather apologetic about being what we are. As a result we don't want to be anything."

Isabel was intrigued. "Ashamed of our history?"

"Yes. After all, we forced ourselves on others. We despoiled and plundered the world. Destroyed cultures left, right and centre."

"Perhaps."

"But we did! No perhaps about it. We did!"

"Well, at least Australia's said sorry," observed Isabel. "I'm not so sure that the West as a whole has. And even if we did all those things, we also invented penicillin and computers and human rights. We don't need to be ashamed of any of that."

Jane sighed. "No, we can't browbeat ourselves for too long."

As she toyed with the salt cellar, Isabel watched her. There was energy there; a controlled energy that was both intellectual and physical.

"An identity can't be founded on guilt," Jane continued. "We have to decide who we are, what we represent, and then defend it."

"Enlightenment values? Defend those?"

Jane nodded. "Probably. Because if we don't, then all is lost. Hobbes's nightmare."

"Of course."

"Self-interest, naked materialism, authoritarian government: all of these are alive and kicking in the undergrowth, ready to take over, ready to fill the vacuum created by the decline of Christianity."

The mention of religion stuck out. The laicisation of conversation—even about major things—had been so complete that religious references seemed inappropriate, almost gauche.

And yet that was what had made us, thought Isabel. That had been at the heart of our culture; it had given our society its fundamental outlook. And could the Enlightenment have flourished in quite the same way in the absence of Christian sentiments of love and cherishing of others? Society may be post-Christian, but could hardly ignore its Judeo-Christian past; we did not, after all, come from nowhere.

"I know this is a bit blunt," Isabel said, "but do you mind my asking whether you have a particular religious position?"

Jane looked at her directly. "Because I mentioned Christianity?"

"Not just that—"

Jane cut her short. "I sometimes envy those who have a strong faith. But in answer to your question, no, I can't believe."

"So you're like most of us today," said Isabel. "I have misgivings about people not having a spiritual life. It's so . . . so shallow. I sometimes think that life without a spiritual dimension must be like being made of cardboard—and as deep and satisfying." She paused. "I feel that there is something there—some force, or truth, perhaps—to put it at its most general. I sense it, and I suppose I'd even go so far as to say that I yearn for it. I want it to be. Maybe that's God. But I find it difficult to accept any statement as to his identity. And as for claims to be the sole interpreter of that force—the sort of claim made by religions that tell you that they have the sole answer—well, what can one say about such arrogance . . ."

"Yet you say that we need religious belief?"

Isabel did not answer immediately. The problem for her was the divisiveness of religion, its magical thinking, its frequent sheer nastiness. Yet all of that existed side by side with exactly that spirituality that she felt we could not do without; that feeling of awe, of immanence, which she knew was very real, and which enriched and sustained our lives so vitally.

"Yes, we need it," Isabel eventually replied. "Because otherwise we live in a world in which there is no real answer to evil."

Jane looked at her quizzically. "Not even a socio-biological one? An evolutionary basis to morality?"

"No. And the point is that we don't want to live in such a world. We would be unhappy if we thought there was no final justice. And so we have to tell ourselves that it exists."

Jane sensed a flaw. "Even if we think it doesn't?"

Isabel hesitated. "The fact that we want something to be the case—that we need it to be so—may be reason enough for saying that it actually does exist."

"Surely not . . . Surely it's more honest to say that arbitrary biological drives compel us to create morality."

Isabel did not think so. Evil had to be combated, and we had to be motivated to engage in the battle. If we did not have a compelling intellectual reason to fight against evil, then it would have free play.

Jane made a gesture of acceptance with her hands. "And so we need a theological perspective to cope with evil? A belief in God is just a tune we whistle to keep our spirits up in the face of something nasty?"

"No," said Isabel. "It's not that simple."

Russell, the proprietor, was at their table, ready to take their orders. "And have you decided?"

Isabel smiled. "About the nature of reality? Or about lunch?"

They placed their order, and the subject of religion was tacitly set aside. It was a debate, Isabel thought, that had taken centuries and would require centuries more.

Jane had an afterthought. "Talking of identity," she said. "A culture requires territory, doesn't it? Or most do. And lots of territory and lots of people make for influential cultures. Imagine if Sweden were massive—"

"It is quite big," suggested Isabel. "Look at a map."

"Population-wise."

"Rather small," conceded Isabel.

"Yes. But imagine that Sweden were the dominant power in the world today. Imagine what a difference it would make. All those wonderful, highly civilised ideas of social democracy and concern for others would have a great army behind them."

A Swedish world. The Swedish century. Isabel had to admit that it sounded attractive, but there was a flaw in the argument, which she pointed out to Jane.

"Of course, if Sweden were massive, and powerful too, then it wouldn't be Sweden. It would behave in exactly the same way as any massive and powerful country behaves."

Jane nodded. "Yes, I suspect you're right. And I suppose that at the end of the day things are the way they are and we have to accept them."

She paused, trying to recall something, then looked directly at Isabel. Her eyes, thought Isabel, have that curious quality of *depth*; eyes that drew you in. Unusual, intelligent eyes; a bit like Jamie's, perhaps.

Jane looked away. She had brought to mind what she wanted to remember. "When I was a young girl there was a poem that I loved—something from A. A. Milne." She closed her eyes—the memory of poetry sometimes comes easier if eyes are closed—and recited:

> *If Rabbit were bigger*
> *And stronger than Tigger*
> *Then Tigger's bad habit*
> *Of bouncing at Rabbit*
> *Would matter no longer*
> *If Rabbit were stronger.*

"That is undoubtedly true," said Isabel; and she thought of A. A. Milne and the Hundred Acre Wood and felt, for a moment, rather sad.

"MADE FROM BUFFALO MILK," said Isabel, as they began their Caprese salad.

Jane sliced off a fragment of the soft white mozzarella. "The real thing." She speared the cheese with her fork and popped it into her mouth. "It was kind of you to get in touch. I haven't really got to know many members of the philosophy department at the university yet. I know a few, of course, but I've been put in the Institute—the Humanities place—and it's a bit tucked away. Good for work, of course."

"I remember how I felt in Georgetown," said Isabel. "I was there as a research fellow and it took me months to get to know anybody."

"Well, I appreciate it," said Jane.

Isabel plucked an olive from the small tub at the side of her plate. Olives made her think of Charlie, who was being looked after by Grace while she came out to lunch. Grace never gave him olives, which she did not consider nursery food, and when Charlie shouted "Olive, olive!" she pretended not to hear. Grace had a tendency, Isabel noticed, of not hearing that which she did not wish to hear. It was a very useful talent.

"Tell me about yourself," she said and immediately apologised. "Sorry, that's a rather intimidating thing to say to anybody, rather like saying to a teenager, 'What are your plans?', when we all know they have none."

"I don't mind in the least. In Australia people sometimes say, 'What's your story?' It's an invitation to go on about whatever one wants to go on about."

Isabel liked Australian directness. "So you can tell them your back-story, as the novelists call it, or just tell them what's been happening that day?"

"Exactly."

Isabel thought about this. It was the back-story that was often the more interesting.

"So if I were to ask you about your childhood, say . . ."

Jane put down her fork. Watching her, Isabel saw a shadow pass over the other woman's face, and she thought: I shouldn't have asked. There was some awful sadness, she felt; some disappointment, some loss. I shouldn't have asked.

"I'm sorry," she blustered. "That was rather rude of me. I wasn't thinking. You can't ask people about their childhood, just like that."

Jane shook her head. "It wasn't rude at all. After all, childhood is one of the most interesting things to happen to people in their lives—probably *the* most interesting. Not that children know it . . ."

"Let's just leave it—"

"No. I'd like to talk to you about it. Do you mind?"

"Not in the slightest. But are you sure you want to?"

Jane smiled. "Listen to us. That's another thing I like about Edinburgh. It's so polite. How does anybody ever get through a door? Everybody would be waiting for others to go through first."

"But that happens," exclaimed Isabel. "There are people who have almost perished—yes, *perished*—waiting for others to go through doors. Do you know that there was an afternoon tea dance in Edinburgh not all that long ago when a fire broke out. Everybody was so polite it was half an hour before anybody went through the door of the fire exit. Half an hour! *You first; no, please you go first; no, after you* . . . The fire brigade turned up and they eventually got in—only after the firemen had said a lot of *You go in first with the hose, Bill, please go ahead. No, after you, Jim* . . . and so on."

Jane looked at her in astonishment.

"Oh, I'm not serious," said Isabel. She had been covering her embarrassment, as she often did: she would ask an intrusive question and then, flustered, go off on one of her odd tangents.

Jane smiled. "I like conversations that drift. But childhood . . . well, the point is that's really the reason why I'm in Edinburgh. I was born in Scotland, you see, and I'm very keen to find out something about my childhood. I'm afraid I'm on something of a quest, even if that sounds a bit ominous . . ."

"It's doesn't sound ominous at all," said Isabel. "It sounds intriguing—which is quite different. So, please go ahead. I'm listening."

CHAPTER FOUR

THAT EVENING Isabel and Jamie went to a concert in the Queen's Hall. It was Jamie who had suggested it.

"We hardly ever go to listen to music together," he said. "When we go it's because I'm playing and you're in the audience. It's not the same as going together, is it?"

She realised that what he said was true. She tried not to miss any of his performances in Edinburgh, but she had relatively few memories of sitting next to him and listening to others.

"No. It isn't. In fact, have we been to anything this year—together, that is?"

He looked at her quizzically. Isabel spent a lot of time thinking about other things; perhaps that was why she forgot events that he remembered quite vividly.

"Yes, we have."

She could not remember. "Oh, well. What was it?"

"That concert in aid of Breast Cancer Research. When they did the Tallis. And Byrd too. They had that counter-tenor. Remember? The one from the Academy in Glasgow?"

It came back to her; it had been four months ago, in February. There had been a snowfall and the streets had been filled with slush. She had got her feet wet as they crossed the street in front of the concert venue, and she had spent the first half of the concert in discomfort. And then the singers had sung "Sumer Is Icumen In" and she had forgotten about her cold feet. And "Sumer" had been followed by . . .

She turned to Jamie. "They sang something I liked. You found the words for me afterwards. It was that counter-tenor."

Jamie had a prodigious memory for music and for the words of songs. " 'Thus saith my Cloris bright.' Was that it?"

"Yes it was."

"You liked it, didn't you?"

She asked who could possibly not like it, and he nodded, reciting:

> *Thus saith my Cloris bright*
> *When we of love sit down and talk together*
> *Beware of Love deere*
> *Love is a walking sprite . . .*

She muttered the words, " 'When we of love sit down and talk together.' " She paused. "Is Love really a walking sprite?"

Jamie was not sure exactly what a sprite was. "A spirit?"

No, it was not quite that. A sprite could be a spirit, Isabel said, but it meant something else in this context. A sprite was elusive, a will-o'-the-wisp, something you grasped at, only to find that it had slipped through your fingers. Love was exactly that.

"So we can never really hold on to it?" Jamie asked.

She did not want to say that one could not. That, she felt,

.s defeatist, but love did not last: at least, not in its intoxicating, overwhelming form. You could not love like that for ever—could you?

She became aware that Jamie was watching her.

"There are so many different sorts of love," she said. "And being in love has a lot of meanings. Affection. Tenderness. Infatuation. Obsession. It's as if love were a disease with a whole range of symptoms."

He was still watching her and she looked away. "This concert tonight, what is it?"

He told her the programme, which was contemporary. "A piece by Kevin Volans. Another made popular by the Kronos Quartet. A cello concerto by Sally Beamish. All interesting."

Grace had stayed to look after Charlie, settling herself in front of the television with a disc of a long-running adaptation of Jane Austen and a large packet of pistachio nuts.

"Heaven," she had said. "No need to hurry back."

They took a taxi to the Queen's Hall and had a drink in the bar before the concert began. Isabel felt a curious sense of joy at being with Jamie, unencumbered by responsibilities, with just music to listen to and nothing else. She thought, *I'm very happy, and this is all that I want in life. Just this.* The realisation surprised her—even shocked her. She never would have imagined that she might have such a simple ambition. She had always wanted to make her mark in philosophy, to contribute to the wider world in some way. She never imagined that she would want only to be with a man, to live a day-to-day life with him. She knew that for many people this was their greatest ambition: to have a partner and a child, to live the domestic life, but she had never thought it would be enough for her. Yet it was.

They went through for the beginning of the concert, finding their seats in the third row, behind a man and woman whom Isabel had seen at concerts before but whose names she had never known. The other couple half turned and smiled at them, and then the man whispered to Isabel, "Richard says this is going to be excellent."

Isabel had no idea who Richard was. "Good," she whispered back. "How is he?"

The man shook his head slightly. "He's doing his best, poor man. It can't be easy, though."

"No," said Isabel. "It can't."

The woman now turned to her. Lowering her voice, she said, "It's not his fault. Categorically not."

The musicians entered, and the puzzling conversation came to an end. Jamie glanced at Isabel and mouthed a word of reproach: *Bad!* She lowered her eyes to the programme; she had not been mischievous; she had been polite.

The concert began. She looked up at the ceiling and let the music flow over her. She was thinking of what Jane had said to her at lunch that day. Her story had not been all that exceptional—there must be numerous people in her position—but it had been told in a way that had engaged Isabel from the start. Now, as she listened to the tones of the cello, she imagined the sadness that such a story entailed. Our tenancy of this world is brief: we come from nothing and go into nothing. In that brief moment that is our life, how disappointing it must be not to know who you are.

In the interval, she said to Jamie, "I don't want to go back into the bar. Can't we sit here together?"

He looked at her with concern. "That's fine. Are you feeling all right?"

She reassured him that she was fine, but wanted just to be with him.

Jamie commented on what they had heard. "That cellist, Peter Gregson, plays wonderfully. He was at the Edinburgh Academy, you know, when I was teaching there. We knew that he would do great things. I love his playing."

"We don't always expect people we know to do anything great, do we? Fame is something that happens to somebody else."

He slipped his hand into hers. "You'll do great things, Isabel. Charlie, too."

She returned the pressure of his hand. His skin was so smooth, so flawless—and he had given that to his son too. "Of course Charlie will. I've never doubted it. The only question is what field will he excel in—which Nobel Prize he'll win."

Jamie knew. "Medicine or peace," he said. "The two best things you can do. Heal people. Stop them fighting."

Isabel wanted to tell him about her day. "You know Cat arranged for me to have lunch with somebody she met? An Australian philosopher."

Jamie nodded. "You mentioned it. How did it go?"

"She told me her story."

Jamie gazed at her expectantly. "Oh yes? Anything interesting?"

"Well, yes. Very. It was—"

Jamie took hold of Isabel's wrist. "Hold on. Is this leading to—"

"I can't ignore her."

He sighed. "Isabel—" He broke off. "All right. Carry on. You can't help yourself, can you? So you may as well carry on."

She looked injured, and he apologised. "I'm sorry. I know that you do this out of a sense of duty. And I suppose that I'm secretly rather proud of you and everything you do. I wouldn't want you to be selfish. It's just that . . ."

"This is nothing risky. It really isn't."

Jamie was about to say more, but the musicians were returning to the platform. "Tell me later," he whispered.

THEY LAY IN BED TOGETHER, covered only by a sheet, as it was June and the evening was warm. It was dark, but not completely so; a chink in the curtains allowed moonlight in, an attenuated silver glow like the light cast by an old and failing projector.

There were shadows: the towering bulk of the wardrobe that had belonged to Isabel's parents, with its twenty drawers and its capacious hanging spaces; the dresser, with its half-length mirror on mahogany spindles, that in the darkness looked like some unlikely legged creature, the mirror its staring face; the chair on which Jamie carelessly threw his clothes; the lumpy chaise-longue at the end of the bed that had been described at auction as having belonged to the late Duke of Argyll—*removed from his castle*, claimed the saleroom note—as if the late duke had said petulantly, *I want that thing out; I want it removed from my castle.* And who could blame him; it was a most uncomfortable piece of furniture, but Isabel, who felt sorry for things abandoned, both animate and inanimate, had decided to give it a home, as a place on which to put clothes, or packets, or books—anything really. It had attracted the sympathy of Charlie, too, who loved to jump off the end of the bed and on to the chaise, before rolling off the edge to the carpeted floor. He would do that time and time again, proud of the endlessly fascinating game he had invented.

Jamie had his hands tucked under his head as Isabel spoke. She lay on her side, facing him, their knees just touching.

"So her mother was a student in Edinburgh. When was that?"

"Forty years ago. Jane told me she celebrated her fortieth birthday in Melbourne just before she came over here."

"And?"

The mother, Isabel explained, studied French. She was called Clara Scott and was the daughter of a doctor and his wife who lived just outside St. Andrews. She was their only child. She went off to university and while she was there— in her second year—had an affair and became pregnant. They were Catholic, and so understandably the pregnancy went ahead and she gave birth to Jane. Apparently they sent her to some place run by nuns in Glasgow for her to have the baby. They sent her away."

"That's what they did then," said Jamie. "It was worse in Ireland, where they bundled them off to special homes. Some of those girls stayed there for the rest of their lives."

"Shameful things happened in Scotland, too," said Isabel. "Let's not get superior. Just because we had a Reformation—"

"And Ireland? What about what's going on now?"

Isabel thought: Yes, that is exactly what has happened in Ireland. A twenty-first-century reformation, only almost five centuries late. It had happened so quickly and so drastically, with the exposure of clerical arrogance and downright cruelty. But nothing had been put in its place: no spiritual renewal—

just puzzlement and distress, an emptiness, the void that goes with believing in nothing other than the material.

And the humiliation of those who meant well, perhaps, was never edifying; all those officials of the old Soviet Union who had done their jobs conscientiously for a lifetime, who had believed that they were doing the right thing, only to discover that—together with the loss of their pension—everything they believed in was suddenly meaningless and actively despised; all those members of Irish teaching orders who had devoted their lives to others, only to find that they were public pariahs because of the abuses of a minority, embarrassed now to wear the cloth of their office.

Was all social change like that: indifferent to individual innocence? Public judgment was rarely finely nuanced; there was no inquiry into the subtleties of a person's position. There had no doubt been good men among the German forces that goose-stepped across Western Europe; good men were prob-·ably among those who pulled triggers, men who had been conscripted and who had no real choice. Yet a uniform makes complicit all those who don it, voluntarily or otherwise. It could not be otherwise because, Isabel realised, life, and its moral assessments, were crude affairs. She might not want it to be so, but that was how it was.

Yet she would never accept things as they were. That was what made her do what she did—practise philosophy—and what made her, and everybody else who thought about the world and its unkindnesses, do battle for understanding, for sympathy, for love; in small ways, perhaps, but ways that cumulatively made a difference.

"She had the baby," Isabel went on. "It was a girl, who was

given up for adoption through a Catholic agency. That baby was Jane."

Jamie was silent for a moment. "Go on."

"Do you know a book called *Empty Cradles*?" she asked. "I've got a copy somewhere. I read it a few years ago."

"No."

"It's by a social worker who lived in Nottingham. She had quite a few people coming from Australia to try to trace their families. As children they had been sent abroad by something called the child migration movement. They came from working-class homes and were thought to have better prospects abroad— or were children who had been in care—and the parents were persuaded to give them up, or they were simply taken away. Lots of people were uprooted and grew up in Australia in the belief that they were orphans. But they weren't. They had been lied to."

"Imagine," muttered Jamie. "Imagine if somebody came and sent Charlie off to Australia. Told him we didn't exist, or what-ever. Imagine."

"No. I can't imagine that."

She could, though, and saw herself, for a moment, standing and looking at a photograph, imagined its being all she had left of her little boy. The greatest pain conceivable, she thought: the loss of a child. Irreparable. A gaping wound in one's world.

"This social worker," Isabel continued, "made it her busi-ness to help these people. She traced their families and they found in some cases that they were not orphans at all. They also found siblings—brothers and sisters who had been left behind in Britain. Think of how emotional that must have been—relatives reunited after decades. What a discovery."

"Jane was one of these?"

"Not quite the same," said Isabel. "She wasn't sent out as an unaccompanied baby, so to speak. She was placed with a Scottish couple who were about to emigrate. The adoption went through just before they were due to leave. He was a plumber, apparently, and she was a nurse. They took her off to Australia and that was that. They brought her up well enough, but they divorced when she was in her final year at high school. She said that the divorce had a curious effect. She had been told that she was adopted and somehow the fact of the divorce changed her feelings for her adoptive parents. She said that relations were cordial enough, but she rather lost touch with them. Both remarried, and somehow the feeling of being a family disappeared as the lives of each began to revolve around the new partner. And neither of these new partners really knew her, or was much interested in getting to know her. She described it as a fading away rather than a rupture."

"Strange."

"It can happen, I suppose. She said that it didn't really worry her too much. They both moved away with their new partners—the father to Hobart, the mother to somewhere in New South Wales. Jane stayed in Melbourne, with a spell at the Australian National University in Canberra and a couple of years as a visiting professor abroad—somewhere in the United States. Rice in Houston, I think she said."

Jamie was listening attentively. He shifted his legs slightly. "Sorry. Carry on."

"She came up for a sabbatical—she's on it at the moment. She decided to come to Edinburgh because she's working on moral sentiments in the Scottish philosophers—Hume and

Adam Smith—and so she thought this would be the place. But she said that it was only when she arrived that she realised that her choice might have been subconsciously motivated by what she knew of her past. She had been conceived in Scotland— this was where she started. That's how she put it to me."

"Understandable enough," said Jamie. "Salmon go back to the exact bit of water where they were spawned. Maybe people want to do that too. It's getting in touch with one's inner fish."

She nudged him playfully. "Do you want me to go on?"

"Yes, of course. It's just the idea of an inner fish . . . We all emerged from the primeval slime, didn't we? Aeons ago?"

"So we're told. Frankly, I'm not sure if *all* of us did, but there we are."

"It's a sobering thought," said Jamie. "It cuts us down to size."

Isabel agreed. It was difficult to see how human pretension, human pride, could survive the knowledge of our fishy past. Professor Lettuce, that great, pompous son of a fish . . . She laughed.

"What?"

"I was thinking of Professor Lettuce as the descendant of a fish. It was very *helpful*." She paused. "I'm sorry. I'm being infantile. It's because the lights are off. If we had a light on, I'd be grown up."

Jamie reached across and touched her cheek. "No, I like it when you talk nonsense. Not that it's real nonsense, it's more . . . fantasy. Or speculation, maybe. You think these things—these curious things come into your mind—and then you just say them. I love it. Listening to you is like reading an amazing book."

There was no reply she could make to that, and so she continued with Jane's story.

Jane knew that she was entitled to trace her biological parents, but had never really felt the need. Not until recently, she had said. Perhaps it had something to do with becoming forty. That was a bit of a watershed, she felt, and perhaps what made her go to an organisation once she arrived here in Edinburgh. It was a charity that put adopted children in touch with their biological parents—and vice versa.

"If both sides want it?" Jamie asked.

"Yes. Children have the right to find out the identity of their natural parents, but the parents can refuse to see them, of course, if they don't want to make contact."

"Some parents want to, though, don't they?"

"Oh yes. Many feel a strong sense of loss, and guilt too. And Jane said something else very interesting. She said that up until after the time she was adopted, many adoptions weren't really freely undertaken. Young women were coerced. They were told that the only option open to them, if they went ahead with the pregnancy, was to have the baby adopted. Apparently this happened a lot. Now we know about it and there are people trying to get the fact acknowledged—a bit late, I suppose.

"Jane said that she started to think about this once she had plucked up the courage to find out about herself, after her arrival in Edinburgh. Imagine coming to a strange city all by yourself and having to deal with this. Anyway, she went to the charity and they helped her. Then, to her astonishment, a few days after they had advised her on how to get access to her birth certificate and to see the court adoption record, she had a telephone call from a woman who worked for the charity. She said that they had something for her, but that they felt it was best that she should come in and get it personally, rather than talking about it on the phone.

"She went, with a lot of trepidation. She had not been nervous before, but now she was. She wondered whether they had found out the whereabouts of her mother—would she perhaps even be there, waiting for her? But it wasn't that. It was a letter.

"One of the things that this charity does, apparently, is hold letters from people who have given children up for adoption. They hold them in case the child should ever come and ask for information. Then they hand over the letter. Apparently they have a lot of them—requests for forgiveness, I imagine. Letters of explanation too: why they did it."

Jamie was quite still beside her. She heard his breathing. He was listening.

"The letter was handwritten and dated years ago, when Jane would have been about five or six. Jane showed it to me. It was very short. It said something like: 'I am your mother and I always will be. I want you to know that I love you and I think of you every day.' That was it—just a few lines.

"Jane said that she wept and wept when she read it, and I could see that this was true: the ink was smudged."

"It gave no details?" asked Jamie. "No address?"

"Nothing. She was shortly to get her mother's name, of course. She was about to go to Register House and see the birth certificate. That told her that her mother was called Clara Scott; occupation: student. And it gave her parental address. There was no father's name, but at least she had an address for the grandparents at the time of her birth."

"She found them?"

"No. This is where it all goes cold, I'm afraid. She went up to St. Andrews and located the house. The people living there had some information for her: they had bought it from the executors of a Dr. Scott, who had died ten years ago. His widow was alive, but was in a home. She suffered from advanced Alzheimer's, they told her, and she had no idea of where she was or even of who she was. There was absolutely no point in going to see her.

"And as for Jane's mother, these people said that they'd heard she had been killed in a road accident years ago, when Jane would have been about eight. So that was the end of her family. It was very disappointing for her."

Jamie moved his arms. "Numb. My arms were getting numb. But she had a father. What about him?"

"She has no idea who he is. None at all." Isabel paused. "She asked me whether I could help her find out about him. She hasn't any idea how to start—she's in a strange city and doesn't know a soul, apart from me and Cat."

"Then you must help her," said Jamie. "You have to."

Isabel had not expected this. "You normally complain if I get involved in other people's affairs—"

"Not this time."

She was curious. "May I ask why?"

"Because I've decided to try to see things through your eyes," he said. "I try to think of—what is it you call it?—moral proximity. And once I do that, I realise that you have no alternative, Isabel. You have to help this woman."

She said nothing, but reached out and put her arms about him, under the sheet. She moved closer. She felt his breath upon her shoulder, his hair against her skin. I have so much, she thought; I have so much, and Jane, it seems, has so little, although that, she saw, was an assumption that was both unsupported by fact and condescending in its implications. Jane was not to be pitied: why should she be? She was an attractive woman who had an enviable job; the fact that she appeared to have no boyfriend or husband was neither here nor there; for all Isabel knew, she might want none. And if she did not know who she was, that was true only in one sense; in every other sense, Isabel thought it likely that Jane knew exactly who she was.

Yet she would still help Jane because she had asked her to do so, and that, for Isabel, was grounds enough. *Ask and ye shall receive.* Yes. But then there was the line that followed, or came soon afterwards: *Or if he ask a fish, will he give him a serpent?*

Isabel was feeling drowsy. "Some knowledge is a fish," she muttered. "Some is a serpent."

Jamie, half asleep too, grunted. She was talking about fish. Was she still on evolution? Fish, he thought. Fish. And then his mind became pleasantly blank and soporific, but aware of the weight of her arm across his naked chest, of the closeness and completeness of their being together in this most intimate of retreats, their bed, their human nest.

CHAPTER FIVE

THE NEXT DAY, a Sunday, passed in contented idleness, but by Monday Isabel could no longer put off attending to the pile of papers that had been growing steadily on her desk. It seemed to be by osmosis, as if the papers were washed up by some tide that lapped across the floor. Of course it was Grace, and her co-conspirator, the postman, who were responsible; Grace took pleasure in receiving large piles of mail from the postman and drawing Isabel's attention to just how many letters there were.

Isabel spent the first part of Monday morning going through submissions for the journal. Her refusal to read on-screen was the subject of mutterings, but subdued ones: as she was the editor, the boot was on Isabel's foot, and though she was careful not to abuse the power that her editorial role gave her, she was adamant that she needed hard copy to give a paper its due.

The issue of editorial power was a sensitive one. Professor Lettuce had shown her how not to conduct herself as an editor. As chairman of the *Review* before Isabel's successful putsch, he had frequently interfered with her editorial discretion and continued to do so, on occasion going so far as to reject articles that authors had mistakenly submitted to him rather than to the editor.

"I take it that you don't object to my saving you the effort," he had recently written in a note to Isabel. "A few articles have ended up in my in-tray and I've sent most of them back. People will insist on sending stuff to me because they see my name at the top of the editorial board list. Anyway, I rather like one of these papers, and have accepted it for publication. I'll send it on to you in due course."

There were procedures for this, and he had ignored them. And the article that he had unilaterally accepted—to Isabel's open-mouthed astonishment—was by a young post-doctoral student, Max Lettuce.

"This Max Lettuce," she wrote back. "Forgive my asking, but is he any connection? It's an unusual name, and I just wondered."

She had wanted to write *It's a ridiculous name* but had stopped herself.

"As it happens," Lettuce replied, "Max Lettuce is my nephew. He took a very good degree at Oxford and is now a post-doctoral fellow in my own department. His work is quite exceptional, as you will see from the paper he submitted. Indeed, we are fortunate to have it."

The paper was not exceptional in any way.

Isabel wrote again:

Dear Professor Lettuce,

How fortunate your nephew is to have you for an uncle! And how good of you to support his endeavours in this way. Many people would be concerned that others might think them guilty of nepotism; *nepos*, as you'll know, of course, translates so very neatly into *nephew*! You, however, have shown that such base imputations should in no way influence the decision as to what should be published or should go unpublished. I really take my hat off to you for resisting any such considerations and for seeking out good and meritorious work even in the efforts of your own family.

But she did not post the letter: there was no point. Lettuce would never change, would never accept that he had acted wrongly. And Max Lettuce, for all Isabel knew, was blameless, no doubt believing that his achievements—the post-doctoral fellowship and the acceptance for publication—were no more than his due.

And there was another reason: sarcasm could be fun, but Isabel felt that it should be a private vice, not one practised in public. It was like swearing: a private expletive, muttered in anger or irritation, could be cathartic and was harmless, unless it reached the point of corrupting the attitude of the person who uttered it; public swearing drew others into one's circle of anger at the world, exposed them to one's antipathy or rage, and invited them to share both it and the view of the world it reflected. That was a different matter altogether.

The morning passed quickly. Jamie, who was at home that day, was going to collect Charlie from playgroup, leaving Isabel free until such time as she chose to break for lunch. By twelve the pile of papers was considerably diminished, even if many of them had been given only a cursory initial glance in anticipation of fuller attention later on.

Several letters had been typed on the word processor and printed out for signature, and a crucial contract with the *Review*'s printers had been read and signed. Printing charges were going up, and sooner or later the cost of subscriptions would have to be raised. She knew what this meant, though: cash-strapped academic libraries, which formed the bulk of the subscribers, would have to consider whether they could afford the new charges. Some would cancel; others would cancel other journals to allow the *Review* to be continued.

It was economic pain of the sort that the politicians had been warning everybody about. Nobody was immune: not even the remote groves of academe in which enterprises like the *Review of Applied Ethics* flourished—or tried to flourish.

Isabel sighed. She would pay the difference out of her own funds if it came to that—she was fortunate enough to have the money, even if the principal source of it, the funds left her by her sainted American mother, were feeling the pinch.

"There is always fat," Peter Stevenson had once said to her. "There is always something that can be trimmed."

Yes, thought Isabel, and for a brief irreverent moment imagined Professor Lettuce, who was considerably overweight, having a diet imposed on him. "There must be cuts," they would say, "and, alas, your waistline has been identified as a suitable target." Not as fanciful as it appeared: she had read somewhere of a very overweight Polynesian monarch—the last king of Fiji, she seemed to recall, who had decided to go on a diet—and had proceeded to put the whole nation on a compulsory diet at the same time. That had happened and quite recently.

Thoughts of money reminded her of the note she had scribbled a couple of days ago. It was still there on her desk, where she had left it. *West of Scotland Turbines*. She picked it up, examined it, and then put it down again. What if the medium were right? What if West of Scotland Turbines was indeed about to do well; and what if she bought a holding in it and then, when the shares went up in value, sold them and . . . and used the money to offset the impact of the increased printers' bills for the *Review*? That would mean that she could avoid any raising of the subscription, and if the shares did *really* well, then she could actually lower the subscription price. Great would be the rejoicing, then, in those struggling university libraries. A *reduced subscription!* The news would spread like wildfire, texted from one librarian to another, from one threatened philosopher to another facing the same fiscal axe. Beacons would be lit on hills to convey the good tidings . . .

She reached for the small blue-bound book in which she kept telephone numbers. Gareth Howlett, who managed her investments for her, was at his desk. His arrangement with her was not to bother her with day-to-day decisions, but to manage things quietly in the background, following a set of ground rules they had established at the outset. No shares in tobacco companies; no shares in fast-food companies; no shares in arms concerns; no shares in the empires of a small list of press barons—a position that Gareth cheerfully described as "broadly ethical."

"Good shares can do just as well as bad shares," said Gareth. "Often they do better. Virtue, you see, has its rewards, Isabel."

Although she left most of the decisions to Gareth, occasionally she contacted him with a particular request. She had suggested an investment in a small company that made disposable syringes—she had read about them in the *Scotsman* and had approved. She had also bought shares in a company floated by a friend—not a good investment, as it turned out—but one that loyalty at least dictated.

"West of Scotland Turbines?" Gareth asked. "Those people over in Paisley?"

"I'm not sure where they are," said Isabel. "But Paisley sounds about right. They make . . . well, I believe they make turbines for hydroelectric schemes."

"Indeed they do," said Gareth. "As it happens, I know the company slightly. They're small—listed on the alternative market rather than the main exchange. We've been looking at their shares. Solid enough, I think, but nothing spectacular." He paused as he typed details into his computer. "In fact, Isabel, I would say that they were rather dull for you. You've always gone for slightly quirkier things—those disposable syringe people, for instance. West of Scotland Turbines is an engineering company. They . . . well, they make turbines. I've actually seen pictures of their products in one of their brochures. Big metal boxes. The water comes in a pipe and goes out another. The turbine is the bit in between."

Isabel listened as Gareth went on to discuss the price-to-earnings ratio of the turbine shares—he had brought the details up on his screen and had the figures at his fingertips.

"They're priced round about right, I would have thought, which fits with what I said before: nothing special, solid; a reasonable choice if you're feeling conservative."

"As opposed to feeling reckless? Risky?"

Gareth laughed. "I can't imagine you feeling reckless. It doesn't quite fit with being a philosopher."

"I'm quite capable of throwing caution to the winds," said

Isabel. "It makes such an exhilarating sound, when you toss caution into the wind. It's a sort of whooshing . . ."

"Isabel? Are you all right?"

"Sorry. Just speculating."

"Well, speculation is something I don't really recommend—when discussing investments. If you're on the lookout, I can come up with a much more interesting option. We had a meeting here the other day—my colleagues and I—and we talked about a company that runs cruise liners. Somebody has come up with a formula to track the relationship between obesity levels and the profitability of cruise lines. Apparently the heavier people get, the better cruise lines do. Interesting."

Isabel laughed. "These are dark arts you practise, Gareth."

Gareth responded that dark sounded better than the sobriquet normally given to economics—dismal—and the conversation returned to West of Scotland Turbines.

"You'd like me to put some of your funds into them? Are you sure?"

"Everybody needs electricity," said Isabel. "And hydroelectricity is as green as it gets."

Gareth agreed. "Well, there's no real reason for me to advise you against it, and so I'll go ahead. How much?"

A brief discussion ensued. Isabel found it awkward to talk figures: she had not asked for all this money, she felt, and she had no intention of letting it dictate the course of her life. She could give it away, of course, but . . .

And there she recognised the contradictions in her position. She did not like to think that she needed the money, but she did. She had the house to maintain. She had to pay Grace. She had all the expenses connected with Charlie—the playgroup charged fees; her green Swedish car would need major surgery, she had been told—possibly a new transmission. There were taxes to pay, insurance, local rates: the list seemed endless. So although she gave generously to a number of causes—Scottish Opera, in particular—she had to keep *something*.

They decided on one hundred thousand pounds, and the telephone conversation came to an end. Rising from her desk, Isabel crossed the room to stare out of the window. She asked herself what she had done. It was absurd, even shameful. She—who had often criticised speculators who played with the currencies and assets of others, those manipulators who did not think for a moment of the victims of their economic games, those financially concupiscent bankers who rewarded themselves with immense bonuses—had behaved exactly the way they did: shifting money about with a view to a quick profit. Shame on you, she muttered. Shame on you.

JAMIE BROUGHT CHARLIE HOME shortly after twelve. The little boy ran into Isabel's study—or tottered, as his running was still a headlong, almost uncontrolled projection—launching himself into her arms.

"And what happened this morning?" she asked, kissing him as she spoke.

He grimaced and wiped his cheek; she could imagine him thinking, *I'm not a baby!* but not yet having the words to express the thought. Boys grew away from their mothers, she understood—but did it start this early? Small boys needed love and cuddles; there would be time enough to be masculine, and lonely, later on.

Charlie seized one of the bulldog clips that Isabel kept on her desk and set about forcing it open. The spring was initially unyielding, and his little fingers were barely up to the task, but he succeeded eventually, fastening it to Isabel's blouse—much to his amusement.

Standing behind Charlie, Jamie signalled to Isabel. "We need to talk," he whispered, adding: "out of range of juvenile ears."

Distracting Charlie with a piece of paper and a red pencil, she rose to her feet and joined Jamie at the doorway of the study. Charlie seemed indifferent to the presence of his parents; a red pencil, applied with force to a blank sheet of paper, was far more interesting.

"What is it?"

Her first thought was of head lice. Every so often a note would come back from the playgroup informing parents that there had been a case of head lice—lice letters went with the territory of being the parent of a small child, people said, and it was no reflection on hygiene: the letters always stressed that clean hair was more attractive to lice. Of course they did not say *whose* hair was affected, much as some parents would have relished getting that information—provided it was not their child, of course. There should be no shame, and yet inevitably there was; one did not advertise the fact that one's child was lousy, in the same way as people did not talk about their colonoscopies or haemorrhoid surgery. In general we love to share our medical conditions with our friends—but not all medical conditions.

Jamie read her mind. "No, it's not lice," he said, his voice lowered. "It's swearing."

Isabel gave a start. "Swearing? Charlie's been swearing?"

Jamie nodded. He was trying his best to be serious, but there was a smile playing about his lips. "Mrs. What's-her-face at the playgroup—the other one, the helper—she said—"

"Mrs. Macfie."

"Yes, her. She drew me aside and told me that Charlie had used what she described as 'a very bad word.' She said it had surprised her and she thought that perhaps she had misheard. But then he said it again. He was grabbing some toy from one of the other children and he uttered this unspeakable word."

Isabel's eyebrows shot up. "Good heavens. Do you have any idea what the word was?"

"I asked her, actually, and she blushed to the roots of her hair. She said it was unnecessary for her to repeat it but she could write it down for me. Which she did. Here's the piece of paper."

He reached into his pocket and took out a folded piece of paper. At the top of the paper was the name of the playgroup and its address: *Little Sunbeams Playgroup, Merchiston.* And underneath was written a word in common usage among builders, soldiers, teenagers and novelists.

"Where on earth did he learn that?" asked Isabel. "You haven't been . . . No, of course not."

Jamie never used even mildly scatological language. He just did not. Neither did Isabel.

"Not me," said Jamie. "Maybe I've *thought* it on occasion; who hasn't? But—"

"The Pope?" interjected Isabel.

"The Pope?"

"You asked: Who doesn't occasionally, even *very* occasionally, *think* such words? I said: the Pope."

"You'd be surprised," retorted Jamie. "Presumably the air turns blue in the Vatican when things get really difficult." He smiled wryly. "Well, perhaps not . . . But whatever the Pope does or does not say, I don't really use language like that, especially around Charlie."

Isabel thought for a moment. "Grace?"

Jamie shook his head. "She doesn't use strong language. It's highly unlikely it was her."

"Then he must have picked it up from one of the other children. Maybe it was . . ."

They both reached the identical conclusion at the same time.

"Algy," said Isabel.

Jamie nodded his agreement. Algy was Charlie's special friend at playgroup—or as close to a special friend that children of that age will have. Friendships at that stage in life are notoriously fickle, and friends will be readily jettisoned over the smallest of things. Algy and Charlie, though, appeared to get on well and their friendship had survived several disputes and the throwing of sand from the sandbox.

"It must be him," said Isabel. "His mother is an actress."

Jamie burst out laughing, causing Charlie to look up with interest.

Isabel smiled sheepishly. "I know it sounds a bit odd, but she swears like a trooper. I've heard her. I assume it's fashionable in acting circles. Or, if not fashionable, at least completely normal."

"So what do we do?"

"Ignore it," said Isabel. "If we tell him not to use that word, then he'll realise that it gives him some power over us. He'll use it all the time."

Jamie thought that this made sense. "But what would people have done in the past?"

"Washed his mouth out with soap, perhaps," said Isabel. "Punished him."

Jamie shook his head. "So we leave it, then?"

"For the time being, yes," said Isabel. "Then, if he uses words like that a bit later on, we can talk to him about it. We can tell him that people don't like to hear that sort of thing."

"Of course, once he's a bit bigger we could stop it in its tracks," said Jamie. "If we told him that if he used that language he'd be struck by lightning or something else pretty severe would happen. His teddy bear would die perhaps. That would work. One hundred per cent certain."

She knew he was joking. "Unwise," she said drily. "Imagine what it would do to his little psyche."

Jamie remembered something. "People used to do that sort of thing. They frightened children. It's just that I'm recalling how when I was a young boy I was eventually cured of . . . Well, I'm a bit embarrassed to say this: fiddling around in public with my hand in my pocket. Small boys do it all the time, you may have noticed. My mother told me it would drop off. I stopped immediately."

Isabel made a sympathetic face. "Oh, Jamie, how awful! Exactly what a mother should not say to her son. Your psychosexual development—"

"I'm still a bit worried about it," he said, with mock concern.

"So you should be," said Isabel, smiling.

Jamie returned to the question of what to do. "Should we have a word with Algy's mother?"

Isabel considered this, and decided not to. "I should hate to seem prudish," she said. "She's very trendy. And we don't really have any proof, do we?" She paused. "I've had an idea. Why don't I say to her that we've heard that Charlie has been using inappropriate words and that we thought we should apologise to her if he's done so in Algy's hearing. We could say that we wanted to warn her that it might come up because we knew that she would be shocked to hear Algy saying anything like that, as he obviously wouldn't come across such words in his own home. We'd get her to think about it—but do so tactfully."

"Brilliant," said Jamie. "As ever."

But then Isabel thought: No, ordinary human issues were not solved by ingenious schemes; in most cases, inaction was the solution, as it was here. Charlie would forget what he had said: he had thousands of new words to learn as he explored the world about him. He would hear things he did not understand, and things she did not want him to understand yet; but for the moment, he should not be lumbered with guilt. There would be quite enough guilt in the future; being human, we all had our share, except for those who never felt guilty about anything because they had no idea why they should. They are a special case, thought Isabel, and I shall get to them later on.

CHAPTER SIX

WE ALL REMEMBER different things, don't we?" Isabel said. "I may remember one thing and you may remember something else altogether. Even if we were both in the same place at the same time."

She was walking across the Meadows with Jane. The morning, having started with a cool breeze off the North Sea, was beginning to warm up as the wind shifted its direction. Now it was from the south-west, a more favourable quarter, and the clouds that had obscured the sun earlier had rapidly dispersed. Isabel had left the house wearing a lightweight raincoat, which she now carried slung over her arm. Beside her, Jane had removed her sweater to reveal a fawn-coloured linen blouse that left her arms bare. Isabel thought this optimistic; the wind could swing back to the east and the temperature could drop, Scottish weather being almost entirely unpredictable and quite capable of producing four seasons in the space of an hour—or even less.

She made the remark about memory because that was what they were now embarking upon: a reconstruction of the past. When Isabel had offered to help Jane to trace her parents, she had not anticipated quite so enthusiastic a response: Jane had not only been effusive in her thanks, but had suggested they start immediately. This had inspired Isabel who, for all her frequent resolutions not to get involved in matters that did not concern her, actually enjoyed the business of intermeddling.

And why not? she said to herself. Of course, helping somebody else, being virtuous, should be its own reward, but it undeniably brought satisfaction in so many other ways. Most of all, it gave the pleasure of discovery—an intellectual pleasure that naturally appealed to the philosopher in Isabel. And not just to the philosopher: within each of us, she felt, there was also an inner Sherlock Holmes, just as there was an inner Sigmund Freud, and an inner . . . She paused. An inner Napoleon?

She had suggested to Jane that she might wish to be involved in the inquiry—though she pointed out that to call it an inquiry rather overstated the case; all she could offer was to use her knowledge of Edinburgh and its ways to piece together such facts as could be unearthed forty years on.

"This isn't exactly recent history," she warned. "Forty years is, well, forty years. People forget. We can't be sure that anybody will now know what you want to find out."

Jane had assured her that she understood and accepted this, but Isabel had her doubts. It seemed to her that, having declined in the past to seek out this information, the other woman was now feeling both impatient and unduly hopeful; hence the precautionary discussion of memory as they made their way across the park separating the Old Town of Edinburgh and its curtilage from the towering stone terraces of Marchmont and beyond.

"Of course you're right," said Jane. "I suppose memory's selective because we have to have a reason to remember something. If we don't have a reason, then the mind doesn't record the memory properly. That's how memory works, isn't it?"

Isabel nodded. She had several books on the philosophical implications of memory and had actually read them, but was struggling to recall exactly what they said. There had been something about memory of dreams . . . Yes, that was it: there was an explanation for why dreams were so hard to hold on to.

"That's precisely why our memory for dreams is so short term," said Isabel. "We remember them for the first few minutes after waking up, and then they go. You must have experienced that. We know dreams aren't worth remembering because they're stories that never happened."

"But they did happen," said Jane. "In one sense a dream is an event; it's something that happened to you, if you see what I mean. The fact of having that particular experience—the thing that happens in your dream—is an event, and a significant one at that."

Isabel frowned. A dog ran across the path in front of them, chasing a ball thrown by its owner. Dogs dreamed, did they not? You saw them sleeping on the floor, their legs twitching in an arrested, stationary run. Yet dogs, by the nature of the doggy mind—and doggy consciousness was a very obscure matter—had no concept of dreaming. The experiences they had in their dream, then, must be absolutely real to them, if they remembered anything on waking up. And how would one be able to tell that? Perhaps by observation: one could watch the dog as it woke, and see whether it looked about as if to locate whatever it had been pursuing in the dream—a rabbit, perhaps, or a cat. If a dog looked for a rabbit, then it must have thought the rabbit was there. One did not have to be a philosopher to work *that* out.

She tore herself away from speculations on canine thought processes and returned to what Jane had just said. Yes, of course dreams were significant because they told us a great deal about what was going on within the subconscious mind; if one forgot everything else that Freud had said, then that, at least, would remain. But did the bundle of responses and strategies within us that dictated the reactive behaviour of the organism—did *it* know that dreams were important and should be remembered? She considered not.

Thoughts of memory prompted actual recollections.

"There's something I've just remembered," Jane said. "You said that our memories alight on different things, sometimes rather arbitrarily. Well, I just remembered a colleague, years ago when I was teaching at Macquarie, who held the most extraordinary grudge. He had lent a tent to another colleague who wanted to go camping up in Queensland. Apparently it was a rather good tent, and it proved to be pretty useful to the person who borrowed it. He had mistimed his trip a bit, and he hit the beginning of the rainy season up north. We call it the wet. Anyway, the tent came in useful, but got pretty soaked."

"I went camping as a girl," said Isabel. "It rained every time."

Scottish rain, she knew, had nothing on the Australian *wet*, but it could sometimes seem like that, particularly in the western Highlands. The whole *point* of those Highlands, some said, was to block the clouds coming in off the Atlantic and make them declare their water—which they obligingly did, sometimes for days on end.

"Well, you may know," Jane continued, "that you have to be careful to dry a tent. This man didn't. He left it folded up when it was still damp and then he handed it back. When the owner opened it to repack it, he found that it had turned mouldy."

"Inconsiderate of his friend."

"Yes. My colleague was furious. *And he never forgot.* He mentioned it for the next twenty years. Often."

"Unfinished business," said Isabel and added, "That tent needed closure."

Jane threw a sideways glance at Isabel.

"In a manner of speaking," Isabel said hurriedly. "Closure has become a bit of a cliché, don't you find? Everybody talks about wanting closure. The concept of closure, perhaps, needs closure."

They were now nearing the point where Jawbone Walk joined Middle Meadow Walk; it was a spot that for some reason seemed popular with dogs and their owners, as natural a meeting place, perhaps, as the *agora* had been in Athens.

Isabel spotted a couple of dog owners deep in conversation while their dogs, waiting patiently at their feet, glared at one another in mute suspicion. Behind them, on the newly mown turf—the sweet smell of freshly cut grass still lingered—a small group of students sat in a circle while one, holding a book, read aloud. The boys were bare-chested, their skin pale in the morning sunlight, the girls with midriffs exposed. One of the girls, she noticed, had a tattoo worked around her navel—a Celtic design, it seemed; all whirls and whorls.

Isabel tried to make out the title of the book from which the boy was reading, but failed. *The* something. *The Prophet* by Kahlil Gibran? They were the right age, she thought; we should all read *The Prophet* before we became too cynical, too jaded to be impressed. Charlie would read *The Prophet* one day, and have a poster of Che Guevara on his wall—if anybody remembered Che Guevara by then.

She touched Jane's forearm lightly and nodded in the direction of the students. "Look," she said. "I expect your mother might have sat right there in her day, just like them."

Jane glanced at them and smiled. "You know something?" she said. "Ever since I came to Edinburgh, I've had the feeling that I'm close to her. I know that it's probably no more than auto-suggestion, but I really do feel it."

They chose the path off to the right, which took them to the southern edge of George Square. Here was a row of old stables, now used as store rooms, and behind them a cobbled road to the one remaining Georgian side of the square. Isabel and Jane did not follow this, but made their way round the back of the University Library, to Buccleuch Place and the premises of the university accommodation service. A discreet blue notice advertised the presence of this office. Most of the buildings in the street belonged to the university and were used for smaller academic departments, the occasional student flat and supporting elements in the academic bureaucracy.

"I know somebody here," said Isabel, as they climbed the narrow stone staircase to the third floor. "In fact, she's a very distant relative on my father's side. A third cousin, or something like that. She's worked here for at least twenty years and is more or less the institutional memory."

A corridor ran off the landing, and beyond that a small internal hall dominated by a large noticeboard. The hall gave on to three offices, one labelled *Assistant Director*, one *Accounts*, and one bearing the simple legend, *Miss Hodge*.

Isabel approached Miss Hodge's door and knocked loudly. A voice within invited her to enter.

"Isabel! And . . ."

Isabel introduced Jane to her cousin, Katrina, a slender, rather concise woman somewhere in her late forties.

"Jane is with us from Melbourne. She's at the Humanities Institute."

Katrina smiled warmly. "Melbourne," she said. "I went there three years ago. I watched the tennis—the Australian Open."

"Katrina is a keen tennis player," explained Isabel. "Almost played for Scotland."

"A hundred years ago," said Katrina. "And not all that almost. Almost almost, I'd say." She invited them to sit down. "When you phoned me, you didn't tell me exactly what it was you wanted to know."

Isabel apologised. "I thought it best to explain in person," she said. "It's rather complicated, but Jane is trying to trace her mother, who's no longer alive. No, that sounds a bit odd. She's trying to find out about her mother so that she can trace her father. That's right, isn't it, Jane?"

Jane nodded her confirmation. "I was born here in Edinburgh," she said. "I was adopted and taken to Australia. I know my biological mother's name and I know that she died when I was about eight. I have no idea of who my father was, but he was probably a student at the same time as my mother."

There was a note in Jane's voice that made Isabel take over the explanation: a note of strained emotion.

"If we could find people who knew Jane's mother," she said, "then we might be able to get further information about—"

"About her boyfriend of the time," said Jane simply. "Her lover—my father."

Katrina nodded sympathetically. "Do you know when your mother started her studies here?"

Jane did and gave the date. "It was 1968. I was born in 1970."

Katrina smiled. "Heady days. The student revolution in Paris. *Sous les pavés* . . .Under the cobblestones . . ."

"The beach," supplied Isabel. "Which meant liberty, I suppose."

"Exactly," said Katrina. "Edinburgh was on the sidelines of all that, and the *pavés* remained in place, I gather."

"We don't do outrage quite as convincingly as the French," said Isabel.

Katrina smiled as she turned to Jane. "Do you have your mother's full name?"

"Yes. Clara Harriet Scott. She came from St. Andrews. She enrolled to read History."

Katrina rose to her feet. "We have the records of everybody we accommodated in that and every other year, going back to 1961. Before that, I believe the files have been scrapped. A pity, I think, for historians and so on. Or for people like you, I suppose." She paused, and looked at Jane enquiringly. "If you're interested in everybody admitted to the university in a particular year, perhaps the best way of checking up on that is the General Council lists. Graduates become members of the General Council—all the names are there. I can give you a copy for the year you're interested in."

"I'd like that," said Isabel. "But it won't tell me where they lived, will it?"

Katrina shook her head. "No. If you want to find out where they lived your best bet is to look in our records. If they lived in university accommodation we'll have a record of where it was."

"And of who else lived there?" asked Isabel. "Which is a way into their lives, so to speak."

Katrina thought about that. "Yes, that's true, I suppose. Students move in packs. They tend to make close friendships with the people they share things with—including accommodation. So yes, those lists could help build up some sort of picture. They're in the records room, if you'd like to come with me."

Jane glanced at Isabel, who could see the hope in her companion's eyes.

"Don't count on anything just yet," she warned. "Your mother may not have been in university accommodation."

"There's a very good chance she was," said Katrina as she led them out of the room and back into the hall. "The university tries to accommodate first-year students. Then they tend to make their own arrangements for their second year and beyond."

She led them back down the corridor. On the other side of the corridor was a locked door, somewhat in need of a coat of paint, thought Isabel. Katrina took a bundle of keys out of her jacket pocket and opened the door.

The room beyond was in darkness, which she dispelled with the flick of a light switch. It was also dusty, the air stale.

"Sorry about this place," said Katrina. "We hardly ever come in here; that's why it looks so neglected. But the records themselves are in very good order. Everything's in exactly the right place."

They found a large section of shelf marked *1968*.

"Now," said Katrina, extracting a sheaf of papers from a box-file, "this shows which students were in university accommodation for all or part of that year. There are separate lists for our various forms of accommodation. This is for the Pollock Halls, for example." She extracted a number of papers that had been stapled together. "Here's S." She ran her eye down the piece of paper. "No Scotts, I'm afraid. So let's take a look at some of our smaller student halls."

Several further lists were consulted without success. Then, holding a much smaller list—a single page of typed names—she pointed to a name.

"Clara Scott," she said. "Here she is. Masson Hall."

Jane reached forward to take the paper. Isabel watched as she examined it; she saw the expression on her face and said to herself: I have done the right thing.

"That's about all we can show you," said Katrina. "You might be able to get academic results if you go to the Registry. Take evidence of the relationship and . . ." She looked apologetic. "Take your mother's death certificate."

Isabel took the list from Jane and addressed Katrina. "Could we photocopy this?"

Katrina looked doubtful. "I'm not sure . . ."

"There's nothing personal in it. It just shows who was there at the time, and that would have been public knowledge. The entrance of Masson Hall would have had a list of residents displayed." She paused. "And it was a long time ago."

Katrina reluctantly agreed. "I suppose so," she said, retrieving the list from Isabel. "We can do it in my office."

WHEN ISABEL AND JANE left Buccleuch Place, the sky had darkened slightly, but the clouds were high and unthreatening. The Institute where Jane was based was only a few yards away in Hope Park Square, a hidden eighteenth-century courtyard, and Jane suggested that they go there for a cup of tea.

The Institute occupied a three-storey stone building that had once been a private house before being converted to offices.

Isabel had always loved the domestic scale of the building and had imagined the Institute's fellows sitting with one another in the common room and enlightening one another with great thoughts. It was not actually like that, she knew; academics as a group thought about the same things as anybody else: what to have for dinner, how to make ends meet, what chances of promotion they—or, more to the point, their rivals—had.

While Jane put on the kettle, Isabel looked out of the window. Below her in the courtyard, a tree, in full summer leaf, was playing host to a couple of thrushes. One of these was on the topmost branch, close enough, Isabel thought, to be touched if one leaned out far enough. The bird was unaware of Isabel's presence and preened itself unself-consciously, puffing up its speckled chest feathers and grooming them with quick movements of its beak. *You use that to kill snails, don't you?* Isabel thought. It was one of the few facts she knew about thrushes: that they killed snails by holding them in their beaks and dashing them against stones.

The bird suddenly stopped its ministrations and looked up at the sky. It was as if it knew it was being watched, the bright eyes seeking out danger, in quick darts of appraisal, before suddenly its throat swelled as it burst into song. The notes were sharp and sweet, a trill and its answer, both repeated. For a second or two after it finished its roll, the bird sang again.

Isabel stood quite still, entranced by the tiny concert performance the thrush had given her. She wanted it to see her now, for it to know that it had been heard, but something on the ground had disturbed it, and it launched itself into flight, closely followed by its companion.

Isabel turned round to see Jane standing in the doorway, watching her.

"There were a couple of thrushes in the tree out there," she said. "One sang."

Jane, holding a mug of tea in each hand, stepped forward. "I watch them too," she said. "Sometimes I watch them for hours. Well, not for hours, I suppose, but for quite some time."

She held out one of the mugs to Isabel, who took it from her and blew across its top to cool it down.

Isabel looked into her mug of tea. "There's a line in Auden about thrushes," she said. "It's in his poem about streams. Maybe you know it."

Jane shook her head.

Isabel continued, "He has a dream in which he finds himself 'in a calm enclosure with thrushes popular.' It's a haunting line, don't you think? A calm enclosure with thrushes popular—that's what your courtyard is."

Jane smiled. "Of course it is. And now that's the way I'll think of it from now on. 'With thrushes popular' . . . yes."

They sat down. There were just two chairs in the room, which had a spartan feel to it—like the room of a scholarly monk: two standard-issue university chairs that had seen better days, a desk, a bookcase. On the wall the only decoration was a print of Allan Ramsay's portrait of David Hume. Jane noticed that Isabel was looking at this.

"Yes, I put that there myself. The good David. I brought that with me all the way from Melbourne. I find that it helps me to have him there when I'm wrestling with some aspect of his writing; it's as if he's, well, somehow encouraging me."

"I've always thought it a fine painting," said Isabel. "It's as if he's amused by something. It's very human."

"Amused by humanity, I imagine," said Jane. "It's a kind face, though, isn't it?"

Isabel nodded. Jane had put the list down on the table and she wanted to examine it. She reached across and picked it up.

"What are you expecting from this?" Jane asked.

Isabel looked up. "From these names? I want to find somebody who knew your mother in her university days, somebody we could talk to."

She returned to her perusal of the list of residents of Masson Hall.

"And here, for example, is one I recognise." She tapped the page. "She—this person here—was a friend of my mother."

"Then we can—"

"Unfortunately she's no longer with us," Isabel interjected. "Breast cancer. She had two young children. It was very sad."

She scanned the list again, watched anxiously by Jane, whose eyes she now met. "Good," she said simply. "Very good."

Jane raised an enquiring eyebrow. "A name you know?"

"Yes," said Isabel. "It's exactly what I was hoping for. There was one Catherine Succoth. See, here she is. She lived in Masson Hall at the same time as your mother."

"And you know how to get in touch with her?"

Isabel nodded. "I know her slightly. We were both on a committee and overlapped for a while." She paused. "I haven't seen her for a year or so, but I've read about her in the newspapers. She's a judge. She presided over a big trial recently—it was all over the front page of the *Scotsman*."

After her earlier disappointment, Jane was beginning to look animated again. "Can we talk to her?"

Isabel hesitated for a moment. "I don't see why not," she said. "But don't get your hopes up too much. The odds are, of course, that she would have known your mother as there were only—what?—thirty women living in Masson Hall. Everyone would have known everyone else, at least by sight." Isabel became more cautious. "But that might be the extent of it. She may have known her only slightly and may have nothing useful to offer us."

Isabel finished her tea, then explained to Jane that she would contact Catherine Succoth and ask whether she would see her. Would Jane care to accompany her when they met?

Jane weighed the invitation. "Do you mind if I don't? This is rather eating into my time and unsettling me. If you wouldn't mind . . ."

Isabel assured her that she was quite happy to see the judge by herself. And, no, Jane should not feel that she was imposing.

"I hope that I'll be able to do something for you sometime," Jane said. "I'm very obligated to you."

It was a slightly clumsy way of putting it, thought Isabel: obligated. It put her in mind of chains, for some reason: heavy chains of obligation. But that was not the way it had to be: obligations could be strangely liberating, light things, a matter of gossamer, as could bonds of love. There was a song about it, she thought; a song about how the people we must carry are not really heavy. It had been a long time since she had heard that sung: it had been during her student days, on a trip to Canada, six glorious weeks of long warm days and sultry nights; a cabin in Ontario, a lake, the smell of barbecued trout; sitting on the deck watching the reflection of the trees on the water; a blond Canadian boy with a guitar; her whole life in front of her. It had been another world.

She left Jane and went out into the courtyard. As she passed the tree *with thrushes popular*, she looked up into the branches, hoping to catch a glimpse of the bird she had seen earlier. There was a movement in the branches, and then stillness; she did not think it was a thrush.

She walked home. The students she and Jane had seen sitting on the grass were still there, the same boy reading from the same book. Isabel slowed down as she passed them, hoping to see the cover sufficiently clearly to satisfy her curiosity as to whether it was *The Prophet*. One of the students gazed back quizzically, and Isabel hurried on her way. But as she made off, she heard the voice of the boy who had been reading aloud, " 'But what is it to die but to stand naked in the wind . . .' "

She smiled to herself. Gibran, she thought, just as I suspected. Such mystical wishful thinking, but beautifully put, as mystical wishful thinking so often is.

CHAPTER SEVEN

ISABEL **WALKED DOWN** Dundas Street the following morning, with the hills of Fife clear in the distance across the Forth. There was a breeze, but not an unfriendly one, and the sky was high and cloudless, a colour that her mother had called "singing blue."

At the junction with Northumberland Street, she turned to the right and began to look at the numbers on the doors. She was in the heart of the New Town, and the stone terraces had all the features of classic Georgian architecture: perfectly proportioned windows, neat astragals, the whole effect being of harmony and pared-down elegance. Judges had to live somewhere—as everyone did—and this, Isabel thought, was a very fitting place for a judge to live: reserved, dignified, understated.

She had phoned Catherine Succoth the previous evening. The judge had seemed a bit guarded when Isabel first spoke to her, but her tone became warmer once she established that Isabel was not contacting her about a professional matter.

"I'm sorry," she said. "But I must ask you whether this is anything to do with the law. I don't want to be unhelpful, but in my position I can't really discuss legal affairs. It's one of the consequences of being a judge—one has to withdraw, so to speak."

"It's nothing like that. It's . . . well, it's about somebody you might have known years ago—in your student days. Clara Scott."

There was a brief silence at the other end of the line. Then, "I remember her. My goodness, that was ages ago. Clara Scott. Yes. Masson Hall."

Isabel could not conceal her pleasure. "I'm delighted you remember her. Could we meet?"

"Of course," said Catherine. Then there was a pause. "I take it that you're aware that she died some years ago? A car accident."

"I know that. But there's something I need to ask you about."

"Come round," said Catherine. "Tomorrow? I'm not in court, so you could catch me in Northumberland Street. Eleven-ish?"

Now, at a few minutes after eleven, Isabel found herself outside a dark-blue doorway on which was fixed the house number in brass Roman numerals. To the right of the door, on the stone architrave, on a discreet brass plate, the size of a playing card, was inscribed *Mr. Rankeillor, Advocate*. The brass plaque had weathered but its inscription was still perfectly legible. This was the Advocates' Quarter, the traditional territory of the members of the Faculty of Advocates, the Scottish Bar, and such brass plates were common up and down its streets. Mr. Rankeillor, Advocate . . . Why not *Miss Succoth, Advocate*, which is what Catherine would have been before she became a judge?

Isabel looked again. There were four neatly filled holes in

the stonework directly below the Rankeillor plate; there had been a second plate, and it had been removed, or fallen off.

She reached for the bell, a large old-fashioned button surrounded by a generous square, also of brass, well polished this time. She pushed it, and it was as if the act of pushing released a memory within. It all came back: the name Alastair Rankeillor had been familiar, and now she remembered.

Of course, it was *that* Alastair, the Alastair who had been a well-known lawyer with a reputation as a philanderer. He had been almost irresistible to women and had taken full advantage of that, leaving a long trail of disappointed girlfriends behind him—as well as a queue of husbands to take issue with him over his seduction of their wives. But there had been one woman to whom he had always returned—one woman who tolerated his bad behaviour and was always prepared to take him back. And, of course, that woman was Catherine Succoth—of course it was: Isabel remembered Roddy Martine telling her about it. Roddy knew all the secrets of Scottish society, and had held Catherine up as an example of female toleration of the waywardness of men.

"It's pretty impressive, isn't it?" he had said. "I could give you a long list, Isabel, of women who have shown the patience of saints—and the same capacity to forgive. Catherine Succoth did this. Forgave him and forgave him. However . . ."

Roddy looked pained.

"However what?"

"However, he eventually brought the affair to an end—after all those years he upped sticks and went off to the British Virgin Islands, where he is today, senior partner in an offshore firm of lawyers, I believe, and doing very nicely. New woman with him, naturally. The widow of a shipping line, you might say. He must be getting close to retiring—at least from the law."

"He must be around that age."

"Yes, but I don't think Lotharios retire from active service in the other department, so to speak. I think they carry on having affairs until they drop." Roddy shrugged. "The injustice of this world, Isabel. Cads, as they used to be called, do very well. They thrive. They live happily ever after. It's enough to make one want to believe in the place below, where they'd get a good roasting for their efforts. It would make the rest of us feel so much better, wouldn't it?"

She pressed the bell and waited. Alastair Rankeillor. She had met him, or at least had him pointed out to her at parties. He was good-looking, certainly, but was he really irresistible to women? Was anybody *completely* irresistible?

Catherine Succoth was, as Isabel's father would have put it, well preserved. Although in her early sixties, she could have passed for a decade or so younger; her hair colour, a light auburn, looking quite natural, and her skin retaining that smoothness that goes with a life spent away from the sun—the skin that comes from living in Iceland, or Finland, or northern Scotland for that matter. She was, by any standards, a handsome woman, with an animated, intelligent look to her that made it easy for Isabel to understand why Alastair Rankeillor, who by all accounts had to fight women off, had remained with her—in his way—for years.

Her greeting was friendly, but with a slight note of reserve. Isabel thought this was normal: the judge belonged to a generation, and a social circle, that was not effusive. There was none of the frostiness, though, that one might have expected from somebody of an even earlier generation, a coldness expressed in the hoary saying that Edinburgh invitations always implied: *you'll have had your tea.*

Catherine led Isabel up the staircase that ascended in a curve from the hall to the floor above. Two open doors gave off the landing, through one of which there was a glimpse of a formal drawing room: an ornate gilt-framed mirror above an Adam fireplace; a sofa and sofa table: altogether an air of quiet comfort. And through the other door was a study; Catherine indicated that they should go in there.

"More comfortable," she said, "and there's a pot of freshly brewed tea, as it happens."

Isabel looked about the study, a smaller room than the drawing room and facing south towards the back of Heriot Row. On one wall there were several pictures, all expressing exactly the taste that Isabel would have expected: a nineteenth-century watercolour of the Falls of Clyde; a Thorburn, or Thorburn-ish study, of grouse in flight; several framed plates from Kay's *Edinburgh Portraits*. There was no photograph of Alastair Rankeillor, but of course there would not be: this was a judge's study, not the bedroom of a lovesick teenager. And yet, thought Isabel, that's what we all are at heart: love-struck teenagers. And every so often the love-struck teenager within emerged to remind us that love is quite as capable of turning our world upside down as it ever was.

The opposite wall was completely taken up by shelves, right up to the ceiling, and they were packed with books, including a long run of green-bound volumes of the *Scots Law Times*. Isabel remembered those so well from her father's library; as a bored teenager she had occasionally paged through them, trying to find interesting nuggets hidden among the arid wastes of legislative news, legal wrangles and obfuscations. There was nothing for a girl there, although she had liked the divorce cases, with their mildly titillating details and, on occasion, their raw explicitness.

She was also amused by the reports from the Court of the Lord Lyon, with their discussions of obscure points of genealogy and heraldry.

"Does anybody actually *worry* about that sort of thing?" she had asked her father, and he had smiled before replying enigmatically, "You will."

Catherine offered Isabel a chair before seating herself on the other side of a small library table. She poured her a cup of tea from a small china pot on the table, then passed it to her.

"You wanted to speak to me about Clara Scott?" she said.

Isabel noticed that the judge wasted no time in getting to the point. The visit, she thought, was not going to develop into a social one; there had been no discussion of the weather, no small talk about the irritations of the interminable work on the city's new tramlines.

"Yes," said Isabel. "I've been contacted by an Australian relative of Clara's who wants to find out about her."

Isabel had decided that she could not reveal the exact nature of the enquiry. She and Jane had not discussed the extent to which Jane wanted her quest to remain private—perhaps they should have done—and she felt that it was best not to disclose everything. To say that she was making an enquiry on behalf of an Australian relative was perfectly true, even if it did not reveal exactly what lay behind it.

The judge did not press for more information. "I told you that Clara and I were in Masson Hall together, didn't I?"

"Yes, you said that over the phone. That's how I knew to come to you. I knew you were contemporaries."

Catherine nodded. "We both spent our first year at university there," she said. "We were not exactly neighbours in our corridor—I was at one end, and she was at the other. But we were pretty close, at least for that year. It was an exciting time, obviously. Everything was so fresh, so challenging. To be eighteen again!"

"And to know, at eighteen, what one knows now."

The judge smiled. "Of course. It seems to me that's a very common fantasy. Most of us think about that, I believe. But to get back to Clara: we were both at Masson Hall for our first year and then, at the beginning of our second year, I went off to share a flat with a couple of other law students. It was in Newington, not far from the Dick Vet. Clara chose to share with a couple of others—another girl who was studying History, and an American student called Emma. The American girl came from San Francisco, or one of those places just outside. She was on a junior year abroad scheme and had picked Edinburgh. She was as happy as a sandboy, as I recall, and not surprisingly; Clara's flat was in the Cowgate—a wonderful atmospheric set-up. *La Bohème* all over. Blackfriars Street. Number twenty-four. I always remember that. Number twenty-four Blackfriars Street."

"That sounds like the student days of all of us," mused Isabel. "Whenever they were."

Catherine looked doubtful. "Do you think so? Do today's students live that sort of life?"

"Probably," said Isabel. "Students are still poor. They still spend a lot of time in bars or at parties."

"Maybe . . . Of course we knew that we'd get jobs at the end of it all. They don't have that luxury today. It never crossed our minds that we wouldn't get the sort of job we thought we deserved. Nowadays they're lucky if they find something that stretches them at all or uses their degree. I suppose it's difficult to be carefree if that's hanging over you."

Catherine paused. There was an air of coming to the point. "What exactly would you like to know about Clara?"

Isabel took a sip of her tea. "She had a boyfriend, I believe."

Catherine did not answer immediately, which made Isabel wonder whether she had heard the question. "Her boyfriend?" she repeated.

There was a further slight hesitation; nothing too marked, but noticeable. Perhaps she thinks this is intrusive, thought Isabel; an enquiry into her friend's sex life; perhaps she's wondering what business it is of mine.

The judge broke the silence. "Yes. There was a boyfriend. She was a very attractive young woman. The boys were interested. Distinctly so."

"Anybody in particular?" asked Isabel gently.

"A boy called Rory Cameron. They met in her second year, or started going out together then—I seem to remember Rory being around in our first year too, but he wasn't attached to anybody. He was doing a degree in Classics, which I thought was a little bit odd, as he didn't strike me as being the type. He was a good sportsman, you see—he played rugby for the university and he was in the men's hockey team too. But there was a very charismatic, well-regarded lecturer in Classics in those days— a man called Francis Cairns. He popularised the subject and everybody appreciated his lectures. I went to one of them myself and rather regretted that I wasn't one of his students."

"What happened to him?"

"To Francis Cairns? He moved to Liverpool, I think. He got

a chair there and then he ended up at a university in Florida, I believe. He wrote a lot. That's all I know."

Isabel's question had been about Rory Cameron, as Catherine now realised.

"Oh, Rory? He was on an army cadetship at university and he went to Sandhurst when he graduated. He was in one of the Highland regiments, I think—not the Black Watch, but one of the others. I saw him years later at the Skye Ball in his full dress kilt. He cut a dash even then. A kilt helps if a man has lost his looks—mind you, he hadn't."

The Skye Ball: Isabel knew people who went to that, but had never been herself. It was not her milieu—the world of Highland society and the more fashionable end of military, and it would definitely not suit Jamie. But unlike some, she did not begrudge socialites their enjoyment. Harmlessness was the test of the acceptability of fun, and spending an evening on the island of Skye dancing Highland reels until four in the morning struck her as being clearly and convincingly on the harmless side.

Catherine continued, "I heard that he left the army. Somebody told me that he didn't like it much, that he got stuck. He got as far as being a major, though, and then he threw it in and took up a post as the secretary of a golf club somewhere near Gullane or North Berwick. Not Muirfield, but one of the others. And that was the last I heard of him."

"He married?"

"Yes. I don't know much about her, other than that she was the daughter of a farmer in Northern Ireland somewhere. She was sporty too. A horsewoman, I think, but I'm not absolutely sure."

She paused. "You seem very interested in Rory. Does this

Australian relative of Clara's actually want to meet these people from Clara's life?"

Something in the tone of Catherine's question—a slight edge to it—made Isabel feel wary; again she wondered whether it was resentment of the intrusion. She did not want to lie to the other woman; she would not do that.

She chose her words carefully. "Yes, she might."

"I wonder why?" asked Catherine. She asked the question quietly, but for a few moments it hung in the air ominously.

"Curiosity about family past," said Isabel. "People want to know about family—and sometimes speaking to friends is the only way of finding out."

Every word of what I have said is true, thought Isabel: every word.

Catherine seemed satisfied with the answer. "Yes, that's quite understandable."

"One thing, though," said Isabel. "Clara left university towards the end of her second year. What happened? Do you know?"

"She took a year out," said Catherine. "She must have had some private reason: her own affair. She came back and completed her degree, of course—she didn't throw the whole thing over. Then, of course, there was that awful road accident. That was only five years after she graduated. A terrible waste."

Isabel was on the point of asking Catherine whether she knew what the private reason was, but there was something in the judge's choice of words that inhibited her. *Her own affair.* That was code for: keep away from this.

There was a final question to ask.

"Were there any other boyfriends?" Isabel said. "Was it just Rory Cameron, or were there others, do you think?"

Catherine did not hesitate. "No, just him. There was nobody else."

Isabel finished her tea and quickly glanced at her watch. "I've taken up enough of your time," she said.

Catherine rose to her feet. "I don't know whether what I've said is of any help," she said as she accompanied Isabel downstairs. "I do hope that your Australian friend feels that she can now fill in the gaps in the family history."

Isabel said that she shared this hope, but as she replied she found herself thinking that Catherine Succoth did not really hope this; that she was indifferent to the quest of this relative and, furthermore, that she was not convinced of the existence of this person from Australia. Judges, Isabel remembered, develop an uncanny ability to tell when somebody is lying or, and perhaps more significantly, telling only half the truth.

Isabel went out into the street, the dark blue door closing behind her. She felt vaguely ashamed of herself, as if she had gained access to another's house by false pretences, and then abused the hospitality she had been shown. It would have been better, she felt, to have told Catherine Succoth exactly why she had come and exactly what Jane wanted. That's what a true Kantian would have done; she, by contrast, had behaved in a way that would not for a moment have troubled the most superficial relativist.

She had walked only a few paces down the street when she turned round and made her way back, decisively, to the doorway she had just left. She rang the bell, firmly, and waited.

"Oh," said Catherine Succoth, as she answered the door. "Have you left something behind?"

"I did not tell you the whole truth," said Isabel. "I am very sorry about that and I apologise."

If the judge was surprised, she did not show it.

Isabel swallowed hard. "My friend from Melbourne, Jane Cooper, is Clara's daughter. She was adopted, taken to Australia, and now she wants to find out about her father. That is why I came to see you."

For a moment Catherine did not respond, and Isabel, holding her gaze, looked into astute, unblinking eyes.

When Catherine spoke, her tone was measured, the few words chosen carefully. "I assumed that," she said quietly.

It took Isabel a few moments to absorb what Catherine had said. It made it far worse, she felt; the other woman had been sitting there throughout their encounter, knowing that Isabel was concealing something.

"I really am very sorry," said Isabel. "I felt that I could not reveal what Jane had told me. I wasn't sure whether she wanted anybody to know."

Catherine seemed to assess this, as she might weigh a defence to an indictment. This, thought Isabel, must be what it's like to be in the dock of a criminal court: to be judged by a rational and dispassionate mind, one that would not be easily misled, nor unduly lenient.

"I see."

"It's a strong desire," Isabel went on. "This desire to know who you are is terribly powerful. I'm only doing this to help her."

It was not much of an excuse, she thought, but it was at least the truth.

"Of course. That's good of you." The judge looked at her watch. "Look," she said. "I appreciate your frankness, and I really don't hold it against you. You were being discreet—which is nothing to reproach yourself for, given that everybody seems compelled to be transparent, so to speak, to the point that . . . well, to the point that nothing remains private any more. So please don't worry." There was another glance at the watch. "But I really must get back to work—I'm in court tomorrow and I have to write something up."

Isabel took a step back as they said goodbye. She felt that her apology had been accepted, but there was something else in Catherine's manner that suggested the door closing behind her was metaphorical as well as real. And who can blame her? she thought, as she began to walk back down Northumberland Street.

CHAPTER EIGHT

JAMIE COOKED DINNER that evening while Isabel read a bedtime story to Charlie. Like most young children, Charlie was conservative in his reading habits, demanding the same book time and time again, and impatiently rejecting any attempt to introduce new fare. Only when a book had collapsed through overuse or had been mislaid—deliberately or otherwise—would he allow something new. Until then, the same text had to be repeated *ad nauseam*, on its young audience's insistence, to the point that Charlie knew every word of the narrative and would protest loudly at the omission of any sentence or paragraph.

The current enthusiasm was a once-suppressed book about a small boy who is stalked by a tribe of frightening tigers. The boy's name, and his description, may not have caused its original Victorian readership to cringe; but a modern reader—at least, one sensitive to stereotype and condescension—might do just that. The story, though, was enough of a classic to remain in print, and was vastly appreciated by Charlie, to whom it was simply a story of a little boy in bright clothes who turns tigers (which is what he called the neighbourhood cats) into butter by making them chase their tails round a palm tree. Tigers, Isabel explained, were rather different from the cats they saw in the street; to which Charlie had solemnly replied, "Cats," and nodded.

After the tigers had turned to butter for the third time, Charlie dropped off to sleep and Isabel was able to join Jamie in the kitchen downstairs.

"White wine, please," she said, in mock desperation. "And please don't mention either tigers or butter."

Jamie had been and was smearing a layer of butter on sliced potatoes in a dish—the beginnings of his potatoes dauphinoise. "I won't," he said, showing her the buttery knife.

Isabel shuddered. "I know it's a classic, but I really have had enough. And it's so full of . . . well, every sort of assumption that we don't want people to make. We're laying them down in Charlie's young mind. Who gave him that book?"

"Cat. She said she'd enjoyed it as a child."

Isabel thought for a moment. Charlie had addressed Cat as "Tiger" the other day, and she had wondered why. It was so obvious, now that she came to think of it.

"Oh well," she said. "There's plenty of that stuff ahead of him. And we can't change—and shouldn't, I suppose—things and books that . . . just were."

"Same with music," said Jamie. "We play what was written, not what we think composers should have written."

"But would you play something with really unpleasant associations? Music can be like that, can't it?"

Jamie laid down his buttery knife. "Perhaps," he mused. "Some people believe that Wagner's tainted. There used to be a tacit agreement in Israel that he wouldn't be played there—and still is, I think, even though Barenboim played Wagner in Jerusalem."

"I can understand how people feel," said Isabel. "And some don't like to listen to *Carmina Burana* for much the same reason. It was wildly popular in Nazi Germany, after all. But it's also pretty vulgar, isn't it?"

She looked at Jamie, expecting a challenge. The concept of the vulgar was not one that everybody accepted any more. And yet some things were vulgar: there was just no other word for them. The houses of overpaid football players sprang to mind in that regard; large jacuzzis; cheap eateries with brightly coloured plastic furniture . . .

Jamie picked up his knife and licked it.

"Don't do that," protested Isabel. "We can hardly stop Charlie from doing it if he sees you. And there's the cholesterol. Not good for you."

He put the knife down again, almost absent-mindedly. "I was thinking about Orff," he said, as if it were an explanation for licking the knife. "I like *Carmina Burana*. That wailing swan. The drums. The sheer viscerality of it." He paused. "Can you say *viscerality*?"

"If you wish," said Isabel. "If you say it with conviction. That's how neologisms get going. Somebody uses a word with conviction. Or shall I say *convictionness*." She remembered the words she had invented as a girl, and smiled. "I don't like to boast, but I came up with some really good words when I was just a little bit older than Charlie. Or so my parents told me. *Hashoo. Oshlies. Gummers.*"

"*Hashoo*? A sneeze?"

She shook her head. "No, a saxophone. I couldn't say saxo-

phone, apparently, and so it became *hashoo*, which is beautifully onomatopoeic, don't you think? *Oshlies* is orange juice—
another good word, if you ask me—and *gummers* are the pads
on a cat's feet. And what else could they be but *gummers*?"

"Delectable words," said Jamie. "I'll use them all. We'll
teach them to Charlie. *Hashoo* in particular: that's definitely
what it is."

"But he might not be able to say *hashoo*," Isabel suggested.
"And then he might say *saxophone* for *hashoo*."

"And if he can't say *gummers* he would have to say—"

"There is no other word for that," Isabel interjected, then
remembered a story. "Your saying that's what it is reminds me,"
she began. "It's a story of English assumptions. Would you like
to hear it?" She did not wait for Jamie to reply before she continued, "An Englishman was reflecting on the different words
that people use for fish. 'Isn't it strange,' he said, 'that the
French say *le poisson*, the Spanish say *el pescado*, and the
English call it *fish*—which is what it is.' "

They both laughed. Jamie, who had been struggling with
the corkscrew while Isabel told this story, succeeded in getting
the cork out of the bottle, and poured wine for Isabel.

"Here," he said, passing her the glass. "New Zealand white
wine. Sauvignon blanc—which is what it is."

The chill of the wine made the glass cold to the touch. She
felt the tiny drops of condensation against her fingers. We forget, she thought inconsequentially, how *wet* air is.

"I suppose we'll have to give it some consideration," she
said.

Jamie returned to his cooking. "Give what?"

"What Charlie reads. It's just such a notion: that there's a little mind there, and we have the power to shape it. That amounts to . . . to making a person, I suppose. What power! And should we try to make him in our image? To think like us? To like the things we like?"

"That's what parents do," said Jamie. "Who doesn't? Children can't choose their own culture—they're born into something."

Isabel saw that this was true; of course it was. "But we can be aware of the sort of message that they're getting, can't we? And this is put across quite subtly in children's literature."

"Maybe."

"No, it is. I'm not one of those hyper-sensitive censors you hear about, but when you look at it, it's there, and you can make out a case. *Babar the Elephant,* for example. It really is crammed full of imperialist notions. Celesteville is a French provincial city inserted into the middle of Africa. And that's not the only bit of aggressive cultural imposition: the elephants, remember, are made to wear Western clothes. And as for Tintin, our friendly boy detective is a really nasty piece of work."

"Surely not," said Jamie. "I rather like Tintin . . . And Captain Haddock. All that whisky and colourful language. He was clearly meant to be Scottish."

"Have you ever read *Tintin in the Congo*?" Isabel asked. "You Tintin enthusiasts pretend that that book doesn't exist, but it does. Tintin shoots whole herds of antelope and his reaction to a rhinoceros, be it noted, is to drill a hole in its back and stuff it full of explosive. And then there's *Huckleberry Finn,* while we're about it, not to mention the entire oeuvre of Enid Blyton."

"Oh well," said Jamie. "Children have to read something."

"They do. And I don't think that we should run around

removing things from Enid Blyton. The fact that Noddy and Big Ears sleep in the same bed, for example."

Jamie thought it ridiculous to worry about something like that. "Of course they did. They were friends."

"But not exactly contemporaries," ventured Isabel.

"Possibly not," said Jamie.

They fell silent for a while. Isabel sipped her wine and thought of her morning; she had not told Jamie about her visit to Catherine Succoth and was not sure whether she wanted to do so. She still felt a pang at the thought of those final moments of the encounter on the judge's doorstep and her admission and apology. Social embarrassment was like that: the memory of some faux pas or gaucherie, of some bit of bad behaviour on our part, brings a sinking feeling later, makes us think, *Was that really us? Did we do that?*

The words came back to her from the general confession of the Book of Common Prayer, on the subject of sins and transgressions: *The memory of them is grievous unto us.* Yes, it was. *The memory of them is grievous unto us.*

Jamie, who had finished his potatoes dauphinoise, was making a mushroom tart. He looked up from his task of chopping the mushrooms. "What did you do today?"

She hesitated, unsure that potatoes dauphinoise went with a tart. But she addressed his question. "I think I found Jane's father. But I must admit I felt a bit bad about the way I did it. I misled somebody."

He did not seem interested in the misleading. "You found him? Already?"

She explained about her conversation with Catherine. "She came up with the name of the boyfriend. Rory Cameron. He became an army officer and ended up as the secretary of a golf club."

"Could be worse," said Jamie. "Jane could have found a father who did something terrible. If she gets the secretary of a golf club, well, it could be far worse."

"Are you being sarcastic? Are you laughing at secretaries of golf clubs?"

He was not. It was, he said, a respectable thing to be. And there was nothing wrong with respectability.

"Have you told her?" he asked.

Isabel had thought about this. She had considered telephoning Jane straightaway, but she had decided against it. All that she had so far was the information that Rory Cameron had been Clara's boyfriend in her second year at university—the year in which she became pregnant. But she did not know how long they had been together. For all she knew, they might have been seeing one another only for a month or two, maybe less. She needed more information, and she needed to find out whether Jane would like to approach him herself or whether she wanted Isabel to speak to him first. An intermediary could be helpful where there was a chance of being rebuffed, and Isabel imagined that there was always a chance of that in cases like this.

"I'll have to talk to her about it," she said. "I'm going to tell her that I have a candidate—if that's the right word. And then we'll see."

"I LIKE YOUR MUSHROOM TART. Delicious. Really delicious."

"Not the usual mushrooms," said Jamie. "I get fed up with

those white button ones you see in supermarkets. I wanted something more unusual."

Isabel manoeuvred a bite of the tart on to her fork and popped it in her mouth. "Chanterelles? Oyster mushrooms? Is that what these are?"

"More exotic than that," said Jamie. "You can get those in the big stores now. They're almost as common as button mushrooms. No, I got these from Cat's. She had a whole box of hand-gathered country mushrooms. All sorts and sizes. I forget what these ones were called."

Isabel swallowed. "All sorts? Really? Who picked them, I wonder?"

"She said it was a friend of hers."

Isabel cut another slice of the tart, but hesitated before putting it in her mouth. She laid down her fork.

"Which friend? Did she say?"

Jamie shrugged. "No. Some person who lives near Perth, who also supplies her with quail eggs. She didn't give the name."

Isabel lifted her fork tentatively. "I hope the friend knew what she was doing."

She stared at the mushroom tart. No, it was ridiculous to worry about that sort of thing: Cat took food safety seriously, surely she would never sell anything at all dubious. She must have been confident in her friend's ability to tell edible mushrooms from deadly fungus.

She put a further slice into her mouth and chewed ruminatively. Everything tasted fine.

"Of course the problem with poisonous mushrooms," Jamie went on, "is that they taste so good. Apparently you can munch your way happily through a whole plateful of death's cap mushrooms and comment on how delicious they are—even as they're doing their dreadful work inside you."

The rhythm of Isabel's chewing slowed down. "Really? Didn't Pope Clement VII die from eating that particular mushroom?"

"Who knows?" said Jamie. "If you suddenly found out that you've eaten the wrong thing, apparently there's very little you can do. You may feel perfectly all right but you're destined for kidney failure. And that can take some time to show itself. You just have to wait. It must be like swallowing a time bomb."

"Oh yes?" She laid down her fork again.

Jamie grinned. "Perhaps I've been a bit tactless."

Isabel tried to smile. "No, not at all—I'm sure that your mushroom tart is perfectly safe." She gave a nervous laugh. "Cat wouldn't want to poison us for any reason, would she?"

It was Jamie's turn to lay down his fork. "Cat?"

Isabel answered her own question. "No motive. None at all."

But she knew that this was not true. Cat had shown considerable animosity towards Isabel after she had gone off with Jamie, who was, after all, Cat's ex-boyfriend. Jealousy lay behind many poisonings, she suspected. And what better way of disposing of anybody than to poison them with mushrooms? There would be no violence and the murder weapon would have been eaten and digested: a very effective way of disposing of it. But Cat would never do anything like that, however questionable her judgement may have been in matters of the heart.

"Let's not think about it," she said. "One is just as likely to be poisoned by lettuce . . ."

She stopped herself: capital letters were vital here. Professor Lettuce had every reason to dispose of her, as did Christopher Dove, both of whom had seen Isabel neatly thwart their plans to seize control of the *Review of Applied Ethics*. What was it that Robert Lowell had written about ambitious professors in one of his poems? *They'd murder for a chair . . .* something like that. Academics were every bit as nasty as anybody else, as red in tooth and claw when it came to the attribution of glory, the division of spoils. *Lettuce, aided by Dove, poisons philosopher*: the newspaper headline was so easy to imagine.

They finished the mushroom tart and the potatoes dauphinoise without the appearance of any obvious symptoms. Dessert came in the form of a piece of shortbread and coffee in a small coffee cup.

"A can," said Isabel, holding up her cup. "That's what these are called—coffee cans."

Jamie smiled at her. "All those lovely words in your head," he said.

This made her laugh. "What a kind thing to say. And in your head? All those notes. All that music."

He ate the last crumbs of his shortbread and rose from the table. Taking her hand, he pulled her to her feet and embraced her. They kissed.

He said: "Let's go and sing something."

She said: "Yes. I'd like that." Then she paused. There was a sharp pain in her stomach.

He noticed and laid the back of his hand across her brow. "Something wrong?"

"A stomach pain," she said. It came again, less insistent now, but enough to make her wince.

"Oh, my darling . . ." Jamie looked at her with concern.

"I'm sure it's nothing," said Isabel, massaging her stomach gently. "Indigestion."

"You don't get indigestion," said Jamie.

"Everybody gets indigestion," countered Isabel. "Sometimes if I eat too quickly, I get a bit of a pain."

"But you didn't eat quickly tonight," said Jamie. "Are you sure you're all right?"

"Of course I'm all right."

She smiled at him, and then the pain returned, more intensely this time. She caught her breath.

"Isabel?" Jamie's voice took on a note of anxiety. "You're not all right."

"Listen, it's nothing. I'll take one of those pink pills in the bathroom cupboard. That'll sort it out."

"They're for acidity."

"Well, that's probably what I've got. Acidity."

She felt the pain again, and it registered on her face.

"Oh no," Jamie said. "It's those mushrooms. Listen, we'll have to go to hospital."

"Nonsense."

"Not nonsense. You can't wait with mushrooms. They have to do something immediately or—"

"You're overreacting. Let's sit down and wait for this to pass, as I'm sure it will."

"This is an emergency. I'm going to phone."

She tried to calm him. "It's not an emergency. It's a bout of indigestion."

But he was not listening. He was telephoning for an ambulance. The call made, he rang Grace and asked her to come round to look after Charlie. It was urgent, he explained, and could she be there in a few minutes' time?

"Of course I can," she said. "I'll get a taxi right away." She paused. "Is it serious?"

"I think so," said Jamie.

THE POISONS WARD at the Royal Infirmary was accustomed to drug overdoses, both accidental and suicidal, but only rarely to cases of mushroom poisoning. In general, they lost no time in dealing with their admissions, washing out stomachs, inducing vomiting, administering antidotes; minutes counted in this branch of medicine, one of the few areas where doctors treated those who wanted no treatment.

When Jamie and Isabel arrived, the doctor on duty was dealing with a young man, jobless and abandoned by his girlfriend, who had sought to end his pain by swallowing an overdose of paracetamol. He had resisted help, but had been brought in by two burly orderlies, proponents of tough love. Now he lay on his bed weeping, shaking his head anxiously, while a nurse stood beside him, holding his hand. The nursing staff kept their voices low, but the drama was being played out in a public ward and could be seen—and heard too.

The doctor finished with the young man and came in to see Isabel in the treatment room.

"Now then," he said briskly. "You think you've eaten a poisonous mushroom. Correct?"

"My . . . my fiancée felt a sudden pain," said Jamie. "We had a mushroom tart for dinner."

The doctor looked inquisitively at Jamie. "We? You too?"

Jamie nodded.

"But you've got no symptoms?"

Jamie realised that in his concern he had simply not

thought about himself. And yet he had eaten the mushroom tart too—and had enjoyed a slightly larger piece than had Isabel.

"I feel perfectly all right," said Jamie.

The doctor was impassive. "Do you know the name of the mushroom in question?"

Jamie shook his head. He explained, though, that he had brought one of the leftover mushrooms with him. He extracted a fleshy brown thing from a small plastic bag he took from his pocket and passed it over.

Isabel sniffed the air. There was a smell of disinfectant— and something else that she could not quite identify. That something was mortality, she thought—or suffering. She glanced through the door of the treatment room towards the young man on the bed. The nurse was still holding his hand, stroking it gently. Isabel watched her and thought: This is the compassionate state in action. The nurse was paid; she was doing a job that attracted a salary at the end of the month—a job that involved the exercise of human sympathy. Money and feeling, it seemed, were not mutually exclusive.

Her gaze returned to the doctor, who was examining the mushroom in the palm of his hand.

"We can identify this quickly enough," he said.

"Do you recognise it?" asked Jamie.

The doctor shook his head. He was younger than Jamie, Isabel realised. "I'm no good with mushrooms," he said. "But we have a mycologist on call. He's the expert."

"You'll get him in?"

The doctor smiled. "The benefits of technology. I'll photograph this and send it to him electronically. I'll get the answer in five minutes—sometimes it comes in less. As long as he can identify it from the photograph, he won't even have to leave the house."

He left them, holding the mushroom delicately between thumb and forefinger. Jamie turned to Isabel. "Is it any better?"

She had not felt any pain since they had entered the treatment room. Now, almost in response to his question, she felt a twinge, although it was less marked than before.

"Less bad," she said.

"I'm sure it's nothing," he said reassuringly.

"Let's hope so," she shot back. She immediately regretted being short with him, and reached out to take his hand. "Sorry. I'm feeling a bit frightened. I didn't mean to snap at you."

She was frightened because she had remembered an article she had read in the press a few years before, of an incident in which somebody in a town near Edinburgh had eaten a lunch of poisonous mushrooms he had found in the woods. He had lost all kidney function as a result and was now on dialysis, hoping for a transplant. It was a tragic story, and it had happened to somebody not far away, somebody she might easily have known. Proximity of that nature brought things home.

"I could die, Jamie," she said.

"Nonsense!" he burst out. "Don't say that."

"But I could. I could be dying right now."

"Don't—"

"Don't die? I'll try not to, but dying, I'm afraid, is not exactly a voluntary act—most of the time."

She tried to smile. Her stomach felt heavy, as if something were pressing down upon it.

She squeezed Jamie's hand, and he moved closer. "If I die—"

"Isabel, please don't talk like that. And what about me? I ate them too. I'm not dying, and neither are you."

"No, I have to speak. If I were to die, from those mushrooms or from anything else, I'd want you both—you and Charlie—to know something: I love you a great deal. I love you with all my heart, with all my heart. It is you I love. And if you have loved me, and I believe you have, then thank you so much for that, my darling." She paused. "And Charlie. If I were to go, would you promise to tell him about how much I loved him? Just tell him, as often as you can."

She closed her eyes. Would it help Charlie to know that? She thought it might, as the memory of love can be as strong, as powerful, as love itself.

He did not know what to say. He tried to speak, but his voice caught and nothing came. And then, behind them, coming back into the treatment room, was the doctor. Isabel saw that the hem of his white coat had come unstitched and was hanging down. He has nobody to look after his clothes, she thought.

"Well, there we are," said the doctor. "Professor Watson identified it straightaway. *Tricholoma* something-or-other. Or Man on Horseback, to give it its common name."

Isabel felt her heart miss a beat.

The doctor smiled. "You'll be all right."

"It's not poisonous?" asked Jamie.

The doctor made an equivocal gesture. "It is and it isn't. It's not very toxic—as far as we know. It used to be considered a delicacy, but it does appear to cause a reaction in some people. Not everyone." He looked at Jamie. "Just some. But even if it does, there are no clear reports of fatalities. I'd consider it poisonous, frankly, and wouldn't touch it. But others take a different view."

Isabel felt immediate, overwhelming relief. She reached again for Jamie's hand.

"Often the reaction becomes psychosomatic," the doctor continued. "If people think they've eaten something that's going to do them harm, the stomach tends to agree. That might be part of the explanation for your rather premature colicky pains."

"Do we need any treatment?" asked Jamie.

The doctor shook his head. "I don't think so. Just let us know if the nausea continues or if you have any other symptoms. But you've probably already experienced the worst it can do to you." He had been addressing Isabel; now he turned to Jamie. "And you—well, those particular mushrooms obviously don't disagree with you. But if you feel any discomfort, you can come back here if you like."

"I'm fine," said Jamie. "I can eat anything usually."

The doctor smiled. "Not the things that people in this particular ward swallow." And to Isabel, "Be careful."

He patted her on the wrist—a strange gesture, she thought: halfway between reassurance and reprimand.

She lowered her feet off the examining couch, feeling for her shoes as she did so.

"Thank you so much," she said.

"That's what we're here for," said the doctor. He stretched his arm out as he spoke, as if relieving it of cramp, and glanced at his watch. "Next time you go picking mushrooms," he said, "just don't. We've had very experienced people in here. Mushroom people are fond of saying, 'There are old mycologists and there are bold mycologists, but there are no old, bold mycologists.' "

The same might be said, Jamie thought, for bikers and pilots and off-piste skiers . . .

"We didn't pick them," said Isabel, in a matter-of-fact tone. "We bought them."

"What?"

"We bought them at a delicatessen."

The doctor shook his head in disbelief. "Where?"

"Here in Edinburgh. In Bruntsfield. The deli belongs to my niece." She hesitated. "I'll tell her immediately. Tomorrow morning."

"You must," said the doctor. "And I think the Environmental Health people will be in touch with you. They'll need to know. We've got your phone number on the admission form, haven't we?"

"I gave it to them," said Jamie. "It's there."

The way out led them past the end of the ward, past the bed where the young would-be suicide lay, fully clothed. The nurse who had been with him had gone off to attend to somebody else, leaving him lying there, staring out. Isabel hesitated when she saw the young man looking at her.

"You go on," she whispered to Jamie. "Wait outside. I'll be with you in a moment."

She approached the bedside.

"I'm Isabel," she said. "What's your name?"

The young man stared at her. He was unshaven, she noticed, and there was a bruise on the side of his head; perhaps he had fallen after his overdose and hit something on the way down.

He spoke quietly, almost too quietly to be heard. "Harry."

She sat down on the edge of his bed. It seemed to her that it was perfectly natural to do this. "I'm sorry that you're here," she said. "I'm sorry that you're unhappy."

He stared at her mutely.

"I'm here," she continued, "because I ate some poisonous mushrooms. That's why."

Harry frowned. "My brother's dog did that," he said.

"Oh dear."

He spoke wearily. "He died."

"Then I've been lucky, haven't I?"

She reached out and took his hand. He did not resist, but it was limp. She felt a sticking plaster.

"We all get luck of various kinds in our lives," she went on. "You know that, Harry? We get a bit of good luck, then we get a lot of pretty bad luck. Sometimes more bad luck than good."

He looked away.

"But it's worth carrying on, Harry. I think it really is."

"You don't know . . ."

She waited for him to finish, but he said nothing more. She pressed his hand. "There'll be somebody who loves you, won't there?"

He did not reply.

She imagined what he thought: *Who is this woman?* But she persisted, "There will be. And there will be things for you to do. There are things for all of us to do."

"I've got no job." He spoke bitterly.

"You'll get one. People do."

He shook his head vigorously. "There's nothing. I'm a plasterer. There's nothing."

She wondered what she could say. There were plenty of people out of work; plenty who felt worthless, unwanted. Platitudes would not ease their pain. One might as well suggest cake, as Marie Antoinette was supposed to have done.

Suddenly, on impulse, she leaned forward and embraced him. He gave a start, she felt it, but then he relaxed. She felt his cheek against hers. His hair smelled stale: of cooking fat, of fried potatoes.

"Harry," she whispered.

He was crying, the tears running down his cheek, and hers too, from its closeness. There was salt at the edge of her lips, stronger now: his tears. She did not mind. He was another person, not much more than a boy, and boys were made of salt and water.

She withdrew, so that she was looking directly into his eyes, still wet with tears, from a foot or so away.

"All right?"

He moved his head slightly: a movement against the pillow; a nod, half-hearted, but discernible nonetheless. She took a step back and then left the ward.

CHAPTER NINE

GRACE STAYED OVERNIGHT, occupying the spare bedroom at the back of the house. She always kept a bag of toiletries and clothes there, just in case her babysitting duty ended too late to bother with the night buses or an expensive taxi.

"You had a very narrow escape," she said to Isabel the next morning. "And now? How are you feeling now?"

"Just fine," said Isabel.

"Diarrhoea?" asked Grace.

Isabel thought this was none of her business. Doctors and nurses could ask questions like that, but one did not go up to somebody and say "Diarrhoea?" just like that.

She shook her head. Grace seemed disappointed by this answer, Isabel decided, and she wondered whether her house-keeper liked the thought that others might have diarrhoea when she did not. It was rather like those who, having exercised restraint at a party, take pleasure from hearing about the hang-overs of those who had enjoyed themselves rather too much. *Schadenfreude* was an odd emotion, but it existed.

"Sounds like you got away with it," said Grace. "And what about Jamie?"

"Nothing at all," said Isabel. "Apparently this particular mushroom doesn't affect everybody."

"Men," said Grace. "Their gut is different. It can handle all sorts of rubbish."

She said this, Isabel thought, with the air of one who had an intimate knowledge of the insides of men. She herself would not presume to pass comments on men's anatomy.

"Oh well," said Isabel brightly. "A lesson learned. There are none left, by the way: I put the ones Jamie didn't use in the bin."

The lesson, though, had to be communicated to Cat, and shortly after nine o'clock, leaving Grace in charge of Charlie—Jamie having gone over to Glasgow for a rehearsal—Isabel made her way along Merchiston Crescent towards Bruntsfield and Cat's delicatessen. Halfway there, she stopped to greet the friendly grey cat that often lay in wait for her at the bottom of its overgrown garden and seemed to have an uncanny ability to know exactly when she would be walking past. She had read that animals were telepathic, but had doubted this. They might *detect* something—as this cat appeared to do—but she doubted whether they could send messages of the sort that human telepathists claimed to convey. What can you convey if you have no language? But then she told herself: animals do pass one another messages, by sound or by visual means, and all that animal telepathy would involve—if it existed—would be the sending of the same *thought* by different means.

She bent down to stroke the animal, now rubbing itself against the railing on top of its low garden wall. Perhaps what a cat picked up was a sort of electromagnetic field, a bleep that indicated that a person was approaching. That was hardly tele-

pathy; that was radar. But if one thought of food and then concentrated on sending a cat the *idea* of food, would it receive it?
She concentrated on an image of a fish laid out on a bowl, pic-
turing it in her mind: a temptation for any cat. Could you send
such an image to a cat?

The grey cat suddenly stopped rubbing itself on the railings
and looked at Isabel with burning intensity. It let out a loud,
demanding yowl.

Isabel tickled the cat under its chin. "Oh," she said. "You got
the message. I have no fish at all, I'm afraid. Sorry."

The cat regarded her disdainfully, before leaping off the
wall, back into the garden. The shift of its attention from Isabel
was immediate and total, as if she were no longer there.

"Fickle," she muttered and continued her journey.

She knew that Cat would be at work when she arrived at
the delicatessen, and she assumed that Eddie's replacement,
Sinclair, would also be there. She had not yet met him and
was intrigued. Eddie was a very unusual young man, and she
wondered what his friend would be like. All she knew about
him was what she had winkled out of Eddie himself—that he
was good-looking, as Eddie, at Isabel's prompting, had confirmed. She had asked about that because she knew Cat well
enough to know that there would be an issue. Cat would not
be able to resist a good-looking young man: it was as simple
as that.

She sighed. It was difficult to keep up with Cat's emotional
entanglements. Her last boyfriend, a teacher, had been dropped
for reasons that Isabel had never learned.

"It's over," Cat had said simply. "I don't want to talk about it,
actually. All I'll say is that it didn't work out."

Isabel had sympathised. "Sometimes it doesn't," she said, stopping herself from going on to say *as I fear you know only too well.*

"We're still friends," Cat had said. "It wasn't acrimonious."

That, again, was typical of Cat. The only bitter break-up that Isabel knew of was the ending of her affair with Bruno, the deeply objectionable tightrope-walker who had shouted at Cat in public and had been got rid of there and then. That was greatly to Cat's credit, thought Isabel, although it was equally not to her credit that she had chosen him in the first place.

She thought of Sinclair. If he was Eddie's contemporary, then he would be twenty, or thereabouts, and Cat was now in her early thirties. If Cat fell for him, it could be difficult for him to cope with the situation, especially if he, like Eddie, was at all vulnerable. Some young men would love an attractive older woman to take an interest in them, but not all, especially if the older woman was their employer. No, Cat would have to avoid falling for Sinclair; she would have to tell herself that he was out of bounds and stick to that, which of course she would not.

Isabel arrived at the delicatessen to see Cat behind the counter, serving a customer. Cat caught Isabel's eye and nodded when Isabel pointed to one of the tables. She would sit and read the newspaper until Cat was free. The first half hour was busy after the shop opened each morning, as people dropped in on their way to work; thereafter things slackened off until noon, when the first of the lunchtime shoppers arrived.

Isabel settled herself at the table. A copy of the previous day's local paper, the *Evening News,* had been placed on the rack and she flicked through the pages of this. A ferry had run

aground in the Western Isles—it happened from time to time—
and there were the passengers on the beach, looking at the
stranded vessel.

"We were very disappointed," one was quoted as saying.
"We thought we were going to Oban, but we ended up here
instead. This is not where we wanted to be."

Isabel smiled at the comment. What did journalists expect
people to say? And when they expressed the obvious—as that
passenger had—then should it even be printed? Of course you
would be disappointed if the ferry on which you were travelling
ran aground, but your disappointment was hardly news.

And she found herself becoming irritated with the passengers too. They should be relieved that they had only run aground
and not sunk. People should not complain about things that just
happened, where it was not necessarily anybody's fault. Ferries
ran aground because the officer on watch misread a chart, or
looked in the wrong direction at the wrong time, or forgot that
the tide was going out rather than coming in; and none of these
might involve actual fault, or at least not fault beyond the normal range of inevitable human error. People made mistakes
because they were human, and there was as much point com-
plaining about that as moaning about the weather. So the man
who told the newspaper that he was upset because he was in
the wrong place should really have reflected on how fortunate
he was to be alive and not to have been travelling on that poor
Egyptian ferry that overturned in the Red Sea and took so many
passengers—hundreds of them—to their watery deaths. That
was what he should be thinking about.

She turned the page: a man who had been convicted of the
assault of a neighbour had been sentenced to three months'

imprisonment. The accused had hit his neighbour with a fence-post, the paper reported, in an argument over a planning application for the extension of a driveway. This sentence had been greeted with outrage by members of the victim's family, who said that three years would have been more appropriate. But of course they would, thought Isabel. Again, if you ask people what they think of the sentences meted out to criminals, they say they are not long enough, an answer you will almost always get from the victim's family.

She was absorbed in the story of an Edinburgh woman whose two daughters and a son had all become opera singers when Cat, who had finished with her customers, came over.

"Something interesting?" asked Cat, as she sat down opposite Isabel.

Isabel put the paper aside. "I was reading about a woman who raised three opera singers," she said. "There was an interview with her and she said . . ." She picked up the paper again and read from the report: " 'I can't sing a note myself,' said their mother, Sylvia, forty-seven, from Inverleith. 'I don't know how this happened. They were just always singing. All over the place—all this singing.' "

Isabel looked at Cat and laughed. But Cat did not.

"And?"

Isabel gestured to the page. "I find that rather funny."

Cat seemed puzzled. "Why?"

Isabel shrugged. It was sometimes difficult to explain just how funny things were, especially to Cat, whose perspective on the world was often quite different from Isabel's.

"It's just the thought of this household with the musically ungifted mother opening a bedroom door and finding a small child singing. Or looking in a cupboard, perhaps, and finding inside a child singing an aria from *Tosca*. Life would be full of surprises."

"Why would a child sing in a cupboard?" asked Cat.

"I don't necessarily think that happened," said Isabel. "Although children do like to squeeze themselves into tight corners, into nooks and crannies. It springs from the desire to get back to the time when they were smaller . . . perhaps."

"A sort of *nostalgie de la boue*?" suggested Cat.

Isabel shot her a glance. "Maybe. Although that usually involves the desire to experience crudity."

And she thought: As well you know, Cat! Bruno had involved *nostalgie de la boue*.

Cat did not like to be corrected. "I thought it meant wanting to go back to something," she said sulkily. "Didn't we all come from the mud a long time ago? Didn't our distant ancestors crawl out of the mud and onto dry land?"

"I find it difficult to see myself as the descendant of a lizard," said Isabel. "You may, if you wish, but not me. I have no inner lizard, I'm afraid. Nor do I feel great affinity for one of those curious salamander things—half fish, half something else."

"Oh well," said Cat. "Evolution's not compulsory."

Isabel smiled at the comment. Surely evolution was not a matter of choice—if you wanted to survive. Of course there might be those who had just done enough evolving. She thought of what such a person might say. *Frankly, I'm not evolving any more.*

"What's the joke?"

Isabel shook her head. "Evolution," she said. "Well, that's

not a joke, of course." She gazed out of the window. "Actually, I was in hospital last night. But only briefly."

Cat was concerned. "Isabel! What happened?"

"Something I ate," said Isabel quietly; she would have to handle this tactfully.

Cat raised an eyebrow. "It must have been pretty bad to end up in hospital." She paused. "Diarrhoea?"

That is the second time, thought Isabel, that somebody has asked me that today.

"No," she said. "No diarrhoea. Just stomach pains—like colic, I suppose. I'm afraid it was a mushroom. Or a number of mushrooms."

Cat greeted this with incredulity. "You didn't go mushroom picking? Isabel!"

"No. Jamie bought them. Here, as it happens. Remember?"

Isabel noticed that Cat's immediate reaction was to blush.

"Here?"

Isabel tried to make it as gentle as possible. "It's not your fault. I'm really not blaming you. The mushrooms were only mildly toxic."

Cat shook her head. "Oh my God, I'm sorry. I really am. Jenny gave them to me. She said they were . . . I forget what it was, but she used a Latin name and she's always been a mushroom picker. She has all those books—"

Isabel sought to reassure Cat. "It doesn't matter. The important thing is this: you haven't got any more, have you? Because if you have, I'd suggest that—"

"No, there aren't any more."

"Well, then there's nothing to worry about."

Cat was relieved. "Good. And you won't tell anybody about

it, will you Isabel?" She did not wait for an answer. "Great. So now let me get you a coffee. It's the least I can do after having half poisoned you—unwittingly of course."

Isabel accepted the offer. "All right. Are you going to be single-handed all day? Where's your new assistant, Eddie's friend?"

Cat looked at her watch. "He usually comes in about now. He'll be here."

Eddie, by contrast, was always there before the delicatessen was opened to customers.

"He's a bit late," said Isabel.

"He lives over near Jock's Lodge," explained Cat.

"Hardly Timbuktu," said Isabel.

Cat ignored this. "He's a quick learner."

"Good." Isabel noticed that the door was opening. "That's him?"

Cat turned round. "Yes."

There was a change in her expression, and Isabel noticed it. We cannot conceal it, she said to herself; we cannot conceal the quickening that goes with sexual desire. Watch the eyes; watch the whole demeanour: it's unmistakable.

Sinclair came up to the table. "Hey," he said.

Cat replied, "Hey."

Isabel said nothing.

"Hey," said Sinclair again, this time to Isabel.

"Hey," she said weakly. She did not like saying "hey"; she saw no reason why she should say "hey" to somebody she had never said "hey" to before.

Cat introduced them. "This is Isabel. She sometimes helps out here."

Isabel inclined her head. She was under Sinclair's gaze, and she felt it. After a moment or two, she raised her eyes to meet his.

"Hey," said Sinclair again.

Isabel stared; it was impossible to do anything else. She tried to look away to avoid embarrassment, but she could not. *Medusa*, she thought, but this was utterly different, of course. Sinclair smiled and two small dimples, perfectly placed, appeared on his cheeks.

"Eddie told me about you," he said. "Eddie thinks you're great."

Isabel laughed nervously. "The feeling's mutual. I'm very fond of Eddie. We all are."

"Eddie's a good guy," said Sinclair, then turned to Cat. "What do you want me to do?"

"Those knives need to be washed," Cat instructed. "And you could also grind some coffee—some of the Kenyan—and put it in the paper bags. Make sure you weigh each one correctly. The label tells you."

Sinclair turned on his heels and walked back to the counter. Isabel fought the inclination to watch him and lost. Cat noticed.

"See?" she whispered. "Stunner, isn't he?"

Isabel could hardly meet her eye. She was angry with herself for succumbing so transparently to physical beauty. She felt like a schoolgirl caught ogling a schoolboy; she was ashamed.

"You can't take him home and put him on your mantelpiece, you know," said Cat.

"Did I express any intention of doing that?"

Cat looked at her in a bemused way. "Didn't I detect a certain . . . frisson?"

Isabel sighed. "He's pretty gorgeous. But he's very young. He's a boy, really."

"He wants to be a model," said Cat. "He's already been in some advertisement somewhere." She glanced at her watch. "You aren't by any chance free for an hour or so?"

"When?"

"Now. I have to deliver a ham to one of my customers. She lives in Trinity and can't get over to this side of town because she's snapped her Achilles tendon playing tennis."

Isabel winced. She coped well enough with pain when she experienced it herself, but not when it was visited upon others. "You go," she said. "I'll stay and look after the shop." She paused. "Can Sinclair manage on his own?"

Cat shook her head. "Sinclair is not all that bright," she said. "He can't add, and I think he's dyslexic. He reads sixes as nines and the other way round." She rose to leave. "I didn't make you your coffee," she said.

"I'll do it," said Isabel.

She made a better cup of coffee, she thought, than Cat did. Cat could be careless, and often served coffee with saucers swimming in foamy milk. And it was exactly that carelessness, Isabel reluctantly concluded, that had prompted her to sell mushrooms of doubtful provenance.

SINCLAIR SEEMED quite happy for Isabel to attend to the few customers who came in over the next hour or so. He stacked plates away, finished the grinding of the coffee and then leaned, a tea towel in his hand, against the door of one of the fridges.

Isabel engaged him in conversation during a lull between customers.

"Cat tells me that you've been in an advertisement," she remarked. "What was it? I could look out for it."

He seemed pleased with the question. "Yeah, I have. It was on a poster. You might have seen it on some of the bus shelters. It was for sunblock. It was really great."

"It must have been exciting for your friends," said Isabel. "I've often wondered what it must be like to recognise some-body in an advertisement."

He had been smiling; now the smile faded and the dimples disappeared. "You couldn't actually tell it was me," he said. "It didn't show my face."

"Still," said Isabel. "It was you, and that's the important part."

"Yeah, that's right. And I'm going for an audition next week. This is a big job, my agent says: nationwide."

Isabel appeared suitably impressed. "You have an agent?"

It was terribly grand to have an agent; she had never had one, and had never been able to say *speak to my agent*. How powerful one must feel to be able to say that!

"Sort of," said Sinclair. "She hasn't quite committed yet, but says she will."

Isabel thought that a commitment to commit was almost as good as a commitment itself, but only in a moral sense, of course, and the world of business was not always constrained by moral sense.

"I'm sure she'll say yes," she said reassuringly. "And I'm sure that you're very good at it. She'll want you."

She wondered, though, how one could be good at being a

model. Models did not have to *do* much; they simply *were*. Perhaps there was some work involved—pulling in one's stomach, or sucking in one's cheeks; but then if you were a good model you would not have much of a stomach to pull in and your cheeks would be just right as they were.

She took another discreet glance at Sinclair. He was at that moment in his life, she suspected, when his looks were at their best: a trace of boyhood and its softness, but without the coarsening that comes with later manhood. In due course he would fill out; his features would become heavier, his beauty fade. Lithesome youths, Ganymedes and Adonises to a boy, became thickset, paunchy men, and quickly. Did he know that? Did he ever think: I shall not be like this for ever? Probably not.

Her question slipped out, as it sometimes did with her: the mind conceived the thought and the tongue made it flesh.

"What will you do when you're older?"

Sinclair frowned. "Older?"

"Yes," said Isabel. "Sometimes people grow old. And models . . . well, models seem to be younger. Most of the time, anyhow."

She thought of advertisements featuring older models: they existed, of course: for pension plans, for comfortable clothing, for funeral insurance. The notion depressed her.

Sinclair chewed on his lower lip. "Oh, for when I'm forty? Well, I thought I might be a golf pro." He clasped his hands together, as if gripping a golf club, and swung his arms. "See."

Isabel raised an eyebrow. "That's interesting. What's your handicap?"

Sinclair shrugged. "I don't play yet. I will, though. Later."

She stared at him. Young children could have unrealistic

ambitions—Charlie, no doubt, would go through the stage of wanting to be an astronaut, but one did not expect it of nineteen-year-olds. Now, watching Sinclair swing his arms again, she thought: This young man is utterly vacuous.

"I hope you find that you can play, once you start. You have to be quite good to be a pro, I believe."

He looked at her almost scornfully. "I know."

"It's just that if you've never played, how do you know that you'll be good enough? I don't want to put you off, of course."

"It's better than working in a food shop," he said, regarding her disdainfully. "Selling cheese and stuff."

Isabel took a deep breath. She was finding Sinclair both vacuous *and* irritating.

"People need cheese and stuff," she muttered.

"Sure, they need it. But I don't want to sell it all my life."

It was clear to Isabel that he assumed that she had devoted her life to the selling of cheese and stuff. The wording of her obituary flashed through her mind: *For many years, she sold cheese and stuff* . . . Such a life would have its dignity and such an obituary would not be anything of which to be ashamed.

"Selling cheese is a better way of spending one's time than being a clothes horse," she said. "Infinitely so, in my view."

She had not intended to engage with Sinclair, and this comment, she knew, was childish and confrontational; but she had to make it.

He responded truculently. "Clothes horse? Who's a clothes horse?"

"Nobody in particular," said Isabel innocently. "I merely illustrate a point."

She looked about her; she wanted to bring this conversation to an end. Picking up a knife to return it to the rack, she noticed that it was still dirty; Sinclair's washing, it seemed, had not been thorough enough.

"You'll have to do this one again," she said. "Look, it's not properly clean at the top there."

Sinclair glanced at the knife. "Looks clean to me," he said.

"Well, it isn't. Look over here. And this bit here too."

"Can't see anything."

"Well, I'm telling you, I can."

He walked away, simply ignoring her, and started to re-arrange small jars of spices on a shelf. She noticed that as he walked he studied his reflection in the window behind him. She turned away, her heart thumping unnaturally within her.

Conflict and confrontation had that effect on her; she had no stomach for it. What a thoroughly unpleasant young man, she thought. She tried to put him out of her mind, but he stubbornly insisted on returning. In her mind's eye she now involuntarily pictured Cat and Sinclair in an embrace, and it was intimate. It was a shocking, unwanted image, and she recoiled from it. It was, she realised, a dirty thought, of the sort that plagues the smutty male mind: *not* what women were meant to think about, or at least in theory. A dirty thought: what a sordid little expression that was, how prosaically grimy.

She closed her eyes, expecting the image to fade, but this merely served to intensify it. They were even more intimately engaged now and she gasped. I must think of something else, she told herself: of cheese, perhaps. She closed her eyes once more. But it was not just cheese that came to mind, in all the innocence that cheese possesses; Cat was offering Sinclair little cubes of Cheddar, popping them into his mouth with practised flirtatiousness.

Such thoughts, she told herself, were not her fault. They

were the product of the subconscious mind, which in all of us, she knew, was a wild, anarchic place, quite capable of doing the most out-of-character things, of dwelling on the most impermissible fantasies, but nothing to worry about, really, because it was not us, not *really* us; or so it claimed, but did not convince. That mind was *us* all right—more authentically *us* than the us we presented to the world. And yet it was an *us* beyond blame and recrimination; it operated in an area of licence, where the rules are suspended.

That suspension of the rules can happen, she thought, remembering how the most rigid systems will allow the normal restraints to be turned on their head, provided this is done at the right time. Years ago, after she had come back from the fellowship at Georgetown, she had paid a brief visit to Moscow and had seen young soldiers there riding down the escalators of the staid and well-behaved underground system, shouting uproariously at a couple of noncommissioned officers travelling in the opposite direction. The sergeants had smiled tolerantly, and she had been told that the young men were on their last day of military service—they had done their bit—and such behaviour was viewed with indulgence by the army, but only on that day. The day before it would have been punished severely: with months in a military prison, perhaps, but not now, within the parameters of this indulgence. So we can think what we like, she told herself, as long as we think in private.

And yet there was a distinctly slippery slope that descended from that particular conclusion. How easy it was to create little areas of excuse in one's life—things that we did, which, we would tell ourselves, were not really our own acts and did not matter. The person on a strict diet who tucks into a poke of crisp-fried potato chips may tell himself that it is not really him eating the chips—but that the real him, the him that counts, is obedient to the doctor's instructions. This was an innocent illustration, but at the other end of the spectrum there is the respectable husband and father, by day the pillar of the community, who by night is the serial murderer. There were plenty of such people, many of whom had two selves that seemed to sit quite comfortably with one another.

She remembered the murderer who had terrorised a whole region of England, who was by day a truck driver, leading an apparently mundane and blameless life, while by night he preyed on young women. Did the truck driver read the newspaper headlines, the reports of his depredations, and think, that's me? No, or, if he did, he must at least have thought *it was a different me.*

CAT TOOK RATHER LONGER than anticipated to return from delivering the ham.

"Sorry," she said. "I had to help her do one or two things in the house, poor woman. Her leg's in plaster, you know. If you snap your Achilles tendon you can't do very much."

"Of course," said Isabel. "You must feel like a puppet with its strings cut."

The simile seemed to interest Cat. "Yes, that's right. It must be a bit like that."

Isabel glanced at Sinclair, who was at the other end of the shop, attending to a customer who was sampling a piece of Camembert.

"I got to know our young friend," she said. "He told me that—"

"Good," said Cat. "He's nice, isn't he?" And then she said

something that surprised Isabel, perhaps even shocked her. "Temptation on legs."

Isabel was not a prude, but this seemed out of place. In saying this, to Isabel it seemed that Cat was inviting her participation in the act of concupiscent looking, and she did not wish to be part of that.

We do not have to reveal to others what we want, thought Isabel. Private desires should be precisely that: private.

"He's certainly nice-looking," she said. "But—"

Cat interrupted her, making Isabel wonder whether her inner reaction to the curious aside had been outwardly visible. "Thanks for looking after him. I think he'll be fine."

Isabel weighed up whether to say something about the knives, and Sinclair's rudeness, but she did not. And as she made her way back to the house, she reflected on it further and decided that she had done the right thing. She should not interfere in Cat's life; any comment that she made about Sinclair, however well intentioned, would not be appreciated and could even have the opposite effect from that which she intended. If Cat was going to fall for this narcissistic young man, then she would do so irrespective of what Isabel advised. And that falling, thought Isabel, had probably already occurred.

She knew the signs by now, and she reckoned they were already there for the reading—the touchiness, the slight air of distraction: this was Cat in love. *Love is blind*: the old adage was absolutely true, as were so many vintage clichéd sayings. And that was precisely why such axioms were popular, and overused: because they showed themselves to be true time and time again. We knew that love was blind because so often we witnessed it obscuring the judgement of others—not our own, of course—

although love was far from blind to begin with. It had its eyes wide open and saw only too clearly the things it was looking for—at least in Cat's case, where looks, it seemed, counted for everything, with Bruno, the tightrope-walker, being the sole exception. Even he, though, must have held some physical attraction for Cat; probably his legs. A funambulist must have strong legs if he is to balance on the wire, and Cat liked men with strong legs. She remembered Toby, who had proved to be disastrous, with his crushed-strawberry trousers; one could not help but notice his legs, and Cat had.

Men's legs, she thought, as she made her way up the path to her front door. An odd thing to think of, but then so much that went through our minds was odd in one way or another: unexpected, unconnected, unimportant; mental flotsam swilling around with sudden moments of clarity and insight. A hotch-potch of memories, plans, dreams, random bits of silliness: the very things that made us human.

CHAPTER TEN

THE ARRANGEMENT HAD BEEN that if Isabel were to be back late, then Grace would collect Charlie from his playgroup. Grace liked this, and Isabel believed that she passed herself off to the other mothers as his aunt—a slightly peculiar thing to do, but harmless, as deceptions go.

She had found this out thanks to a remark made by Algy's mother, the actress, who had said, in the middle of a casual conversation that she and Isabel were having, "As I said yesterday to Charlie's aunt . . ." and then drifted off into some remark about something unimportant. Isabel had been momentarily nonplussed: Charlie's aunt?

And then she had realised that she must mean Grace, and had said, "Actually, she's not his aunt."

Algy's mother had paused and said, "She said she was. I'm sure she did. But it doesn't matter, does it? The more aunts one has in this life, I would have thought, the better."

It did not matter, of course; it was a tiny, irrelevant thing. And yet it was poignant, Isabel thought, that Grace should want to have a more formal connection—an auntly one—with the little boy of whom she was undoubtedly so fond. Grace had her own family—she frequently mentioned cousins and other relatives, telling Isabel about their doings and their foibles—so why should she claim kinship with Charlie? Unless it was simply a matter of love; after all, that was exactly how families expanded: through love.

And Grace loved Charlie: that was touchingly evident, as well as being exactly what Isabel expected and wanted. She and Jamie loved him to distraction, and it seemed only natural that others should do so too. Charlie loved them back, and showed it in the grasp of his tiny hand and the way he nestled his cheek against the face of the one carrying him, and in the odd little gifts that he would suddenly give: a crust of bread from which the butter and jam had been thoroughly licked; a feather he had picked up in the garden; something he had drawn, a scribble that was a house or the sun or a person, it was impossible to tell. So if Grace claimed to be his aunt, it was done out of love, and was a compliment.

They were in the kitchen when Isabel came back. Charlie ran to her and flung his arms around her knees. She bent down and embraced him. There was something sticky on his face—strawberry jam, probably; Grace gave him it as a treat—but she did not mind its being transferred to her skin, not from him, because he was, she realised with sudden clarity, *her*. That was the miracle of giving birth to another person, the existential miracle of motherhood. Your child was *you*. It was as simple as that.

But that conclusion, of course, gave rise to all sorts of moral hazards. Your child might be you, but would not want to be you for ever. It was all very well with a child of Charlie's age, who snuggled and cuddled and wanted to be part of his mother, but already there were the seeds of separation. And the desire of the child to be himself should not be resisted; parents had to let go, and if they did not, then they were building up for themselves resentments and distortions that had the capacity to ruin the child's life.

What we do to our children, they do to the world, thought Isabel. If only Hitler had been loved more as a little boy and as a young man too—given a few prizes, told by some woman that he really was a wonderful lover, and so handsome; if only somebody had taken Stalin and kissed him and made him feel good about himself. Or was that all too simple? Was the massive psychopathy of the mass murderer something that sprang from an entirely different psychopathology? Perhaps some monsters are monsters because they feel *too* good about themselves; perhaps, but love could still have made such a difference, even to the likes of them. *Amor vincit omnia.*

She was not sure whether it was Virgil or Horace, but whoever had coined the phrase was being . . . She paused. Was it *omnia vincit amor*? One could so easily change the emphasis if one cleared one's throat at the end, thereby by adding an *em*, and misremembered, or misheard, the verb. She smiled at the notion. *Omnia vincunt amorem:* all things conquer love. The problem with which Romeo and Juliet, and many other star-crossed lovers, had to contend. She smiled again as she drew the inevitable conclusion: don't clear your throat when completing a pithy saying in an inflected language!

Grace was staring at her. "Did I say something amusing?" she asked.

Isabel shook her head. "Sorry. I was thinking."

Grace continued to stare at her, as if waiting for an explanation. Isabel knew that the other woman considered it rude to smile to oneself and not say why. Grace had once alluded to that when she remarked that secret jokes were unnerving to those who were not party to them. "People may think that there's something odd about their appearance," she had said. "They might think that the other person is laughing at them. Well, not laughing, actually, but smiling—and that can be as bad. You don't want to walk down the street and see people smiling at you, do you?"

"Don't you?" asked Isabel. "I would have thought that it would be rather nice. Reassuring."

She thought for a moment. She had recently spoken to a politician friend, a member of the Scottish Parliament, who had said that he had decided that we should smile more at others as a matter of principle and should be readier to greet strangers in the street as a matter of courtesy.

"Why should we lead our lives as if we're surrounded by complete strangers?" he had asked. "If you go into the country or a village maybe you'll find that people say good morning to one. They may not have a clue who you are, but they still say good morning, which is how it should be."

"Yes," Isabel had said. "Of course."

And she wanted to add: but we are *not* moral strangers to those we see in the street. We are not.

But her friend continued: "Mind you, it doesn't always work." He went on to explain, "I tried it out the other day in Morningside Road, which is in my constituency. As I walked down the street one morning I said good morning to everybody I encountered."

"And it didn't work? Did you get a series of scowls in return?"

He smiled at the recollection. "Two of them stopped,

looked me in the eye and said, 'I'm not voting for you, you know!' "

They both laughed. "And if you say good morning to a child," she added ruefully, "it will scuttle off, or call the police. Such is our paranoia."

She had wanted to say to Grace, when she had raised the issue of smiling to oneself, that if one were completely secure, one should not mind if another smiled. But who among us was completely secure? Who would not naturally wonder, even for a moment, if one's buttons were undone or whether one's make-up had run, or, if one were a child, somebody had put a KICK ME sign on one's back? Children used to do that to one another and think it hilarious, but of course now it seemed that the consequences could be draconian. Had not a nine-year-old boy been suspended from his school in New York for doing just such a thing? How absurd. *Of course* boys thought it funny to put KICK ME signs on others; there would be something *wrong* with them if they did not. In most cases it was not real bullying, although it could become easily that if the targets were subjected to regular indignities. But you could not stop boys doing things; boys threw snowballs too, and balanced books on the top of doors to fall on the heads of those who entered. That would seem extremely funny to a boy. And for adults to overreact to these childish pranks was to kill the fun of childhood stone dead.

But now she was in the kitchen with Grace, who was clearly still waiting for an explanation.

"It's nothing to do with you, Grace," said Isabel. "I wasn't smiling at anything you said or did. I was smiling because I was thinking of the Latin expression *amor vincit omnia*, which is actually incorrect because it should be *omnia vincit amor*—at least, I think it should. And then I thought if you inadvertently added an *em*, through clearing your throat at the wrong time, you could turn the meaning of the phrase on its head. Provided you changed the verb to the third person plural."

"Love conquers all," said Grace. "Love conquers all—em?"

Isabel struggled not to smile at that. "*Amorem,*" she said.

She was surprised: she had not expected Grace to know the meaning of the Latin phrase, but she immediately realised that her assumption was condescending. It was as if she had said to herself: housekeepers don't know Latin. And in general, they did not, but it was wrong to imagine that somebody who happens to have such a job in life should not know such things. And that, surely, was what education was all about: it should make it possible for everybody to have the consolations of literature—and Latin, too—to accompany them in their work, whatever it turned out to be. The bus driver who knows his Robert Burns, the waitress who reads Jane Austen or who goes on her day off to look at an exhibition of Vermeers: these are the quiet triumphs of education, Isabel thought. It's why education was justified for its own sake, and not as a means to some vocational end.

"I was wondering whether love really does overcome everything," Isabel continued. "Do you think it does, Grace?"

Grace, who had been wetting the corner of a towel under a tap in order to wipe Charlie's face, shrugged. "I don't know. Maybe in a very general sense, in that good overcomes bad in the long run. Maybe then. But otherwise, no. There are plenty of cases where people never get the person they want because things are stacked against them. There's an aunt of mine, for instance. And then . . . ."

She did not complete her sentence, and Isabel understood that Grace had been thinking of herself; and her heart went out to her, and she wanted to put her arms about her and comfort her, but did not, because it would have embarrassed Grace. Regret is sometimes best left unspoken.

"Oh well," said Isabel. "These are big issues, and Charlie will need his lunch. I'm going to give him sardines, I think. He's discovered that he likes mashed sardines, and he can't seem to get enough of them."

At the mention of sardines, Charlie gave an excited yelp. "Yes. Yes. Charlie's sardines."

"Charlie's sardines indeed," said Isabel.

AFTER CHARLIE was put down for his nap, which he took reluctantly that day as he had his own plans for the afternoon, Isabel went into her study. She had done no work that day, she reminded herself, and if she allowed herself to do the *Scotsman* crossword, three o'clock would come and she would have made no progress on the papers that had piled up on her desk. She glanced at the newspaper, aware of the temptation, and thought that if she did just one clue she could start on her real day's work a few minutes later and feel virtuous at having resisted the diversion.

Five down: *He enjoys female company and gives authority* (8). That took two minutes, and then "mandates" came into her mind. He was like Cat, she thought; she liked dating. How would one compose a clue for Cat? *Feline plays the role of prize, we hear; her love life is certainly this!* (11). Catastrophe.

She immediately felt guilty. Compiling crossword clues like

that about her own niece showed, she feared, a great lack of charity. She should support Cat, rather than make up crossword clues about her. So she tried something different: *Give feline a pick-me-up*, she thought, *the opposite effect! (9)*. Catatonic. *Bed for a feline, a use for string (4-6)*. Cat's cradle. *As many append-ages as it has lives, punishing! (3-1-4-5)*. Cat-o'-nine-tails.

Hours might be wasted like this, she thought, and she put the newspaper down firmly on a table. Now, to work . . .

She eyed the stack of manuscripts. There was only one way to deal with it, and that was to mine one's way through the pile. Sighing, she picked up the first one and read the title out loud: "On Good and Bad Diversions." She looked at the synopsis that the author had typed on the title page.

"There are some leisure pursuits that are intrinsically bad," he had written. "They may not have consequences in the real world, but they encourage character traits that could well have deleterious results. The playing of electronic games that simu-late the death of others is one example."

Isabel sat down. This intrigued her. Of course amusing one-self with the death and destruction of others was bad for the character, and yet that is precisely what electronic games were all about. She glanced at the author's name: William Blandford. He was courageous to make the point; people mocked those who spoke in favour of gentleness and the virtues. And the moment there was a whiff of censorship . . . Yet how could one stop the peddling of these things, if not by banning the sale of games that glorified and rewarded violence? The makers were incorrigible; millions of pounds were at stake and if the market wanted cruelty and death, then that was what they would provide.

"So what should society do?" asked William Blandford towards the end of his paper. "Do we not have an obligation to help people to become better? And if we shrug our shoulders over the corruption of so many minds by violent entertainment, then are we not failing in this duty? Civilisation involves moral effort—on our own behalf and on behalf of others. Without that moral effort, there can be no civilisation." On that note he concluded.

Isabel read the comments that had been attached to the paper by the two members of the editorial committee who had read it. "A stout defence of the paternalist position," wrote one, "but lacking, perhaps, an adequate justification of paternalism itself."

The other comment was more succinct: "The author refers at many points to *we*. We must do this; we must do that. But who, may one ask, are *we*? The author in the plural?"

While Rome burned, thought Isabel, putting the paper to one side. While Rome burned, philosophers fiddled with concepts. The reference at the end to civilisation had caught her attention. Few philosophers spoke about it now—few *people* spoke about it—perhaps out of embarrassment. In the past, talk of civilisation had perhaps been too frequently accompanied by guns pointed at those on whom it was being imposed. But had there ever been any civilisation of note that had not been based, at least in the beginning, on force? Civilisation required organisation and cooperation—the works of Bach could never have come into existence in chaos—and without authority, which was usually ultimately based on force, would people ever be organised and cooperative?

She rose to her feet and walked over to the window. There

was a garden outside, and a garden was, in a sense, a tiny corner of civilisation, or at least an allegory of it. Gardens were all about the imposition of order through force. There were weeds to be rooted out. There were paths to be made. There were shrubs to be planted, lawns to be nurtured. All of this involved hacking and pulling and forcing into shape. Lines written by Robert Burns about ploughing up the home of a field mouse came to her. It was there in her memory, deeply buried, as it was in the minds of so many Scots who had learned Burns as children.

> *I'm awful sorry man's dominion*
> *Has broken Nature's social union . . .*

Exactly. Force. Somebody, somewhere, has to believe in something sufficiently to force it upon others. If that belief was in justice and human flourishing, then, well and good: that produced civilisation. Or well and good—but only to an extent. Civilisations expanded by suppressing other, weaker societies. There were plenty of ruined temples and cities that, if one looked for them, reminded us of Darwinian rules in this respect. One person's vision of the good lost out when a more confident vision of another good came along.

She sighed. She was not an historian; she was a philosopher, and that was quite difficult enough without adding to the intellectual tasks it entailed. And yet everybody had to be an historian, at least to some degree, because life was a long . . . What was the metaphor, she wondered: a long narrative? A long film? Yes. Human life is a long film, which can be fully understood only if one looks at what went before. It was no good looking at a single still picture, or even a few frames; one would end up scratching one's head over that; as one did when one turned on the television—not that Isabel possessed one—and found one-self in the middle of a scene in a film that one simply could not understand. Why were the characters in that particular room, saying those particular things? Why was there an air of menace?

A movement in the garden distracted her. Clearly visible from her study window was a large clump of rhododendron bushes, the home of the fox she knew as Brother Fox. He was a shy creature, not as emboldened as some urban foxes had become, and he did not flaunt himself. This appealed to Isabel. A friend who lived in another part of Edinburgh had told her of their local fox, who was, she said, redder than other foxes and altogether more dashing.

"He walks down the street in broad daylight," she said. "In his fine red fur. Extremely well turned out—as if he's going down to Princes Street to do some shopping. Very pleased with himself."

A *nouveau riche fox,* Isabel had thought, but did not say it. Her friend lived in a street that was full of rather flashy houses, and it was not at all surprising that they should attract a fox like that.

Brother Fox would never approve of such conduct, she decided. He was a fox of the old school, and appreciated the importance of keeping to the shadows and the undergrowth. Foxes should *never* be too visible, she pictured him saying. We are not dogs, after all. But they were, she thought, although she would not argue that point with him, of course, because he could simply end the discussion by saying: "Whose categories, Miss Dalhousie?" That was how she imagined he would address her if he were ever given the power of speech. He would be formal, and perhaps use slightly old-fashioned, gamey expressions like "old chap" or even the wonderful, now largely retired expression, "old bean."

A movement in the rhododendrons could be the wind—the branches of the trees were moving slightly—or it could be Brother Fox. She stared at the foliage: rich, green, waxy. It danced against the darkness of the shrub's interior. And then a nose: tiny, black.

"Brother Fox," she whispered.

She gazed at him. The nose had been followed by a head and now the forequarters. He stopped, as if deciding whether he had forgotten something. And then another, unexpected movement, and a small bundle of fur teetered out unsteadily. A cub.

She drew in her breath. Brother Fox had a son.

The telephone rang, taking her away from the window. She picked up the receiver, still thinking of the cub. He was so beautiful, so perfect, just like one of Charlie's stuffed toys.

"Isabel?" It was Gareth Howlett. "A moment?"

She answered vaguely. How old would Brother Fox's cub be? He looked as if he was only a few weeks old.

"I'm calling about those shares," said Gareth. "West of Scotland Turbines."

"Of course. Yes. You bought them, I take it?"

"Fortunately," said Gareth. "You must have some pretty good sources of financial intelligence, Isabel. They've appreciated by forty-two per cent in the space of a few days. Extraordinary."

She smiled. Pretty good sources of financial intelligence? The best, in fact. Direct from the other side, as Grace would put it.

Gareth explained that he thought that it might be best to sell them and take the profit. "I'm not sure that they will necessarily keep their current value," he said. "Let's err on the side of caution."

Isabel was still thinking of foxes. Where was Brother Fox's mate? Had they split up, perhaps? Incompatibility? Would she leave him with the children? Some women did that. It was rare, of course, but it happened. Did foxes divorce? Absurd idea. In the animal world you chose a mate and you stuck to him or her, at least for the season. It was not conversation that you were interested in, after all.

"Of course you'll have a capital gains tax bill," said Gareth. "But you'll end up with a pretty tidy profit."

Isabel thanked him, and the conversation came to an end. She had already decided what that money would be used for: relieving financially stressed libraries of the cost of their subscription to the *Review of Applied Ethics* for a couple of years. It would be free for them. She would write to them about it.

She returned to the window. Brother Fox had vanished, as had his son.

CHAPTER ELEVEN

WHEN ISABEL PHONED JANE, the phone was switched through to the secretary, who said that she thought that Dr. Cooper was in St. Andrews for the day and would be back very late in the afternoon. Isabel left a message, and it was not until that evening that Jane returned the call.

"I've had the most gorgeous day," she said. "A meeting of the Scots Philosophical Club that lasted only two hours. Then I went for a walk and to a seafood restaurant and . . . I'm sorry, you've probably been at your desk all day."

"I've barely sat at it," said Isabel. "Distractions."

Jane sounded apologetic. "Not my . . . enquiry, I hope."

"No. Not today. But I do have some news on that."

There was a silence at the other end of the line. Isabel sensed the anticipation; telephones, she felt, could transmit more than mere words.

"I think I may know who you're looking for," she said. She could have said *I've found your father*, but she thought that would sound excessively melodramatic.

Jane said nothing.

"Are you there, Jane?"

"Yes. Sorry. This is a bit surprising, that's all."

"I can understand," said Isabel. "Anyway, there was a young man called Rory Cameron who was your mother's boyfriend at the relevant time. I found out by—"

Jane cut her short. "Is he alive?"

"I think so," said Isabel.

"Oh my God—" She broke off, and Isabel heard what she thought was a sob.

"I know this must be rather emotionally overwhelming for you. Do you want me to come round to see you? I could, you know."

Jane thanked her. No. She would cope; she was fine; she needed a minute or two. Now she asked Isabel what the next step would be. "May we go and see him?"

"That's up to you," said Isabel. She had offered to help, and now she was running things. It had happened before; it always happened. "You decide what you want. All that I'd be inclined to say is that it might be better for me to go and see him first. I could break the news and see what his attitude is." She paused. "He may not want to see you, you know."

She knew that was not an easy thing for anybody to hear, in whatever circumstances. Of course people would want to see *me;* how could they not? That was what most people thought, although there were those who were realistic to the point of self-effacement; those who said too quickly, "You won't remember me, of course."

Jane seemed unconcerned. "I know that," she said quickly. "We don't know whether he's even aware of my existence."

Isabel doubted that. "He may not know who you are, but surely he knows that there was a baby. Surely . . ."

But as she said this she saw what Jane meant. In those days—and today—people could deny pregnancy. She had met somebody who had gone through a concealed pregnancy and then, to the astonishment of all, had excused herself one day, gone into the bathroom and given birth. This woman had been pointed out to Isabel at a wedding reception: she sat demurely at the edge of the room with a toddler at her feet.

"That woman," Isabel's companion had whispered, "went into the bathroom one day and *had a baby*. That very child at her feet. Not a soul knew. Not her doctor. Not her parents. Presumably not the child's father. Can you believe it?"

It was the sort of story which people loved, which brightened their lives, in fact. That somebody should do something like that in defiance of the framework of a benevolent state, with its nurses and health visitors and information leaflets: it spoke of rebellion, of self-determination on a heroic scale. Or of shame, which itself was becoming rarer and rarer.

Nobody felt very much ashamed of anything any more, Isabel thought. You could do what you liked and then speak about it at great length on a confessional television show and nobody would bat an eyelid. And while that revealed a healthier attitude when it came to dealing with things that were better unconcealed, or with things that should not involve shame at all, it also meant that one of the main reasons for social restraint had been removed. Isabel recalled reading an article on homicide by a psychologist who argued, somewhat obviously, that shame and feelings of guilt were the main reason why people were hesitant to murder one another: a self-evident point, but one that perhaps we might need to remind ourselves of. The hesitation could so easily be removed and then anything might be done, and was.

And then she thought: How does the sense of shame get dismantled? One way suggested itself immediately: *Get children used to killing.* Yes. And how? *Let them play games about killing. Let them do it on their computers!*

"Isabel?"

"Yes, I'm still here. I was just thinking, you're right: Clara . . . I suppose I should call her your mother . . . Your mother may well not have told Rory. She may just have gone off and had the baby." She hesitated. "Perhaps she didn't want Rory to be involved because she didn't want to continue to be involved with him. Perhaps it was all an accident. She might not have loved him. It might just have happened and then been regretted."

It was not the silence at the other end of the line that stopped Isabel; it was her own realisation that what she was talking about here were the facts of another person's coming into existence. We all like to imagine that we do so in the most romantic of circumstances, to the accompaniment of music, by candlelight. But for most of us it may well not be like that at all—not that we like to dwell on it. Freud was right in suggesting that what he called the primal scene was disturbing; of course it was. Our parents could surely not have done that sort of thing.

And here she was suggesting to Jane that she was an accident. She had more or less spelled it out: a student party in a shabby flat, with two people having had too much to drink, perhaps, and ended up fumbling about in a cluttered bedroom, and hey presto, a new life is conceived. And then self-reproach and horror and embarrassment, and the new life is concealed and shunted away to Australia with a new set of parents.

"I'm very sorry," she muttered.

Jane seemed surprised. "About what?"

"About suggesting that . . . that your conception was accidental."

"But I'm sure it was. How many of us are planned? Some, maybe, but many aren't."

"You're very matter-of-fact," said Isabel.

Jane laughed. "I'm Australian. We don't go in for hypocrisy about these things."

"Clearly not." Isabel paused. "But here in Scotland we do, do we?"

"I wouldn't put it that way. But people here are a bit more . . . subtle, perhaps. It comes from having to be careful not to tread on too many toes. You people say an awful lot without actually saying it, if you know what I mean. That's a talent, maybe, rather than a fault."

Isabel brought the conversation back to its original purpose. "So shall I try to see him?"

"Yes," said Jane. "Exactly. If you don't mind."

Isabel assured her that she did not. "And I'm not being subtle," she said. "I'm really not. I've become interested in this. I want a happy ending, you know."

"Don't we all?" said Jane.

"Yes. But it doesn't always happen that way."

"That depends on how you write the story," said Jane.

MIST HUNG OVER the fields of East Lothian, the rich farming land that lay between Edinburgh and the North Sea coast. There was a local name for this, for the rolling banks of white that came in off the sea, drifting across the low ground, filling valleys, lapping at the feet of hills; this was the *haar*, a word that

Isabel had always found onomatopoeic. If the *haar* made a sound, which it did not, it would be "haar," a soft breathing out, an exhalation of slightly moist air from the depths of the lungs.

Now, at ten o'clock in the morning, the *haar* was still in evidence, although it was quickly being burned off by the sun to reveal the countryside beneath: the orderly fields, dark green in their summer clothing but with earlier crops here and there already golden. She drove past a large field of hay that had been cut a day or two previously, the circular bales dotted about where the harvester had disgorged them. She saw a tractor halfway up a slope, driven by a man who was waving to another man on the ground; she passed a field full of pigs with their curious, domed pig arks like the tepees of some tribe of plainsmen. She thought: All *this* happens to support all *that*—that being the life of the cities, all those people who were ignorant or indifferent to the life of the countryside and to their agricultural roots. Music and art and philosophy are ultimately based on the premise that this man on his tractor, and these pigs, and the swarms of bees that fertilise the crops, will all continue to do what they do. And every philosopher, no matter how brilliant his or her insights, needs a portion of this field—how much? Half an acre?—to support him if he is to survive.

She followed the back road that led through the village of Longniddry and then along the railway line towards Haddington. Years ago while this had been rich agricultural land up above, it had been mining country down below. Thick seams of coal ran directly beneath these fields and out under the North Sea. The mining had stopped, but had left its mark on the land and on the people too, who, some of them, had hard work stamped on them like a badge.

It had not been difficult to find Rory Cameron. Isabel had phoned a friend who lived in Gullane, a village on the coast that was surrounded by golf courses. Did she know anybody called Rory Cameron who had been—

"He was the secretary of one of the golf clubs," her friend interjected. "Years ago. That Rory Cameron? He was married to an Irishwoman, I think."

Isabel held her breath. She had not expected it to be quite as easy as this. "He's still alive?" she asked.

Her friend had laughed. "Why should he be dead?"

"Because we all die," said Isabel. "Didn't you know that?"

"I had my suspicions," said her friend. "No, that Rory Cameron is alive and kicking. I saw him a week or two ago in the village. I don't really know him very well—but you know what this place is like: everybody is *aware* of everybody else even if they don't actually know them. I've met him once or twice at drinks parties."

"And?"

"And what?"

"And what's he like?"

There was a moment of hesitation. "More or less what you'd expect. A bit unusual maybe."

Isabel waited for her friend to explain. When she did not, Isabel asked in what way.

"There's an air of unhappiness about him. Not what one would expect in the secretary of an East Lothian golf club. They're usually . . . well, you can imagine what they're like. Brisk and sociable. And he was also an army officer. You expect army officers to be rather brisk, don't you? You don't think of them as being tormented by doubts."

Isabel could not help but imagine an army officer plagued by doubts. *Quick march, or maybe not. Left-flanking attack, or maybe right. Move forward, but perhaps not quite now.*

Isabel made a remark about avoiding stereotypes. "The army recognises that there can be all sorts of officers. And the British Army, surely, has had some very unusual soldiers in the past, hasn't it? Look at Lawrence of Arabia. Or Montgomery. He was a much more complex character than people think."

She mulled this over as she neared Gullane. Rory Cameron had been polite on the telephone. She had explained that she wanted to talk to him about somebody he had known at university. She did not mention Clara's name, even when he had asked.

"Do you mind if we don't go into the details over the phone?" she said. "I'd much prefer to talk to you about it in person."

He had seemed more bemused than suspicious. "I don't see why you can't say who it is," he said. "It's hardly state secrets we'll be discussing." He paused. "What's it to do with, then? You should at least be able to tell me that."

"Somebody has asked me to find out more about a parent," she said. "Somebody from back then."

He had remained good-humoured. "I'm sorry; do I know you?"

"We have a mutual friend."

She gave the name of her friend, and he said, "Ah, yes," before going on to say, "All right, I could see you if you wish, as long as you make it relatively early in the morning. Ten-thirty tomorrow? I'm playing golf in the afternoon and I can't change that."

THE CAMERON HOUSE, which Isabel found with some difficulty after a few wrong turnings, was at the end of an old farm road, rutted and potholed from years of neglect. The fields on either side, shielded by unruly hedgerows, were still in use, with one being occupied by cattle clustered about a gate, watching her balefully as she negotiated a particularly muddy patch of the track. The cattle were expecting their feed, and one or two of them poked their heads through the bars of the gate.

"I'm sorry, I have nothing for you," she muttered, and then thought, *It's come to this at last: I'm talking to cows.*

The house itself was organised in the typical way of the more prosperous Scots farmyard, with a rambling barn, or steading, behind it, a block of storerooms and a walled vegetable garden. The steading had been worked on and had a set of freshly painted doors; at several points along the roof, an uneven structure covered with warm red pantiles, modern skylights had been added. Ranged against the steading wall were four large kennels, each with a tiny roof tiled to match.

The house was larger than one might expect to find on a working farm, and Isabel imagined that a century or two ago it might have been occupied by a family with pretensions to being part of the gentry: not quite there yet, but on the way. The original family had clearly gone, but might have held on until the 1960s or 1970s, when a new generation might have lost interest in farming and pursued careers in Edinburgh or Glasgow. The land would have been let—it probably still was—to a neighbouring farmer and the house would have been bought by somebody exactly like Rory Cameron.

If that is what he really was like, as Isabel reminded herself as she made her way to the front door. She had him pigeon-holed: he would be fit and good-looking, still; he would wear cavalry twill trousers and one of those sweaters from the Borders wool mills; his shoes—brown brogues, of course—would be well polished. No, she reminded herself: do not stereotype people. And yet, and yet . . . people stereotyped themselves: they were the ones who chose to follow the part assigned to them.

"Don't use the front door," came a man's voice from above. "Everybody comes in the back door. And don't mind the dogs. They don't even bark, let alone bite."

There was an open window directly above her, but no head poked out of it.

"All right," she called out and made her way round to the back of the house. There she found an open door and beyond it, on a floor strewn with blankets, two Irish wolfhounds lay sleeping.

A woman appeared in the doorway. "They're very old," she said. "They sleep all day."

Isabel looked at the woman who had appeared to greet her. She was somewhere in her fifties, she thought, which would make her a few years younger than her husband—if she was, as she suspected, Rory Cameron's wife. She had a rather angular face, but any severity in her features was softened by an unusually warm smile. She was dressed comfortably, but with a touch of country elegance—exactly as one would expect a woman living in such a place to be dressed.

"I'm Georgina Cameron," she said, holding out a hand. "And you're Isabel Dalhousie, aren't you?"

Isabel nodded and shook the proffered hand. The skin was dry: the hand of a woman who groomed horses, or worked in the vegetable garden? The accent, she could tell, was Northern Irish.

"Rory will be down in a moment. You caught him in the middle of a telephone call."

"I'm sorry. I'm a bit early."

Georgina smiled. "Actually you're a tiny bit late. Not that it matters, but Rory will have to keep to half an hour on the clock."

"He told me," said Isabel. "Golf."

"Yes."

Georgina led her from the hall and into a large, well-lit kitchen. At the far end of the room was a wide Aga stove, with a capacious kettle on one of the hotplates. On a pine table in the centre of the room a white china teapot had been set out with three cups and saucers. There was a plate of shortbread beside this and an opened copy of that morning's *Scotsman*.

In the background, one of the dogs gave a growl.

"He talks in his sleep, that one," said Georgina. "Dreams of past glory, I suppose. Same as all of us."

Isabel found herself taking an immediate liking to this woman. It was the smile, but also the accent. Isabel liked Northern Ireland and its much misrepresented people. "Charming people, when not actively shooting one another," a friend had once said, which was so unkind but, like so many unkind comments, had a grain of truth in it. They *did* shoot one another and had been doing so for centuries. They did bicker over and brood on long-dead history—or history that should be long dead. The problem with history was that it refused to lie down and die.

"You're from Northern Ireland?" Isabel asked.

"I am that," said Georgina. "Belfast." She paused, a smile showing in her eyes as well as on her lips. "You know it?"

"A little. I've been there a few times and I liked it."

Yes, she thought; yes. She liked it because John Liamor, her Irish ex-husband, hated it.

"A grand place," said Georgina. "But I've lived here in Scotland for so long that when somebody asks where I'm from, I say Scotland. Which, in a sense, is historically true. I'm an Ulster Protestant—that much maligned category. My people went over from Scotland in the seventeenth century. The plantations."

"Nothing to be ashamed of. Protestantism in those days stood for the rejection of the old dark ways—the ways of corruption and superstition and so on."

Georgina nodded. "Maybe. But we were still settlers, weren't we?"

"But there have been all sorts of settlers. The Irish settled in Glasgow in the nineteenth century. Look at all those Irish names there. And London too. So it worked both ways. People move in and out. We're all mixed up in these islands."

Georgina thought this was right. "I'm not apologetic. I just want us all to . . . well, make our peace, which we have more or less done now—or started to do. We have more in common than we think."

"Except a flag," said Isabel. "You differ on that."

"And what does that matter?"

Isabel raised an eyebrow. "For some people, it matters a great deal, I suppose. Not particularly for me, but for many."

"It doesn't matter to you because you're under the right flag—the one you want to be under. It's not quite the same if you find yourself under the wrong flag. Then it matters a lot."

A slightly edgy note had entered the conversation. Isabel realised that she had gone straight to the issue on which Northern Irish people, of whatever persuasion, might be expected to feel strongly. One should not do that, she thought. She remembered her mother's aunt, a redoubtable matriarch from Mobile, Alabama, who insisted on raising the Civil War in any meeting with a Northerner, and would persist with the conversation, pretending to be too deaf to hear any defensive sallies made by a visitor. Age and a generally forbidding manner meant that she got away with this for years, until eventually a spirited New Englander, who had called at the house, seized a yellow legal pad and wrote in large letters: YOU WERE ON THE WRONG SIDE. PERIOD.

The story had passed into family history and was now used extensively by Isabel's American cousins in any dispute. "You are on the wrong side. Period," was a very effective way of closing down a wide range of arguments from the political (decades ago one branch of Isabel's family had strayed from the time-honoured family position and had been sent a telegram: WRONG SIDE. PERIOD.) to disagreements about the best recipe for clam chowder, the right way of training dogs, or the relative merits of New York hotels.

Rory's appearance changed the subject. "I'm sorry to have kept you," he said. "I was talking to a neighbour on the phone. There's going to be a new road and that means everybody's up in arms. We all have cars, of course, but other people's cars are very annoying, aren't they?"

They shook hands and Isabel took the opportunity to study her host, discreetly, of course. He was precisely as she had thought he would be: he was not wearing the sweater she had imagined for him, but the shoes were exactly right, as was the face. Although he must have been in his mid-sixties, Rory had kept the features of a man in his early forties. Open air, thought Isabel; all that walking around windswept golf courses. And something else too, perhaps; people like that usually had a secret: a diet restricted to dried cranberries and hazelnuts, or something of that sort. Or, in the case of the late poet, Hugh MacDiarmid, the best part of a bottle of Glenfiddich whisky a day. That, of course, was hardly recommended, but had seen him through to his mid-eighties in remarkably good shape. Scottish poets, though, were a special case.

Rory joined them at the table, and Georgina started to pour tea.

"Have you seen Kirsty recently?" he asked. "She hasn't been very well, I hear."

Kirsty was their mutual friend in Gullane.

"She had an operation on her knee," said Isabel. "I saw her just after that. She's made a good recovery."

Rory nodded in satisfaction at the good news. He regarded Isabel steadily. "I was rather intrigued by your telephone call," he said. "It's not often that somebody rings up and wants to talk about something they won't divulge on the phone."

Isabel smiled weakly. "It's easier sometimes . . ."

He made a gesture of understanding. "Of course it is. Phone calls can be stilted. And you can't always judge the effect of what you have to say if you can't see the other person."

"True," said Georgina. "I don't like speaking about anything really important on the phone."

They both now looked at her expectantly, and Isabel's heart began to hammer in her chest. She had not thought this through. She had imagined that she would talk just to Rory—how stupid of her: of course there was always a possibility of his wife being present. And now she wondered whether she could even raise the subject.

She glanced at Georgina. "I'm very sorry," she began. "I know it sounds ridiculous, but I imagined that our conversation . . ." And here she turned to Rory. "I imagined that our conversation would be confidential. It's a rather delicate matter."

Georgina and Rory exchanged glances. He frowned. "We have no secrets from each other," he said formally. "We are husband and wife."

Isabel noticed that Georgina winced at this. It was a fleeting reaction and immediately suppressed, but she saw it and wondered. Was it his choice of words: the cliché of having no secrets, the formality of the declaration? Or was it something else altogether: the response of one who hears something said that she knows to be untrue? If that were the case, then who harboured the secrets? It could be him, in which case she might wince at the untruth; or it could be her, in which case she might feel regret, or embarrassment, perhaps, at knowing his trust to be misplaced.

"Please forgive me," Isabel said. "That was most tactless of me." She realised that she could hardly stop now. "I've come to talk to you about somebody called Clara Scott. I believe you knew her a long time ago."

"Clara Scott?" said Georgina. "No—"

"It's me," said Rory. "Of course I knew her. We were at university together in Edinburgh back in the . . . year dot. She was, in fact, a girlfriend of mine, for a short time."

"Oh, her," said Georgina. "You showed me—"

"A photograph," said Rory. "Yes, I have several photographs.

Georgina doesn't mind. We have photos of all our old friends—and why not? Mine is of me and Clara in York. We went there once with the university chorus."

They waited for Isabel to say something. But before she could do so, Rory added: "You know that she died a long time back? Poor Clara. It was six or seven years after she left university—maybe a bit later. A road accident."

"I know," said Isabel. "Her daughter told me."

This was greeted with silence. Then Rory said, "Her daughter? Clara didn't marry, did she?"

"No," said Isabel. "She didn't."

There was a further silence. One of the wolfhounds mumbled in his sleep again.

"She had a daughter," Rory muttered, almost under his breath.

Isabel nodded. She noticed that Georgina had glanced sharply at her husband, but quickly looked away again.

Rory seemed to be somewhere else altogether. "Why didn't she tell me?" he whispered, not to anybody else but to himself.

"The daughter was adopted," Isabel continued, "and taken to Australia. She lives there now."

Isabel saw the effect of this on Georgina. There was a visible relaxing of posture; clearly some anxiety had been defused.

Only to be rekindled. "But she's in Edinburgh at the moment. That's why I'm here. She wants to find out more about her mother . . ." A half-truth that I must correct, she thought. "And her father too."

That brought even more of a reaction. Georgina sat bolt upright and for a moment or two closed her eyes; Rory stared at Isabel in what appeared to be complete astonishment. For her part, having delivered the shocking news, even if she had not spelled out, Isabel sat quite still. She was uncertain what to do now, but it occurred to her that it was too late for tact.

"It's possible, I suppose, that you're the father," she said to Rory. "That is, if the relationship was a close one."

"It was," he muttered, half looking at Georgina. She closed her eyes again. "But she didn't say anything. She didn't. Why on earth would she not . . ." He shook his head. "Why not say something?"

Isabel tried to answer. "People sometimes don't. I know it seems odd, but when one's young, and frightened too—"

"She had no need to be frightened," Rory interjected. "I would have . . ." He left the sentence unfinished, silenced, perhaps, by a look from Georgina.

"One thing I'd like to ask," Isabel went on, "is whether there might have been somebody else. Were there other boyfriends?"

He thought for a moment. "I don't think so. She didn't sleep around, you know. She was Catholic."

"So you're convinced there was nobody else?"

He became more confident. "Definitely. As I said, Clara wasn't the sort."

Isabel nodded. "I'm very sorry to spring this on you," she continued. "We—that is, Jane and I: Jane is her name, you see—we decided that it might be easier for you to hear this from a third party, rather than her turning up—"

"And saying: 'You're my father'?" Rory asked.

Isabel noticed that he was beginning to smile. She was still cautious. "Possibly."

Rory now stood up and clasped his hands together in a curious, almost praying gesture. "I'm a father," he muttered. "I have a daughter. I have a daughter." He turned and looked at Georgina, as if suddenly reminded that he had a wife. He placed a hand on her shoulder. "My darling, please forgive me. I'm . . . well, I'm overwhelmed."

She reached up and put her hand on his—a touching gesture of support, of reassurance. "That's good, darling. Very good."

Isabel thought that she should leave them alone and began to rise to her feet.

"Don't go," said Rory. "Please."

"No," said Georgina. "Please don't go."

"Does she want to see me?" asked Rory.

Isabel nodded. "She does."

"Today?"

Isabel was a bit taken aback. "We had no plans. I'm sure that she will want to see you soon, but perhaps you should give her a day or two to prepare herself."

"A sensible idea," said Georgina. "We all need to adjust." She turned to Isabel. "I think it would be best if Rory met her alone. I'd love to meet her too, of course, but I think the first meeting should be just the two of them."

Isabel agreed, and then Georgina suggested that she would show Isabel the garden while Rory collected himself. It was obvious to Isabel that her intention was to have a private talk, but Rory appeared to be quite content with this. They went outside, into the sun that had now dispatched the *haar* and was bathing the garden in a thick summer light, an impasto of gold.

"PERHAPS YOU SHOULD KNOW something about my husband," said Georgina. "He's a disappointed man."

They were walking around the perimeter of the walled garden. There was a line of lavender bushes, old and gnarled, in need of pruning, and a row of espaliered apple trees.

"I had heard him described as a bit unhappy," said Isabel.

Georgina raised an eyebrow. "Really? Well, that's very perceptive of whoever it was—Kirsty, I imagine."

Isabel was hasty to point out that Kirsty had not been critical. "All she said was that she felt Rory was a bit unhappy. She didn't run him down."

"Of course not," said Georgina. "And she's right, anyway. He is." She paused and bent down to pick up a stick that had fallen across the path. "Most of us are unhappy to a degree—if we have anything between our ears at all. It would be impossible to be completely sanguine about the world, don't you think? Not with the state that it's in."

"Yes," said Isabel. "Hardly anybody can be completely happy. And who would want to be, anyway? A life without moments of unhappiness would be monotonous, I would have thought."

"Exactly," said Georgina. "But for poor Rory the prevailing emotion is unhappiness, I'm afraid. He's never been happy with what he's been doing. Never."

Isabel said nothing. Was the marriage unhappy too, she wondered?

"You see," Georgina continued, "he was sent off to boarding school when he was eleven. That was the start of it, I think. He went to one of those places where all sorts of cruelties were practised. They've closed a lot of those places down now, or they've changed of their own accord. You can't bully these days—but when Rory was at school bullying was written into the life of those places. It was a tradition.

"And so his unhappiness started. He told me that before he was sent back to school at the end of each holiday he would cry until he was sick. Actually throwing up. And then he was subjected to all sorts of indignities and, well, I'm sorry to have to say this, sexual abuse. The older boys. Nothing was done about it. Nothing. The younger boys didn't dare mention it or report it because they knew it was hopeless.

"Then he got a place at university but went on to choose the wrong career. He went into the army because his father was keen that his son should join his old regiment. He was in a Highland regiment, and you know how family-oriented those are. Well, Rory joined and found that he did not like it at all. But rather than resign his commission and upset his father, he stayed put. I hated it too. I found the company of the other officers' wives insufferable—I know that sounds snobbish, but they were the snobs, not me. I hated the whole thing and tried to live my life as if the army didn't exist.

"And then he had to do something that really upset him. He's never told me exactly what it was, but I know that it distressed him greatly. I don't like to think about it, of course, but sometimes I dream about it. I see him . . . Well, I shouldn't burden you with that, I really shouldn't.

"At long last he left the army and looked for another job. A post at a golf club came up and he applied for that. It was not a well-known one—a rather poor club, and in fact it's no longer in business. He went there and I think he was good at what he did. But he did not enjoy golf in the slightest. And yet he found himself being drawn into the game. Now he has friends who expect him to play regularly and he goes along with it—he pretends to enjoy golf. It's every bit as inauthentic for him as the army was."

She sighed. "His whole life has been spent doing things ~~he~~ didn't really want to do. What a complete waste."

"I'm sorry to hear that."

Georgina shook her head. "He shouldn't have let it happen. But then, quite a few people do, don't they? They live lives that are all wrong for them."

She turned around. Isabel's eyes were drawn to a brooch that she was wearing—an art nouveau twirl with a peridot in the centre. There was something intensely poignant, she thought, about the little things we do to adorn ourselves, to present a face to the world; our tiny vanities; our desire for the beautiful. How human.

Georgina resumed. "What you told Rory this morning will be terribly important to him, you know. I expect that he's thrilled. But we must be careful about it—the whole point of my speaking to you as I just have done is that he is very vulnerable, believe it or not, and this is a very emotional area for him. I've been unable to have children, you see."

Isabel drew in her breath. "I'm so sorry. I didn't mean to barge in like this—"

"But you did the right thing," said Georgina. "It's just that we must be quite tactful with Rory. That's all I'm saying." She stopped for a moment, as if weighing up what to say next. "In fact, there's something that perhaps I should . . ."

Isabel waited, but Georgina had evidently decided not to say whatever she had on her mind.

"Yes?" she prompted gently.

Georgina shook her head. "Let's get back to the house," she said.

CHAPTER TWELVE

Isabel had told Grace about Gareth's telephone call. "That medium was spot on," she said.

Grace looked puzzled. There are so many mediums in her life, Isabel thought; perhaps one séance fades into another and she becomes blasé. And so many spirits jostling to communicate; after all, the other side must be pretty crowded by now . . .

"The one who told you, the audience—"

"The meeting," Grace corrected primly.

"Yes, told the meeting about that firm West of Scotland Turbines. That one. Well, I bought some of their shares and I'm happy to say they've gone up in value tremendously."

Grace smiled. "I told you so," she said.

You didn't, thought Isabel. *You never said anything about the shares.*

But Grace was determined to claim whatever credit was available—or to claim it on behalf of the spirit world.

"They're usually absolutely right," she said. "I can think of hardly any occasions when they've been wrong."

Isabel could. She very clearly remembered the spirits being

reported—through Grace—as having predicted the outcome of a French presidential election entirely wrongly; the spirits, it appeared, tended towards a conservative view of politics and the victory had gone to the socialists. And she remembered, too, when one of the spirits had said that an Irish horse was going to win the Grand National when it was an English horse owned by an Arab sheik that eventually romped home. The spirits had also warned Grace about a volcano in the Canary Islands that they said would explode within two months. That was eight years ago. And while seismologists may get it wrong from time to time, spirits surely could get it right, given their location, as Grace often put it, beyond the constraints of our ordinary human time and place.

The conversation about the rising share price of West of Scotland Turbines had taken place the day before Isabel went to see Rory and Georgina. Isabel had not thought much of it and certainly did not expect the outcome that Grace revealed to her when she came back from East Lothian.

"I've invested in West of Scotland Turbines," Grace said, as Isabel came into the kitchen.

Isabel frowned. "When?"

"This morning," said Grace proudly. "You remember that legacy I got from my father's cousin? The one who lived in Aberdeen? The twelve thousand pounds?"

Isabel nodded weakly.

"Well, I had that in the bank and it wasn't getting much interest with these rubbishy interest rates these days. So I spoke to the bank on the phone and they have a stockbroking service that buys shares. I told them to buy shares in West of Scotland Turbines. They've done it for me."

Isabel tried to sound a note of caution. "You have to be

careful," she warned. "Just because something has gone up, it doesn't mean that it's going to stay up."

"But you made a profit," said Grace. "You told me so."

"I did," said Isabel. "But you have to remember that the stock exchange is volatile."

"But yours went up," said Grace.

"I know," said Isabel patiently. "But yours may not."

"Are you saying that they're going to go down? Is that what you're saying?"

Isabel tried to reassure Grace that she was not suggesting this. She was careful: Grace was touchy about a whole range of matters, and money was one of them. It was not that Grace resented Isabel's financial position; she did not. It was more a question of independence, which was something that Grace defended assiduously. She did not like Isabel to advise her on anything, and even when it seemed that advice was exactly what her housekeeper was looking for, Isabel knew better than to offer it. And that, she felt, was precisely what many people wanted who sought advice. They did not want you to tell them what to do; they wanted you to confirm that what they intended to do was the right thing.

"I'm sure that everything will be fine," said Isabel soothingly. "There is never enough electricity, is there, and so West of Scotland Turbines should hum along nicely."

"I think so too," said Grace. "That's why I did it."

"And I'm quite sure that if there is any danger of a real dip in their value, the other side will give you adequate warning."

Grace looked at her suspiciously. She was very defensive of the spirit world and she was not sure whether Isabel's comment was serious enough. One mocked the spirit world at one's peril, in Grace's view.

The subject of stocks and shares was put to one side. Charlie had received a lunch invitation—his first—and did not need to be collected until three o'clock. Grace had offered to do the collecting, as the house of Charlie's new friend was only a few streets away.

"You can work," said Grace. "The morning post was massive, I'm afraid."

Isabel groaned. "Manuscripts?"

"They looked like it," said Grace. She smiled at Isabel. "Why do these philosophers do it?"

Isabel was not sure what this meant. "Do what? Philosophy?"

"Write all those articles. Surely there isn't much new to say. Surely it's all been said before."

Isabel thought about this. Had it all been said before? A lot of it had, she decided, but that did not mean that it was not worth saying again. And even when something has been said before, there was some point in its being said again by different people, and said *to* different people.

She was about to say this when Grace changed the subject. "A man telephoned," she said. "He left a message."

Isabel wondered whether it was Gareth Howlett, who had said that he would call her to confirm the sale of the West of Scotland Turbines shares.

Grace shook her head. "No. I know Gareth. I didn't know this one."

She waited for Grace to retrieve the piece of paper on which she had written the details of the caller. Grace's notes were laconic, but enjoyable for their sometimes astringent comments.

Now Isabel listened as Grace read from her aide-mémoire:

"Max Lettuce. Is in Edinburgh today and tomorrow. Would like to see you, if possible. Could you phone him on his mobile? Full of himself. Thought I would know who he is. Did not say please. Asked if I was cleaning lady." Grace regarded her balefully. "That's the message," she said. "I wrote down the number of his mobile—not that I wanted to, but I did anyway."

She passed Isabel the scrap of paper, on which the mobile number had also been noted.

"This is rather unexpected," said Isabel.

"Not the Lettuce I met?" asked Grace. "That big—"

"Slug," said Isabel quickly. And then immediately retracted her comment. It was wrong; it was uncharitable. "No, I didn't really mean that. Professor Lettuce may not be everybody's cup of tea; in fact, I suspect he's nobody's. But we should not belittle him."

Grace was more robust. "But he *is* a slug," she said. "That describes him perfectly."

Isabel ignored the encouragement. "This is his nephew. The lesser Lettuce."

Grace laughed. "I assume he's taken a leaf out of his uncle's book."

Isabel could not help but smile. "*Let us* not descend to puns," she said. "Even good ones." She paused. "I suppose I have to phone him."

Grace did not see why. "You don't have to phone people back. Why should you?"

"Because they've addressed you," said Isabel. "If somebody said something to you in the street, would you not feel that you had to reply?" As she asked the question, she realised its complexity.

For Grace, the answer was simple. "No. Not really. If a stranger comes up and says something that you don't want to hear, you don't have to say anything. Why should you?"

"Because . . ." Isabel shrugged. "It's to do with minimal moral obligation."

"And what about minimal disturbance?" retorted Grace. "I'm entitled not to be disturbed when I'm going about my business, aren't I?"

Isabel nodded. "Yes, I suppose you are."

"Well then," said Grace, with the air of one who had won her point.

Grace was right about being entitled not to be disturbed, but even if the people doing the disturbing were in the wrong, it did not mean that they ceased to be of any account: it all *depended*, as everything did. If you were in a great hurry, then you might be excused for ignoring a stranger who addressed you. But if you had time enough, then surely you could at least say no thank you, or sorry, or something of the sort; that was surely easy enough. After all, the other person—the stranger— shared those attributes that made each of us, every single one of us, so interesting, so morally significant: a life; a particular set of experiences; emotions; hopes; a family. In each of us there is something of human value, some grain of wisdom. If that did not count for something, then nothing, she thought, counted.

"I think I should phone him," she said, looking at the piece of paper.

Grace frowned, disapproving. "Of course," she said. "If that's what you want to do."

Isabel left the kitchen. She felt rather irritated by Grace's attitude. Her housekeeper was entitled to her opinions, and of course she should express them. But there were tactful ways of doing so and when you were sharing space with somebody—as she and Grace were—then you had to avoid too many disagreements. The relationship between Isabel and Grace was, after all, a working one. They were bound together by circumstance, and Isabel always treated Grace with consideration, but surely she was entitled to stand in her own kitchen and not be contradicted quite so firmly.

It was the same with friendship. Disagreement between friends—and spouses, too—had to be carefully handled. If the time you spent with friends was consumed by disagreement, then there was no room for the essence of friendship, which was a sharing of the world. And that sharing involved seeing things the same way, or at least seeing things through the eyes of the friend. That, surely, was why friends tended to be of the same general view. Jack Spratt, of nursery-rhyme fame—he who notoriously could eat no fat—could hardly have had a very comfortable marriage to his wife, who could eat no lean. And yet, of course, they proved to be a good team, as the last two lines of the nursery rhyme made clear:

> And so between the two of them, you see,
> They licked the platter clean.

The rhyme, then, was about how opposites may complement one another for practical purposes. But they may still be unhappy, of course.

Isabel's irritation with Grace did not last; it never did. She knew that Grace would do anything for her, and she would do anything for Grace. It was just that, on some subjects, they did not see the world in quite the same way. And Isabel was sufficiently self-aware—and modest—to know that this was not because she, Isabel, was always right. She was, in fact, often wrong—and knew it. Life became difficult when those who were often wrong did *not* know it.

She went into her study and dialled the number that Grace had written down. At the other end, the telephone rang only once or twice before being picked up.

"Max Lettuce."

Isabel gave her name in return.

A short pause followed. "Oh, yes. Of course. It's very kind of you. I just phoned on spec. I didn't expect you to call me back."

Why not? wondered Isabel.

"My uncle," Max continued, "said that I should contact you when I was in Edinburgh."

Why? Isabel asked herself. But what she said was: "How nice."

There was another short pause. "I was wondering whether we could meet. I'm in Edinburgh for a rather short time, but . . ."

I don't really want to meet you, she thought, but said: "I'd be very happy to see you."

Max asked whether that same day would be possible, and Isabel replied that it would. Where was he? She had been thinking of going into town and could meet him, if he wished, at Glass & Thompson. She would buy him coffee.

"No, you must let me do that!"

"We'll sort that out when we meet."

The call ended and Isabel frowned. Why had she done this? It would have been simpler to tell him that she was busy and that she hoped they would have the chance to meet the next time he came to Edinburgh, whenever that would be. But she realised that Max Lettuce's telephone call was a perfect illustration of the point that she had made to Grace. Max was the stranger addressing her in the street, and thankfully she had replied in exactly the way she had said one should reply. So at least she was being consistent.

Yet she did not want to do it. Max Lettuce, she was sure, would embody all the worst qualities of his uncle: he would be ambitious and scheming, an academic *operator*. He would be impossible, and she should not have agreed to meet him. And yet she had readily and without hesitation done just that; the internal moral automatic pilot had taken over and she had put herself out, and ruined her day—or so she suspected—by being obliging when she was fully entitled to protect her time from encroachments. She sighed. It would be simpler, she thought, to stop thinking.

She went into the kitchen to check with Grace on the arrangements for collecting Charlie. She would be back, she hoped, not long after Grace picked him up. He might need a piece of bread and peanut butter when he came back; it depended on what he had been given for lunch.

Grace nodded. "Sometimes they don't eat," she remarked, "when there are other children around—they're too busy playing."

The telephone rang. Isabel answered it on the kitchen extension. It was Gareth Howlett.

"Isabel? I said I'd call back to confirm that we'd got rid of West of Scotland Turbines. That went through fine. And, as I anticipated, you made a pretty good profit."

"Well done."

At the other end of the line Gareth laughed. "And we were just in time."

She looked across the room. Grace was wiping the counter with a cloth.

"Oh? Why?"

"They fell badly," said Gareth. "A couple of hours after we sold. That sometimes happens when there is a bit of completely unexpected bad news."

Isabel was silent, her gaze resting on the back of Grace's head. That money had been the other woman's nest egg. I have so much, Isabel said to herself, and Grace has so little. And yet it is I who have made the profit.

"Isabel?"

"Sorry. It's a bit of a surprise, that's all. Tell me what happened."

Gareth explained. "They were counting on the success of their new equipment. It had performed brilliantly in tests, which accounted for the rise in value of the shares. Everything seemed to be going the right way, but now one of the turbines has failed dramatically—it blew up, in fact—and that's set them back several years, I'm afraid."

"I see. Well, I suppose we should be grateful that we sold just at the right time."

She tried to keep her voice down, but Grace suddenly turned round and looked at her directly. Isabel closed her eyes. She said goodbye to Gareth hurriedly and put down the phone.

Grace moved her cloth slowly over the surface of the counter, but her heart was no longer in cleaning anything. "Is that West of Scotland Turbines you were talking about?"

Isabel could not lie, nor did she want to. "Yes."

"So if you sold yours at the right time, that must mean I've bought mine at a bad time."

Isabel nodded miserably. "I'm so sorry, Grace. I wouldn't have recommended you to buy them had I known. But I didn't . . ." She trailed off lamely.

Grace stared down at the surface of the counter. "It's my own fault," she said. "I've been greedy. I saw the chance of a quick profit and I went for it. I'm getting what I deserve."

"You're not," said Isabel. "You don't deserve to lose anything."

Grace appeared uncomforted by this. "There's no difference between gambling and playing the stock market," she said. "They are much the same thing. You may as well take the money to somewhere like Las Vegas or Monte Carlo and put it all on the tables."

Isabel was about to refute this but she realised that this was not the time. One could play the stock market quite morally because one was providing capital for companies to put to use. There was nothing wrong with that. The real villains were the people who made money out of manipulating people's currencies or took aim at companies in order to cripple them and profit from their distress; they were even worse than ordinary gamblers, she thought. They wore suits and ties and worked in plush offices, but they were muggers, really—no different from the criminals who lurked in the shadows and leaped out to relieve people of their wallets.

She knew, though, what she must do.

"Let me make it up for you," she said. "The profit I've made will more than compensate you."

Grace would not countenance this. "No," she said immediately. "It's very kind of you, but it's my own fault. I took the risk and I must pay for it."

"Please," said Isabel. "Please let me."

Grace shook her head.

"I have more money than I need," said Isabel. "And I'd feel much better if you let me do this."

Grace faltered. "I don't have much else," she said. "I've never been a great saver."

Isabel pressed home with her offer. "Good. Then that's settled."

"But what can I do for you in return?" asked Grace.

"Carry on being who you are," said Isabel.

ISABEL WAS RARELY in a bad mood, but when she arrived at Glass & Thompson she felt angry, with herself—for agreeing to go; with the as yet to be encountered Max Lettuce—for being a Lettuce; and with West of Scotland Turbines—for allowing their shares to tumble. There were other, lesser things that had irritated on her trip into town: a young man with extremely dirty dreadlocks sitting directly in front of her on the bus—she was sure that she saw his hair *moving*; a vapour trail across an otherwise unclouded sky—why must we spoil even the sky with the signs of our presence; and a newspaper billboard announcing a secret plan to impose a local income tax on Scotland.

How dare politicians have secret plans, she said to herself; if you intend to do something, then you should be honest about it and not seek to keep it secret from the people who will be affected by your plans. And if the government imposed heavier and heavier taxes on the population then presumably there would come a point at which anybody in a position to leave would do so. Well-off people were resented, of course, because human beings were, by nature, envious. But there came a point at which we had to accept that shaking out the pockets of the wealthy would simply drive them away. And after their pockets had been shaken out, who would there be to invest in schemes to create further wealth?

She went into Glass & Thompson and looked about her. The café was reasonably busy, although there were one or two tables free. Behind the counter, the bow-tied proprietor, Russell Glass, was cutting a large quiche.

"Your friend is over there," he said, nodding in the direction of one of the tables at the back.

"Not my friend," muttered Isabel.

"Oh!" said Russell. "He said he was."

Isabel checked herself. "I'm not in a good mood, Russell. Everything is—"

"Going pear-shaped? Oh, I know the feeling. Let me get you something to sort all that out. A bit of this almond tart? Almond tart has amazing restorative properties."

She smiled. "Thanks, but I'll resist."

"Very restrained of you. I'll tell you what, friend or no friend," said Russell, "he made some very nice remarks about New Zealand." Russell was a New Zealander and was receptive to compliments.

Isabel made her way towards the back of the café. There was no mistaking Max Lettuce, who had the same sandy hair as his uncle, but cut shorter, and the same nose.

As she approached the table, Max stood up. "Dr. Dalhousie?"

They shook hands. "Please don't call me Dr. Dalhousie. Isabel."

"Isabel," he said, as if savouring the name. "I'm Max."

"I can tell," she said. "You are not entirely dissimilar to your uncle."

Max looked down at his hands. "So I hear. I thought I resembled my father, but my father obviously looks like his brother."

"Most of us don't like to be reminded of family resemblances," said Isabel. "We like to feel unique, don't we?"

Max agreed.

They sat down and Max pointed to the menu chalked up on the board behind the counter. "That's if you need something other than coffee. I didn't have lunch and thought that I might have something light."

While he read the menu, Isabel sneaked an appraising glance. He did look like Professor Lettuce, she decided, but was less fleshy, less ponderous. Would that change? Was this merely a young Lettuce who would become an old Lettuce in due course and be like all the other old Lettuces—assuming that all the other old Lettuces, whom Isabel had never met, were all alike?

Her attention moved to his clothes. Professor Lettuce always seemed to wear a tweed jacket and flannels—hopelessly old-fashioned attire that flapped about him like a tent; Max, by contrast, was wearing a blue linen jacket and black denim jeans. She noticed that his shoes were made of soft blue leather, an effective match with the jacket.

He turned to face her and smiled. Isabel smiled back: that old, instinctive human exchange, the signalling that overcomes initial distrust. In this case, what needed to be overcome was her preconceived irritation, which now seemed to be fast dissipating.

"It's good of you to see me at zero notice," said Max. "Thanks so much."

Isabel made a gesture to indicate that it had been no trouble. "I like to get away from my desk," she said. "Any excuse will do." That, she thought, sounded rude, and she corrected herself. "I wanted to meet you anyway. Now that we're about to publish you, it seemed a good opportunity to put a face to the name." And that name, she could not help but think, was Lettuce.

Max's eyes widened slightly. Isabel wondered if he had picked up on her hostility. Did he know, perhaps, that his uncle was, if not an enemy, then at least an adversary of hers? It occurred to her that Max was some sort of plant, an agent provocateur dispatched by Professor Lettuce from his London fastness to weaken the redoubts of Edinburgh. Was this a trap?

"I'm very grateful to you for accepting the article," said Max.

Isabel thought: *I didn't.* But she had no intention of telling him that.

"I'm sure that it will attract attention," she said. "And I remember just how important those first publications were in my own career."

He was staring at her, as if troubled by something. Isabel questioned whether she had alarmed him by saying that his article would attract attention. It would not, of course; she was simply being polite—or optimistic.

"Your uncle and I have worked together for a long time," she said. "He's made a major contribution to moral philosophy, in one way or another. I'm certainly looking forward to his Hume book—how's it going, by the way?"

Max shrugged. "It's taking him a long time. But he's very thorough."

"Of course he is," said Isabel. *Thoroughly unscrupulous*.

Their order was taken. Isabel stuck to a cup of coffee although she relented to the extent of asking for a small bowl of olives. "They don't go with coffee," she said. "But I feel like them anyway."

"Then why not?" said Max. He ordered the smoked mozzarella salad; she approved.

"All those buffaloes," remarked Isabel. "Contented in their watery fields, or wherever it is that buffaloes wallow. They do wallow, don't they? That's why mozzarella is so liquid."

Max looked at her sideways.

"Please forgive me," said Isabel. "Sometimes I find that I go off at a bit of a tangent. I know it's annoying for other people but then other people annoy us in different ways. We all, I suppose, have the capacity to annoy one another." She paused. "And civilisation, I suppose, is the structure that helps us to minimise the annoyance."

This seemed to amuse Max. "I suppose we're all in favour of civilisation, just as we're in favour of motherhood and apple pie."

Isabel observed that there were presumably some who were *not* in favour of apple pie, but she felt that they were probably decently reticent about this. As she made the remark, she realised that she *liked* Max Lettuce, and that was a lesson. I had judged him even before I met him, she thought. The sins of the uncle should not be visited upon the nephew; of course they should not.

"Dr. Dalhousie . . ."

"Yes?"

He seemed to be struggling with something. "Look, that article—"

She interrupted him. "If you need to change anything,

please don't worry about that. Nothing's gone off to the printer yet, far from it."

He shook his head. "No, it isn't that. Not at all. It's . . . well, it's much more serious."

She waited for him to continue.

"Yes," he said. "You see . . . you see, I didn't write it. It's not by me."

It took her a moment or two to absorb this. "You didn't?"

"I didn't write it. It was written by my uncle Robert. Oh, he asked me to write a few sentences here and there, but the bulk of it was him. Then he put my name on it and sent it off."

She sat quite still. One of the assistants now placed her coffee in front of her and offered her the sugar bowl. She did not notice, and the assistant, after shooting an enquiring glance at Max, moved away.

"May I ask why he did this?"

Max grimaced. "I feel really awful telling you this. In fact, you'll have no idea what an effort it's been for me to spell it out—actually to find the words."

"I have every idea of that," Isabel snapped. "A confession is never easy."

He looked at her anxiously. "You despise me?"

The bluntness of the question disarmed her. One could not answer yes to somebody who has the honesty to ask.

"No," she said. "But please explain a bit further."

"It's the least I can do," he said.

She waited.

"My uncle is not the easiest man, but he's always been very good to me. My father, you see, his elder brother—he's twelve years older than Uncle Robert—suffers badly from depression.

It ruined his career—he trained as an architect—and it meant that he could never get a really good job. He was too unreliable and there would be long periods when he couldn't do anything. He attempted suicide twice, once when I was twelve and then again a couple of years ago.

"Because of all that, we were pretty hard up. He's sixty now and he has no pension, none at all. Uncle Robert, though, has money from his first wife, who came from a family that owned quite a few commercial buildings in Leeds and New-castle. She died. Did he ever mention her to you? He was very much in love with her and I think he still misses her, even if he remarried. Uncle Robert has kept my father going for years. He gives him a monthly sum—I don't know what it is—but it keeps my parents going. Without him, they would have been out on the street.

"Uncle Robert also paid for my education. He persuaded me to study philosophy, which I enjoyed anyway. He introduced me to the professor I did my post-graduate work with. He set everything up. I was grateful—who wouldn't be?

"Then he arranged for me to get that post-doc post in his department. I was more worried about that, because I knew that there were a whole lot of people after the post and I'm sure that some were better qualified than I was. But I took the job any-way. I shouldn't have, but I did."

He paused as the assistant reappeared and placed his moz-zarella salad in front of him. The assistant glanced at Isabel. "Did you order olives?"

"I did."

"I just wanted to be sure."

"Well, I did."

She went off to the kitchen, to return a few moments later with a small bowl of olives in oil. "Enjoy," she said.

Out of earshot, Isabel said to Max: "I wonder if that's mandatory. It sounded like it, don't you think?"

Max was too immersed in his confession to appreciate the remark. "Yes, maybe," he said vaguely. "So I took the job and then he was very good to me. If an invitation came to go to a conference that he couldn't attend, he would often put my name forward as a substitute. Normally I would never have got that sort of thing, but I did. I went to Oslo. I went to a conference of the American Philosophical Association in St. Louis. I went to a UNESCO philosophical meeting in Paris. Everything was going really well.

"Then he said that I should publish something. I started to work on an article, a version of a paper I had given at a conference, but he said that it wasn't right. I tried something else, and he said the same thing. I thought that he was becoming a bit concerned, and I was right. He took me out for a drink and told me that I really had to get something into print or I might find it difficult to get the next job—the post I have in his department is for three years, you see."

Isabel was familiar with the situation Max was describing. The life of the untenured academic was less secure, she knew, than the life of the junior plumber—different, maybe, and more privileged, but without the same prospects of a career. It was all very well becoming a philosopher—that was perhaps the easiest part; it was remaining a philosopher that was the challenge. Not that philosophers, or academics of any discipline, should complain too much; there were people whose career path was even steeper and more slippery. Isabel had known professional singers who had for years clung by their fingernails to the lowest rungs of the singing world, stuck in the choruses of obscure opera companies, understudying roles for principals who were distressingly healthy, who never developed last-minute laryngitis or suffered allergic reactions between Act Two and Act Three.

"It's not easy," said Isabel.

So Lettuce—the elder one—was a cheat, a practitioner of academic fraud, no less. He should bear most of the blame for this, she thought, rather than his nephew. It was a classic case, the sort of thing one read about all the time in newspaper court reports. Fagin and the Artful Dodger: a young man corrupted by an older one. It was an ancient story, and a tawdry one.

"Then he gave me an article he had drafted. He said that I should add a few footnotes, but that in essence the piece should be published as it was. I didn't know what to say. I should have given it right back to him. I should have said that I assumed that he was joking. I should have shown some moral courage. I did none of these things. I took it off and read it and did what he told me to do."

He paused. He was staring down at the table, his mozzarella salad untouched. For a moment Isabel thought that he was about to burst into tears, but he did not. He looked up at her, his face full of misery and self-reproach.

"Why did I do it?" he asked. "It wasn't for the job—I really don't mind too much about that. It was because I knew that if I rubbed my uncle up the wrong way, it could mean a falling-out between him and my father. I know what my uncle's like. He can be vindictive and I didn't want to do anything that could threaten the status quo. I have to remain on good terms with him for my parents' sake. Uncle Robert has got this mixed-up thing about me—he sometimes calls me the son he never had, but he can be very ambitious for me, overweening, bullying even."

Isabel regarded Max with sympathy, wanting him to know that she understood.

"So there you have it," said Max. "My confession. I'm sorry that I did it. And now, I suppose, you'll have to take it up with him." He suddenly sounded like a boy caught out. "Everything's ruined."

"In what way?"

"He'll be furious with me for telling you. But I had to speak about it. How could I continue in the knowledge that you were being deceived?"

He seemed to expect an answer. She looked at him, thinking: I had written this man off. Now he reveals himself as flawed, weak and repentant, as we are, all of us: flawed and weak, if not repentant.

"Max, what you've just done is very brave. It isn't easy to confess to something like that. You've done it and I admire you for it."

He seemed astonished. "You admire me?"

"Yes," she said gravely. "All of us do things we regret—that's part of being human. And sometimes, I think, moral quality reveals itself not so much in what we do, but in what we later say about what we have done. Do you see what I mean?"

"Maybe. But—"

Isabel stopped him. "But nothing. Of course you were in awe of Lettuce . . . I mean, your uncle. He was supporting your indigent parents; he was indirectly supporting you. Money is so powerful, isn't it? Those who have it can control the lives of those who don't. And they do just that—with arrogance and selfishness in some cases." She paused. "I'm sorry, but what you've told me about your uncle doesn't endear me to him. In fact, I must say that my previous dealings with him haven't done that either."

He appeared suddenly crestfallen, and Isabel doubted whether she should continue. Did he still *like* Lettuce after what he had done to him? He must have admired his uncle; did that feeling persist?

She decided not to say more. "But that's irrelevant now. What we need to think about is what he's involved you in here. We can't leave things as they are, can we?"

He shook his head. "No. So can I just withdraw the article?"

She thought about this. There was a way out and it was just beginning to show itself. But there was something that did not seem to make sense and she needed to ask a question first.

"May I ask you something?" she said. "Why did your uncle suggest that you come to see me? Was it just because you happened to be in Edinburgh?"

He took a moment to answer. "He didn't suggest that I come to Edinburgh. I was here anyway to see somebody—a friend who's taken a job here. He said that I should seize the opportunity to meet you since you were going to publish my article. And . . ."

"Yes?"

"And he said that he wanted to get me on to the board of the *Review*. He said that he had an idea of how he could."

Isabel sat bolt upright. "Did he now?"

"Yes," said Max.

"And how did he propose to do that? You do know, don't you, that I own the *Review*? I'm not just the editor—I'm the publisher."

Max nodded miserably.

"Well?" Isabel pressed.

"I've started telling you the truth," said Max. "I have to carry on."

"Yes please," said Isabel. "I'm listening."

"It's not easy to say this."

"Evidently not."

He sighed and looked away. "He hinted—just hinted."

"Yes?"

"He wanted me to seduce you."

CHAPTER THIRTEEN

JAMIE LISTENED with growing anger. Isabel had not seen him angry before, and she reflected on how strange it was that even at this stage in their relationship she had never observed the effect on him of that most common of human emotions.

"He said *what*?" he exclaimed.

She repeated Max's disclosure.

Jamie's face reddened. "I'm going to sort him out."

Isabel frowned. "Sort who out?"

"Lettuce," Jamie snapped back.

"Which one?"

"The older one. That creep down in London."

She felt touched that Jamie had reacted in such a protective, if clichéd masculine way. Was that what men should feel in circumstances where somebody makes an approach to their partner? And what did *sort out* mean? It sounded physical, but surely Jamie was not planning to assault Lettuce; he was far too gentle for that. She had never really thought about it, but had she been asked whether he was capable of physical violence, she would have answered that he was not.

Indeed, there had been the occasion when they had witnessed a military parade outside St. Giles' Cathedral—one of those occasions when the Scottish establishment dressed up and carried flags from point A to point B with immense solemnity; the Earl of This and the Duke of That and the Hereditary Keeper of the This Thing and That Thing, all bedecked in tartan, with feathers in their bonnets, were rendering homage to an ancient Scotland that still haunted the present. On the edge of this ceremony had been a platoon of kilted soldiers, simple working-class boys from worlds so far from those of the grandees. These boys had real rifles with bayonets attached, and the bayonets had glinted in the slanting Scottish sun.

Isabel had whispered to Jamie, "Could you ever have done that? Could you ever have put on a kilt and carried a rifle with a bayonet?"

And he had glanced at the soldiers and she had seen something like sympathy, and sorrow, in his expression, and he had said, "Never. Never."

He had been about to add something, but the bagpipes had begun to play and their wailing sound had drowned all speech, as it was meant to do.

No, Jamie was too gentle to sort anybody out, and even now, immediately after issuing the threat, he had calmed down and begun to look sheepish.

"You don't mean it, do you?" she asked.

"What? Sorting Lettuce out?"

"Yes."

He started to smile. "I'm not sure if I'd know how to."

She leaned over and kissed him. "I'm sure you wouldn't. And just as well—I couldn't live with somebody who sorted other men out. It just wouldn't seem right."

"It's still an awful thing for him to have said," Jamie muttered. "It's a sort of violation. By proxy."

Isabel shrugged. "Lettuce. He's dreadful. He always has been."

"And that nephew of his?"

Isabel thought very carefully. She had already done Max an injustice by condemning him before meeting him; she was keen not to do the same thing again.

"He's a bit weak, I suppose. He certainly let himself be led astray by Lettuce. But beyond that, we have to remember that he came clean. That takes courage. And now he's all for accepting responsibility for the whole situation."

Earlier on she had explained to Jamie about the article. It was fraud, he suggested, and she had agreed. Go to the police, he had said, but she had considered that something of an overreaction.

"The police would hardly take it seriously. They've got murders and muggings to look into. I'm sure they don't have the time for a couple of philosophers getting hot under the collar about who wrote what. And anyway," Isabel continued, "I've decided what to do. I'll write to Lettuce to say that I've declined the article on the grounds that I don't think it's the work of his nephew. I'll say to him that I think it reads like the work of a more experienced writer."

"He'll kick up a fuss."

"Of course he will, but I'll stand by my guns. I won't tell him that I think it's him, but I'll say that if he wishes, I can hand it over to one of those stylistic analysts. They're people who use computer programs to identify the frequency of the use of certain words and constructions. They can detect a writer's fingerprint, so to speak. I'll suggest that we run the article against something by him—by Lettuce—and see how it looks, just to show him how it works. Of course that'll alarm him and he'll drop the matter because the computer program would probably come up with the conclusion that he wrote it."

Jamie smiled at her ingenuity. "But why not just confront him?"

"Because it will harm Max and in my view he's relatively—not entirely—innocent in all this. He agreed to go through with it only to save his parents from Lettuce's wrath."

She paused; an idea occurred to her. She would encourage Max to write something that was authentically his. She would publish it if it was up to scratch, which it probably would be: Max struck her as an intelligent young man, even if he was a Lettuce. He would go away a friend rather than an enemy, and not only was it therefore the right thing to do in itself, it would also negate the elder Lettuce's scheming.

She explained her plan to Jamie: "I'm going to ask Max to write something without any involvement from his uncle. It'll help him to get free of his influence."

Jamie looked disgruntled. "So Lettuce gets away with it? He gets away with that crude plan to—"

"To seduce me? That's just laughable. It shows how much Lettuce knows about women. He assumed that any woman could be persuaded to fall for any good-looking young man who turns up. What an insult!"

Jamie smiled. "Can't they?"

She gave him a scathing look—but with irony, of course. "Can any man be persuaded to fall for an attractive woman who makes a pass at him?"

Jamie took some time to answer. "Sixty per cent of men could," he said. "No, seventy."

She chided him. "Where do you get those figures?"

"Intuition," he said. "I know what men are like. First-hand experience. I am one."

"But you're not part of that sixty or seventy per cent?"

"No. I promise you I'm not. Just you. You're the only one who could seduce me."

She laughed. "But I've already done that," she said.

"So you have," he said. "Utterly. Completely. Totally." Then he became serious. "You do remember that we're going to get married, don't you?"

"Yes, of course."

"When?"

She replied with a question of her own. "When would suit you?"

"Two weeks' time?"

"Why not."

He took her in his arms. "Good. I'll make arrangements."

THAT NIGHT Isabel had a visit from Jane Cooper. She came unannounced, shortly after half past nine, finding Isabel alone in the garden. The midsummer evening, only a couple of days away from the solstice, was still lit by a sun not yet set; there would be a good hour of light left before the gloaming proper, that hazy, fuzzy time of soft edges and gentle, washed-out colours. And it remained warm; Isabel wore a blouse with no cardigan or sweater, the friendly air about her at a perfect temperature.

She saw Jane before Jane saw her. The other woman was walking down the street, on the other side, and had slowed down when she drew level with Isabel's house. She hesitated for a moment before crossing the road, peering up—presumably to see if lights were on—and then started to make her way up the garden path.

Isabel, who had been examining a camellia bush, a mug of tea in her hand, called out: "You needn't press the bell. I'm here."

Jane spun round, almost guiltily, and made her way across the lawn to where Isabel stood.

"I was passing by," she said. And then, "Well, actually, I wanted to see you, but I felt—I don't know—I felt that I didn't want to pester you. So I thought if I took a walk and just happened to bump into you . . ."

Isabel sought to put her at her ease. "You can come and see me any time," she said. "I'm not one of those formal people who expect every visitor to phone in advance." She gestured to a bench at the side of the house, near a clump of lavender. "Why don't we sit there? I'm just finishing this tea—I could get you a glass of wine. An excuse to have one myself."

Jane accepted, and Isabel went off back into the house to fetch the glasses. She came back out and handed her visitor a glass of chilled white New Zealand wine. They exchanged toasts.

Isabel went straight to the point. "You've met him?"

She knew immediately from Jane's expression that the meeting had been a success. "Yes. Earlier today. We met for lunch in that restaurant you recommended to me. The Café St. . . . I forget its name."

"St. Honoré," Isabel prompted.

"Yes," said Jane. "There."

Isabel sipped her wine and then held the glass up to gaze

through it at the sky. The pale, attenuated blue became green through the yellow of the liquid; the colour of our world, she thought, is mediated by our lens.

"And it was a success?"

She imagined Jane entering the restaurant and looking about her—for the father she had never met. What would one say in such circumstances, without appearing melodramatic. *Father?* Too restrained; too reminiscent of the dialogue of an old-fashioned repertory play. Noël Coward. Or Oscar Wilde, with discussions of handbags and railway stations. Perhaps such a first contact today would be wordless, or maybe feelings would be closer to the surface and there would be unashamed sobbing and unrestrained emotional histrionics.

Jane smiled. "It couldn't have gone better. It was very . . . moving, I suppose. He was so kind to me."

Isabel, who had become tense, relaxed. This was an intervention on her part that had worked; it was a very satisfactory conclusion, which was not always the case with what she called her *involvements*. Jamie would be pleased; he was always concerned that she might make matters worse. Well, she had not done that in this case; far from it. She had facilitated happiness.

"We talked for hours," Jane went on. "I went there at twelve—we were the first people in for lunch. In fact, I think I was there at ten to. He came along fifteen minutes later, and we stayed until three. They started brushing the crumbs off our table very attentively—the signal, of course. At dinner they can turn the lights off if they want to give people the message."

Isabel smiled at the recollection of her own experience of the ways of restaurant staff understandably anxious to get away. She had once been in Paris, at a philosophical congress, and had had dinner with two loquacious Milanese philosophers. They had enjoyed their conversation so much that eventually a waiter had felt obliged to whip the tablecloth from under their elbows—a feat of dexterity requiring, no doubt, years of practice if it is to be done without causing seismic disturbance to the table arrangements. Nobody could fail to get that message, and the Italian philosophers had risen to their feet, unfazed, continuing their debate as they left the restaurant.

"You must have had a lot to talk about," she said. "Your whole life. And his, too, I suppose."

She wondered how one began such a conversation. The bare facts of a life can be compressed into a few pithy phrases summing up school, job, marriage, interests, but those would hardly do in such a case.

"He told me a lot about himself," Jane said. "To begin with, I thought that he would be reserved. You know there's a certain sort of man who . . . well, I suppose, strikes one as being buttoned up. Military people are often like that. He had that about him, and then suddenly, all in a bit of a rush, he opened up and started talking about his feelings. I hadn't expected it, but I suppose I had no idea what to expect."

Isabel knew what she meant. So many men were starved of the opportunity to discuss their emotional lives, put off by inhibition, by the expectations of others, or by male denial: so much so that some felt they had no such life, that there was simply nothing there: a desert of the heart. Auden had said that, she remembered: *in the deserts of the heart, let the healing fountain start . . .*

"A healing fountain . . ."

Jane was listening attentively. "Exactly. That's exactly what I felt. The pain started to come out, but even as it emerged you could see—really see—him feeling better. He started to smile. He started to talk about his future."

Isabel was interested in that. "Did he say he was going to give up golf?"

Jane was puzzled and listened intently as Isabel explained. "I had the impression—from something his wife said—that he played golf but did not actually enjoy it. He was trapped, in a way."

Jane became animated. "Yes! Yes! That's exactly the word he used: trapped. He didn't say that he was trapped by golf, but he did say that he had been trapped all his life by people who expected him to do things he didn't really believe in."

"And that's pretty common," said Isabel. "Have you ever known a priest who doesn't believe in God?"

"John Knox knew a God who didn't believe in priests," Jane replied.

Isabel laughed. "Jokes about the Scottish Reformation are so rare," she said. "And all the funnier for it. But, tell me: have you? I have. I had a university friend who became a priest because he came from a devout family and there was a lot of pressure on him to go off to a seminary. Subtle pressure—nothing crude—but it was there. He half believed to begin with, and then he persuaded himself a bit more, but eventually he lost what little faith he had. But by that time he was a fully fledged priest with a parish and people relying on him and so forth. And all the time, he was just going through the motions."

"Which many of us do, don't we?" said Jane.

"Yes. More people than we imagine. There must be police-men who don't believe in the law—or don't identify with it, rather. There must be personal trainers who don't see the point in being fit." Once the theme was broached, the examples flooded in. "Or politicians who are in the wrong party, whose careers have been based in a particular party and they have to see it through or they'll be out of a job." She paused. "And philosophers who would far rather be doing something else. Making money, perhaps. Or doing something practical."

Their eyes met for a moment, and then Jane looked away. "Me," she said. "Sometimes."

"And me too," said Isabel quickly. "Sometimes. Not very often, but sometimes. I help my niece in her delicatessen, you see—you met her, Cat. And when I do that, I sometimes find myself thinking: wouldn't it be far less *complicated* to have a job like that? To sell things? To order cheese and salamis and all the rest and not worry about what we should do and how we should do it?"

Jane said that she could identify with that. "My moments come when I'm on the beach. I have a beach near my place and I walk there at weekends and I see women with their families. The women have their jobs cut out for them. Where are the kids? Who hasn't put on sunscreen? Who hasn't had their sandwich yet? All that sort of thing. And I think: imagine if that was your *life*. Wouldn't you be happier dealing with all that rather than worrying about whether one understands exactly what Hume was getting at?"

"And yet we choose to do what we do," said Isabel. "Maybe it's the same for everybody. People may have to do quite a few things that they don't want to do—that aren't them, so to speak—and then they have the things that they do like to do, and they fit these into the interstices of all the obligations and chores."

Jane returned to Rory. "In his case, there doesn't seem to have been much opportunity to be what he wanted to be."

"And what's that, do you think?"

Jane fingered the stem of her glass. "We didn't go into the details. He just said that he wished he'd gone down another path altogether. He wanted different company. He did say that, at least. He said something about needing new friends and not finding any."

"Not uncommon. Don't you . . ."

Isabel did not finish. She was ashamed of what she had been about to say. She was going to admit to wanting new friends, but she did not want to sound disloyal or shallow.

Jane was intrigued. "No," she said. "I can't say that I particularly want new friends. Or at least I don't go out of my way to meet them. What I'd really like to do is to spend more time in the company of the friends I've got, especially the old ones."

Isabel wondered whether Jane could be described as a new friend of hers. She liked her, and she had sensed that the two of them thought in the same way about a number of things. This conversation had only confirmed her in that view. But they had met just a few times and she was not sure that one could call a person one has met merely a few times a friend.

Friend was a powerful word in Isabel's view. It was not to be conferred lightly because, if one did that, it weakened the concept of friendship. If casual acquaintances were friends, then how could one distinguish them from those with whom there was that more sacred, important bond?

"That priest you knew," Jane suddenly asked. "What happened to him?"

"He carried on with it. He never revealed to anybody else, he said, that he had lost his faith. He told me in an unguarded moment and I think he regretted it. I told him that his secret was safe with me."

Jane smiled mischievously. "And yet you've told me."

"I've anonymised it," said Isabel. "It's not a breach of confidence if you give no clue as to who it is you're talking about and the person can't possibly be identified."

"He'd say it was," said Jane. "He would never tell you—even anonymously—what anybody had said to him in the confessional, would he? They're serious about those secrets." She put down her glass. "We've rather forgotten about Rory."

"So we have. What now?"

"I'm going to take him and Georgina out to dinner in a couple of days' time," said Jane. "Then we're going up to Pitlochry at the weekend. There's a theatre there and I want to see a bit of the Highlands. And when I go back home, they're going to come and visit me. I'm really pleased about that. I want to show them Australia. He's always wanted to go but has never done so. I've got air miles. I'm going to get them a ticket."

Isabel said that she was pleased that Jane was so happy. Jane replied that she was: very happy. And he was too, she said. They had found one another; they had found a whole future.

"I know who I am now," she said, reaching out to touch Isabel on the arm. Isabel reciprocated. She took Jane's hand briefly and pressed it.

"Good. Very good."

Jane got up to leave. As she did so, Isabel asked a question. "One thing I was wondering about: are you going to have a DNA test? Just to confirm?"

Jane was silent for a few moments. Then she replied, "No, we won't."

Isabel made no comment on this.

Jane looked at her. "You obviously think we should."

"No," said Isabel. "I have no views either way."

"Well, I don't want one," said Jane. "Why test something that's so perfectly obvious anyway?"

"Of course," said Isabel.

She led Jane to the gate. *You are not his daughter*, she found herself thinking. *You are not.* She did not want to think that; she wanted to believe quite the opposite, just as, no doubt, her priestly friend had so wanted to believe. But we cannot choose our convictions; they come to us unbidden, prompted by intuitive understanding of what is and what is not. She was convinced that they had made a mistake. She was not sure why she thought this, but it seemed an inescapable conclusion to her, and she was saddened by it. And Jane knew this too, she thought.

CHAPTER FOURTEEN

YOU CAN'T LEAVE IT like that," whispered Jamie. "Definitely not."

They were in the Greyfriars Kirk, waiting for a concert to begin. The church was a well-used venue for musical events—a great barn of a place in the Old Town of Edinburgh, its churchyard sloping down towards the Grassmarket. It was steeped in Scottish history, which meant that it was redolent of suffering and hardship, of fanaticism and stern refusal to budge. The defenders of Presbyterianism had signed their Covenant here, signalling their defiance of Charles I's—and his son's—attempts to impose royal control over religious practices. People had died here, starved to death by implacable authorities, martyrs to their beliefs. They lay cheek by jowl with common criminals, with pioneers of geology, with poets and artists—all brought democratically together in the best of Scottish traditions of rough egalitarianism. And what is more egalitarian than the embrace of the soil?

"Don't bury me here," Jamie said. He felt uneasy; the memorials were so final, so uncompromising.

"I'm not going to bury you anywhere."

He smiled and kissed her lightly on the cheek. "I *am* going to die, you know," he warned. "One of these days."

"Don't talk about it," she said. He had told her, after all, not to talk about death when she had been in hospital with mushroom poisoning.

"On the grounds that the things that we don't talk about won't happen?"

She shook her head. "No. On the grounds that we have to live our lives without thinking of those things that will render those lives pointless. We have to conduct ourselves as if everything is going to be all right and that the things we know today will still be around in hundreds of years. Otherwise . . ."

"Otherwise what?"

"Otherwise we wouldn't bother. Why build buildings that we think will last indefinitely? Why have museums and galleries and cultures, for that matter, if these things are not going to last? And they won't. Why have countries, even?"

"Countries?"

"Because even those are not going to last. Do you think there will be a country called Scotland in five hundred years?"

"It's been around for the last five hundred."

"A few decades ago would people have betted on there still being a Soviet Union at the turn of the twentieth century? I would have. I would have thought it a very safe bet."

"That's different."

"No it isn't. Nothing lasts, Jamie. But we have to convince ourselves that it does. We have to make certain assumptions, certain pretences, otherwise . . ."

"Otherwise?"

"Otherwise we wouldn't bother. Would I marry you if I thought you weren't going to last?"

He stopped in his tracks. They were walking through the churchyard towards the door of the church. He looked at her with incredulity.

"I can't believe you just said that."

She realised that he had misunderstood. "Listen," she said. "I would marry you even if I knew that our marriage would last five minutes. I'd marry you *for* those five minutes. I was speaking *generally*—not for me, but for people, and marriages, in general. When I said 'I,' I didn't mean me, and 'you' didn't mean you."

They continued towards the door. "You worry me sometimes," he said. "You talk about things in a way that makes me wonder whether . . ."

She had her arm in his and squeezed his elbow. "Don't listen to me," she said. "I think aloud. I think unusual thoughts. It's not what I really mean. It's because I'm a philosopher. The important thing is that I love you to bits—to absolute bits. I want nothing else in this world other than to be with you and Charlie. That's all, and it's quite enough for me. Forget these . . . these musings. I'll say something else soon. Think of that."

They entered the church. Jamie knew the young woman taking tickets at the door; she was the secretary of Edinburgh Studio Opera, and he had played for them in their production of *Cavalleria Rusticana* and *Pagliacci*. She glanced at Isabel, who correctly read her appraising, only half-disguised, look: *the older woman she had heard about—Jamie's older woman.*

Only a handful of people had arrived, and Jamie and Isabel found seats in the second row. Jamie settled down to read the programme notes while Isabel looked about her. She liked Greyfriars; she liked the simplicity of it, which she thought was probably one of the things that those Covenanters had died for; out there in the kirkyard, huddled in their misery, but still refusing to yield to the foppish Stuarts who would impose their will on the people of Scotland. Freedom of body—and of conscience: it was such a sustaining brew, even for those who existed on gruel, and she felt suddenly proud of the fact that these were her people, these determined Scots—at least on her father's side.

On her mother's side—those gutsy American forebears who had scraped a living from their farms until things had gradually turned good for them—they had been like that too, she imagined: in nobody's pocket; they too would have known what freedom was about. Their freedom, of course, and not necessarily that of others. Her mother's aunt came to mind, and the spirited cousin from New York: *Wrong side. Period.* She smiled.

Jamie prodded her gently in the ribs. "What's the joke?"

She shook her head. "History."

"Hardly funny."

She agreed. "Yes, of course. But what we think about it can be."

He folded his programme and glanced at his watch. "We're far too early."

"You're the one who wanted to—"

He changed the subject. "What about that Australian woman? What are you going to do?"

It was now a few days after Jane's evening visit. Isabel had told Jamie that night about what Jane had said to her. She did not mention her misgivings, though, and he had not seemed to be particularly interested in the matter.

"It's good that she's happy," he said. "And it sounds rather nice for him too. Well done, Isabel."

She would have basked in his praise, had she shared his

view of the outcome. Now, she decided to tell him. She explained about Jane's reluctance to have a DNA test, which Isabel said had contributed to her own conviction that Rory was not the father.

"Surely he must have known that she . . . what's her name . . . was pregnant?"

It was the point she had already discussed with Jane, when she had first heard the story.

"Clara. No. Not necessarily. You would think that she would have told him, but remember her circumstances. What if he had wanted her to end the pregnancy? What then? Remember that the Scotts were Catholics. She might have been frightened of his reaction. She might have imagined that he would pressure her into something that she would not want."

"Maybe."

He picked up his programme distractedly, glanced at it and then put it down again. A woman had taken the seat beside them on the pew. She smiled at Jamie, who returned the smile. More or less every woman who sees him smiles at him, thought Isabel. What a blessed state in which to go through life: to be smiled upon. And he doesn't notice it. It must be like the weather to him: just something that happens, that is always there.

Aware that they could be overheard, he dropped his voice to a whisper. "You can't leave it like that. Definitely not."

"But I may be quite wrong. And anyway, I'm not sure that I have any right to interfere. I've done what she wanted me to do. It's over to her now."

He looked at her half in surprise, half in reproach. "I didn't think I'd hear you say that. You've always said that you have a duty to help people you come into contact with. What's that phrase you use? Moral proximity? Well, you've got moral proximity with that woman. You've got moral proximity a mile wide."

"Proximity is narrow, not wide," she corrected.

"Narrow, then."

"Well, what do you expect me to do? Go on, tell me."

He was silent.

"See?" she said. "It's not simple, is it?" She slipped her hand into his. "Thank you, anyway."

IF EITHER OF THEM had felt tetchy, the concert put them both in a good mood. When they came out at the end it was barely ten o'clock and there was still light in the sky. Swallows were darting about the trees in the churchyard like tiny fighter planes, disturbed, perhaps, by the crowd of people spilling out of the church.

"I don't want to go home just yet," said Isabel. "Grace is staying the night. We don't have to keep an eye on the clock."

Grace had agreed to look after Charlie and, as sometimes happened, would be staying the night rather than going home afterwards. She liked going to bed early, often before ten, which made it more convenient for her to stay. She also liked the breakfast that Jamie made for her when she did this: scrambled egg with smoked salmon, generous racks of toast and lashings of milky coffee.

Jamie shrugged. "I don't mind. We could go somewhere for a drink. Sandy Bell's? Or that place behind the Museum?"

Isabel considered these possibilities. "Or we could go for a walk."

"Where? Holyrood Park?"

"No. What about just around here? We could go down Candlemaker Row and then along the Cowgate."

He seemed unenthusiastic. "I'm not sure that I want to go down there."

The Cowgate was the basement of the Old Town, a narrow road that ran below the towering tenements and bridges of the extraordinary early feat of engineering that Edinburgh was. Walking through it, you were aware that life was going on above you, on the streets under which the Cowgate ducked and weaved, or in the streets that ran off on either side: steep cobbled alleyways, twisting in either direction up towards the light.

"Come on," said Isabel.

"Why?"

"I want to go to see something."

He looked at her quizzically. "Such as?"

"Blackfriars Street."

He was puzzled. There was nothing to see in Blackfriars Street, he thought; was there anything there? Bannerman's Bar at the bottom and a place that sold folk instruments and Scottish fiddle music. And . . . there was nothing else, he thought, unless one counted the tenement flats. It made for, of course, an attractive enough stroll, but there were plenty of places more interesting than Blackfriars Street, and if Isabel were prepared to be imaginative, a much better walk could be concocted.

"You aren't planning—" Jamie began.

"I want to look at a place from the outside," said Isabel. "It's the flat where Clara stayed at the time that this happened. Catherine Succoth told me about it. She said it was number twenty-four Blackfriars Street."

Jamie did not object. "All right. If you insist on playing the investigator."

Isabel reacted playfully. "That's rich! Who told me not much more than an hour ago that I couldn't leave things as they were? Sound familiar?"

He accepted her point gracefully, but added, "I don't see the point, but if you want to, then all right. But Isabel, may I ask one thing: what do you think you'll find?"

"I'm not looking for anything in particular," said Isabel. "I just want to remind myself of what it must have been like. That's all."

They left Greyfriars and made their way along the sharply descending street that curved down towards the Grassmarket. The roadway at the top was bounded on either side by buildings of ubiquitous Edinburgh stone, modest in scale here—a few floors at the most, comfortable in their simplicity. The façades of these buildings were punctuated by low doorways that led to the flats above, the highest of which looked over the kirkyard towards the Castle. The street was not busy; a group of young people—students by the look of them, thought Isabel—had spilled out of the Greyfriars Bobby Bar and were making their way down the hill ahead of Isabel and Jamie. Two boys and two girls were conducting a conversation that echoed off the walls.

"She didn't!" one of the girls exclaimed.

"She did. I swear she did."

"Joe doesn't make things up, do you, Joe?" This from the other girl.

"No, of course not. It's true. Seriously true. She met this guy right under Alan's nose. He was one of his flatmates. She started sleeping with him when Alan was out of the flat. Two-timed him."

The first girl again: "And you look at her and think . . . and then you realise that—"

"Same as anybody," said Joe. "She's just more up front about it."

"Except to him? Yeah?"

"True, except to him. He thought that this other guy was his friend. And he was laughing at him all the time. Then he came back from lectures one afternoon and there was little Miss What's-her-face having a seriously nice time with this guy and so Alan gets his stuff and throws it out the window. Yeah, he did. And there was this neighbour who was walking out the door and . . ."

There was laughter, drowning out the rest of what was said. And then they stopped at a door to a shared stairway and disappeared.

A few yards back, Isabel looked at Jamie and raised an eyebrow. "*La Bohème,*" she said. "Contemporary version."

"Yes, except *La Bohème* is completely different."

"I mean the student life."

Jamie smiled. "I had a flatmate like that at music school."

"Like her—or him?"

"Like him. He was hopelessly in love with this girl from Aberdeen. She had about six boyfriends at the same time, and he never seemed to have a clue what was going on."

"Six?"

"A bit of an exaggeration, maybe. Certainly three or four. She just liked sex, I think. It was . . . well, it was her hobby, I suppose. Like stamp collecting. She collected boys."

Isabel wondered why the Aberdonian girl bothered to keep Jamie's flatmate in the first place. "Was your flatmate her regular boyfriend?"

"He was meant to be."

"But why did she bother?"

"He was a terrific cook," answered Jamie. "He made her these fabulous meals."

"That basic," sighed Isabel.

"That basic," agreed Jamie.

Isabel wondered what had happened to this *enthusiastic* young woman. And she could not help but compare her with Cat, whose emotional entanglements were innocence itself by comparison.

They reached the bottom of Candlemaker Row and turned into the Cowgate itself. Directly under the high arches of George IV Bridge the street became tunnel-like. They passed the Magdalen Chapel, a sixteenth-century almshouse, in shadows and darkness. A voice called out, a rough, guttural sound: a drunk, a man sleeping rough and having a nightmare.

Then they came to the back entrance to Sheriff Court, with a door large enough to admit the vans that brought prisoners into court. Isabel had walked past it a few months ago on her way to have lunch with a friend who worked in the Scottish Parliament at Holyrood, and she had been obliged to stop as one of the prison vehicles—the Black Maria, or the paddywagon, as her mother used to call it—had nosed its way out after that morning's trials. It had passed so close to her that she had glimpsed, through the narrow, barred window, the face of a young man inside—a youth really—and seen that he was crying.

We create misery for each other, she had thought, such misery, as this young man had probably done. He would have assaulted somebody, or stolen somebody's car, or done something dark and horrible to another human being, and now, fresh from the passing of sentence, he wept as the state set about imposing its own brand of misery in retribution. But it had to—it had no choice. If he went unpunished, there would be more misery in store as, undeterred, he did once more whatever he had done already. And those whom he had wronged would feel outraged that nobody had attended to their pain . . . She had watched him briefly and then, quite unexpectedly, she had lifted a finger and wagged it at him. His eyes had widened and the vehicle had borne him away.

She had stood where she was, astonished at her own action. What had possessed her to do that? What had made her suddenly take on the role of the disapproving, tut-tutting *tricoteuse*, admonishing this youth for whatever he had done? It had happened so quickly, almost without her realising that she was doing it, and now he had been carted off and she could not apologise—as she wanted to do—for adding to his humiliation.

Perhaps it was just that she had had enough of hearing about people who spoiled the lives of others. She had read that morning in the newspaper of a man in London who had had bleach thrown in his eyes by a mugger. No, he had not known his attackers. Yes, he was going about his ordinary business. Yes, his eyes had been damaged. Was that why she had shaken her finger in a trite, populist way: because the young man *deserved* to be censured?

"Isabel? You still with me?"

They had walked almost halfway along the Cowgate now, while she had been deep in thought about justice and retribution and showing one's condemnation like an *echt* Mrs. Grundy.

"Grundyism," she muttered.

"What are you talking about?"

"I was thinking of people who set themselves up as the

guardians of conventional morality. Who spend their time disapproving of others. There's a name for it apparently—Grundyism, after Mrs. Grundy, a character in a play, who was the epitome of propriety."

"Oh. Well, we're almost at Blackfriars Street. You did want to walk up it, didn't you?"

She did not.

"I'm sorry, Jamie, I've changed my mind. Let's go home."

He was puzzled. "Why? I thought you wanted to—"

She took his arm. "Come on. Let's get a taxi and go home. I've thought of something, that's all."

They had no difficulty in finding a taxi. The driver mumbled something about the road being up in the Grassmarket and took them by a circuitous route up the narrow cobbled road past the city morgue. *In the midst of life we are in death:* those final harrowing words, in the unsurpassed English of the King James Version, as desolate as language can be. *Man that is born of a woman hath but a short time to live . . . he cometh up, and is cut down like a flower; he fleeth as it were a shadow, and never continueth in one stay.*

She reached across and took Jamie's hand in hers. He had been looking out of the window, but in the opposite direction so that he had not seen the morgue. She wanted, suddenly and absurdly, to protect him; she did not want him, or Charlie, to have to think about these things. If reality had to be faced, then she wanted to do it for both of them as well as for herself, so that they might think, with untroubled hearts, of things that were as light and free and lovely as they themselves were.

CHAPTER FIFTEEN

BROTHER FOX had been digging. Isabel had a bed of alliums—her ornamental onions as Jamie called them—and Brother Fox had taken an interest in them, scratching away at the spoil to expose the bulbs. These he had then gnawed, or simply discarded on the neighbouring lawn.

"Odd behaviour for a fox," observed Jamie, as they surveyed the damage the following morning.

Isabel bent down to pick up a felled plant with its mangled bulb. "If it was Brother Fox," she said. "We have no proof." She looked at Jamie sheepishly. "Sorry, that's very lame. It must have been him."

Jamie said in mock reproach, "You always try to protect him. To excuse him. He's a bad fox, and you just want to let him off the hook."

"A fox can't be bad," said Isabel. "I'm not sure whether any animal can. They just are as they are: neither good nor bad."

She stood up, the bulb in her hand, a small drift of soil, a wisp, falling from between her fingers. She realised that she did not believe this—although she had said it. We can say all sorts of things without believing them, she thought. The apologists of appalling regimes—the ambassadors of tyrannies—are called upon to defend their governments when quizzed by journalists; they know, thought Isabel, they know; and yet they speak with such conviction, denying the obvious, the manifestly true reports of wrongdoing. She had often wondered how it must feel to have to say things you knew were untrue; to say that your employer, your political boss, was as pure as driven snow when you knew just how bloody his hands were. It was easy, she decided; saying one thing while you thought quite another was the simplest thing in the world. All you did was open your mouth; actors showed us how easy it was when they spoke their lines as if they believed them.

"Actually, that's probably not quite right," she said. "Perhaps animals can be good and bad."

"Exactly," said Jamie. "That dog round the corner is obviously good—you know the one? The one who tries to lick your hand."

"Moby-Dick," mused Isabel. "Whales . . ."

"They're good," said Jamie.

"Not Moby-Dick," said Isabel. "He showed malevolence."

"He didn't exist," said Jamie. "You can't pay any attention to the emotions of fictional characters, especially if they're whales. All you're doing there is reflecting what the author thinks."

"But if Moby-Dick behaved as real whales do, then you can. He stands for all whales, or even just for a number of whales."

Jamie said nothing. In his mind, Brother Fox had done it because he was naturally mischievous: Isabel might dote on the fox, but Jamie did not. Isabel was silent too; not because there was nothing more to be said about the moral lives of animals, because there was, and she had just received a book for review that dealt with just that topic and bore that precise title: *The*

Moral Lives of Animals. She was wondering, now, whether a whole issue of the *Review of Applied Ethics* might be dedicated to that topic. She could contact Peter Singer at Princeton, perhaps, one of the first philosophers to deal with the implications of attributing greater moral status to animals. She could contact some of the others who had taken up the issue since then. She could give it a catchy title perhaps: "Was Moby-Dick a Malevolent Whale?" Or possibly, "Are All Dogs Good?"

That last question raised profound issues. Dogs were evidently capable of being helpful—sheepdogs and guard-dogs were; they were also capable of showing affection and friendliness to their owners and others. Those surely would be good acts if performed by human beings, but were they good if performed by an animal? That depended on the reasons for which they were performed. A person who does the right thing is not necessarily being good, as Kant was at pains to point out; this could be a moral accident, if we did something good only because we were told to do it. And that meant that dogs were never truly good, at least in Kantian terms, because it was instinct, or even fear, that made them do what they did. So no dog really deserved a pat on the head then, nor a medal, nor thanks . . . and no fox deserved opprobrium for eating alliums.

Isabel let the allium bulb drop from her fingers and recited:

> *There once was a fox called Macallium*
> *Who enjoyed the occasional allium.*
> *When they said: Oh how bad!*
> *He replied: I'm not sad*
> *As I'm not a fit object of opprobrium.*

Jamie stared at her. "Macallium?"

"Macallum is a perfectly common Scottish name, and

therefore Brother Fox, were he to be graced with a name, could well be called Macallium. Surely the composers of limericks may take the occasional liberty with names."

Jamie smiled. "I can't set it to music," he said. "The rhythm of a limerick is just too strong. It would take over. And besides—"

"Besides, it's a piece of nonsense. At least Lear's limericks had something poignant to say about human aspirations—and human loneliness."

They began to walk back into the house.

"And yesterday," he said. "What about yesterday? What are you going to do? Are you going to speak to Jane?"

She shook her head. "No. I want to speak to somebody else. To a judge."

"Catherine Succoth? The woman you told me about?"

"Yes."

Jamie placed the palm of his hand against his forehead, the gesture he invariably used when admitting failure. "Oh, I'm sorry. I forgot."

Isabel looked at him enquiringly.

"She phoned," Jamie said. "I meant to tell you. She phoned yesterday."

He was always forgetting to pass on messages to her; it was a male failing, she thought. John Liamor had been the same—although he may have done it out of perversity, being jealous of her friends, though it was far from clear to her why this should have been so, when his feelings for her must have been so shallow, so loveless. And her father never passed on telephone messages, although that was vagueness, she thought, and a curious belief he entertained that nothing of any real consequence was ever said on the telephone.

"And?" asked Isabel. She forgave him this; she forgave him everything.

"She wanted you to phone back. She left her number."

"Nothing else?"

He shook his head. "Nothing. Interesting, though. There was something about her in the *Scotsman* the other day. Some big trial in Glasgow—she was the judge. Some big Glasgow hood who had a yacht that he used to run drugs from Spain. She gave him a real dressing down and then sent him off to prison for nine years."

"Deservedly, no doubt."

"Apparently he started to rant and rave after the sentence was passed and he shouted out that he would get her some day. I thought: You have to be brave to be a judge."

Isabel agreed. "Yes. It can't be easy."

"And then you go home afterwards, after dealing with all that stuff, and you have to do ordinary things like preparing dinner and paying bills and things like that. And you know that there's this character, going to his bunk in Barlinnie Prison or wherever, and starting his nine years—and thinking of you as his Nemesis."

Isabel reflected on this. "No doubt you compartmentalise. Doctors do that, don't they? They do the difficult things they do—telling somebody that they're terminally ill, for instance—but they can't let it stop them leading their own lives. They switch off, I suppose."

She thought: *What about me?* She had to do the occasional unpleasant thing—rejecting unpublishable papers, knowing how much the author might have invested in his or her work. And in some cases, when the paper came from somebody struggling to keep a job, the rejection of the paper might be the thing that means the end of a career. Yet you couldn't think about it; you couldn't, because there simply was not enough room on the page for everybody who felt that they had something to say.

They reached the house. Jamie opened the door for her and then remembered. "Oh, and there was another call."

She glanced at him reproachfully. "Yes?"

"Today. Somebody from the council. Environmental Health, he said. He gave a number too. He said you should ask for the food safety officer on duty."

Isabel frowned. "Food safety?" And then she realised what it was. Mushrooms.

SHE CALLED the council first, using the kitchen phone, and was put through to a Mr. Wallace. As she had imagined, he was interested in mushrooms.

"We follow up on cases of food poisoning," he said. "It's usually restaurants, but occasionally we get unsafe products being sold by retailers. The hospital informed us that you had mushroom poisoning. Is that correct?"

"I felt a bit ill," she said. "But it wasn't anything serious."

There was a brief silence at the other end of the line: a silence of censure, of disapproval. Then: "Any case of food poisoning is serious, Ms. Dalhousie."

"I didn't mean to make light of it," Isabel said. "It's just that I was only very mildly ill. Hardly anything life-threatening."

Mr. Wallace passed over this. "We'd like to know where you bought these mushrooms," he said.

"I bought them from . . ." Isabel hesitated, remembering Cat's keenness to gloss over the incident.

"Yes?"

"From a delicatessen."

"That doesn't surprise me," said Mr. Wallace. "The supermarkets are very careful about these things. Which one?"

Isabel thought quickly. She could say that she had forgotten, but that would be a lie, and she would not do that. Cat would, she suspected; but she would not.

"Does it really matter?" Isabel asked. "I've spoken to the person who runs it and she's assured me that there would be no prospect of this being repeated."

The irritation in Mr. Wallace's voice was now unmistakable. "Of course it matters. Some shopkeepers will tell you anything. We have to make sure that they understand the importance of knowing their suppliers." He paused. "I could tell you some hair-raising stories about food impurity, Ms. Dalhousie. Yes, right here in Edinburgh."

"What will be the consequences for the delicatessen?" asked Isabel.

"We'll visit them," snapped Mr. Wallace. "We'll check up on their arrangements. We'll discuss the situation."

She hesitated.

"It's for the best, you'll agree," came Mr. Wallace's voice again.

She did not like being pressed in this way. Others might be so sure of their position as to answer directly and determinedly, but it was not her style. Isabel thought about things; she weighed them; she saw dimensions to a question that others might not. And in these circumstances, faced with a question that could incriminate a relative, some people might suffer a convenient lapse of memory, or tell an outright lie. But that, again, was not her way.

"What if I ensured that it didn't happen again?" she asked.

There was only the briefest pause at his end of the line. "What do you mean? How could you?"

She kept her voice steady. "I mean exactly that. If I were to make sure that the person who sold me those mushrooms never again obtained their supplies from those people in—"

Mr. Wallace interrupted her. "So you know where they came from? You know the supplier?"

A *foss,* she thought. I have fallen into a foss of my own creation. The word came to her because it had occurred in a crossword—no other letters would have fitted—and she had gone to the dictionary to find its meaning. It was a hole, and she had dug it for herself: a metaphorical foss, but a foss nonetheless.

She realised that she could not avoid telling him. It was her duty to do so, of course, and she knew it, but she felt reticent for the most human, most understandable reasons. "It's my niece's delicatessen," she explained, giving him the address. "And that makes it a bit complicated."

The tone of disapproval deepened. Isabel was now, by her own admission, almost complicit. "I can see that," he said icily. "But thank you for this information."

They said goodbye and she replaced the handset in its cradle. Jamie, who had been standing in the doorway listening in to this conversation, raised an eyebrow.

"Bureaucrat," said Isabel.

Jamie looked sympathetic. "I'm sorry."

She took a deep breath. She should not have called him a bureaucrat, even if that was what he was. There had to be bureaucrats; there had to be people who investigated cases of mushroom poisoning, and to dismiss them as bureaucrats was wrong—it was a word which so often tended to be used with contempt that it might be described in the dictionary as a term of abuse. Mr. Wallace was only doing his job; he was paid to protect people and was entitled to expect cooperation. No doubt it was not easy, no doubt he encountered obstructiveness and mendacity at every turn. And now he was planning a head-to-head with Cat, who could be difficult at the best of times.

Jamie was thinking much the same thing. "Rather you than me," he said. "Cat's not going to like that."

Isabel defended herself. "I had no choice."

"Of course you didn't," agreed Jamie. "But I still say that Cat's not going to be pleased." He looked uncomfortable. "They could fine her."

"Do you think so?"

"Oh yes. Or close her down for a while. I know somebody whose butcher was shut for two weeks by those food hygiene people."

Isabel winced. "If that's going to happen, then it's going to happen. Remember that I'm the victim here, not Cat. I was the one who was poisoned."

He nodded his agreement. "Yes, but also remember that Cat doesn't always see things in quite the same way as others do."

Isabel knew that was true. "We'll see," she said.

"Yes," said Jamie. "But, look, don't worry. She can't bite your head off."

"She can try," said Isabel.

Jamie glanced at his watch and pointed upstairs. Charlie would wake up from his afternoon sleep in a few minutes, if he had not already done so, and Jamie was planning to take him down to the canal at Harrison Bridge. A small flock of over-privileged ducks, fed to bursting point by visitors, had established itself along the canal bank, and Charlie loved throwing them bread. Afterwards, Jamie planned to take him into town by bus; Charlie delighted in travelling on the top deck of buses and would do so, uncomplainingly, for long periods, fascinated by this first-storey view of the city.

Isabel consulted the scrap of paper on which Jamie had noted Catherine Succoth's number. She was not sure whether the judge would be at home in the mid-afternoon, but she could leave a message if she was out. The number, though, was not her home one, being answered by a court secretary. Yes, Lady Succoth might be available; he would check.

Isabel was put through. "I'm sorry I didn't call back yesterday," she said. "I got your message only today. My . . . my fiancé forgot to tell me."

The judge laughed. "Men."

"Yes, men."

Isabel waited.

"Would it be possible to see you?" asked Catherine. "I can imagine that you're very busy but there's something I'd like to talk to you about."

Isabel wondered whether the judge really believed that she was busy, or whether she was just being polite. It was easy to imagine the judge thinking that a philosopher would have time on her hands; most people thought that, after all, and Isabel had given up explaining that editing the *Review of Applied Ethics* was a real job that made real demands on her time. And she ran a house, too; made meals; looked after a young child, even if she had a housekeeper, which for most people, again, sounded like the height of privilege, of self-indulgence. It was not really; Grace was a high-maintenance housekeeper and Isabel kept her on because she believed that it was her duty to do so, Grace having worked for her father. It was her business, anyway, how she spent her money, and her time, and she had no obligation to justify herself . . .

"Dr. Dalhousie?"

"Yes, I'm still here." She noticed the use of the doctoral title. Had the judge been checking up on her?

"Would you mind if I popped in to see you?"

Isabel assured her that she would not mind at all.

That afternoon—was there any chance of seeing her that afternoon? It was no notice, of course, but the judge was not sitting in court and could come to see her if Isabel had a few minutes, just a few minutes.

Isabel suggested that they meet for a cup of tea in the Elephant House, a café on George IV Bridge that was close to Parliament Square, where the judges had their chambers. She had been planning to call in at a bookshop on South Bridge and she could kill two birds with one stone. In using that metaphor, she wondered whether it would eventually be replaced by something else. People no longer killed birds with stones—or not in Scotland. People fired at them, or blasted them out of the sky, but did not kill them with stones. Metaphors were so bloody: people shot messengers, flogged dead horses, cut the throats of their competitors. Perhaps that was life; perhaps that was what it was really like.

Catherine sounded grateful. Isabel was going to ask her

what it was that she wanted to discuss, but held back. She imagined that it had to do with Jane's search. Did the judge want to find out the outcome? She had revealed that it was Rory Cameron who had been Clara's boyfriend; was she now curious as to what had happened? Or did Catherine want to speak about something altogether different?

Was she perhaps going to ask Isabel to serve on some committee? People were always looking for volunteers to serve on the committees of their various causes, and Isabel did her fair share of that. She had no idea what Catherine Succoth's charitable interests were, but she was bound to be the chairman of something or other. The lifeboats? Too obvious. Everybody supported the lifeboats, which raised vast amounts of money without having to do much persuading. It was because Britain was an island, perhaps, and its inhabitants felt a deep-seated need to know that there were lifeboats at the ready. Donkeys in North Africa? There was widespread outrage at the way donkeys were treated there, and the donkey charities did very well. There would be donkey committees in Edinburgh, no doubt, and they needed members, but again she did not quite see Catherine Succoth becoming exercised over the discomforts of Tunisian donkeys.

What about distressed gentlefolk? They, too, had their charity, which gave stipends in appropriate cases—a worthy cause, of course—even if quaintly named. She pictured the distressed gentlefolk, a rather quiet, uncomplaining group of people, looking slightly pained at their distress but not wanting to make a fuss, lining up politely for their stipends in their increasingly threadbare tweeds and outmoded skirts.

She decided to walk. The day, which had begun in a blustery fashion, had turned still and somnolent. There was a buttery feel to the air—or so Isabel felt; Jamie had heard her describe summer weather in those terms and had been puzzled.

"Butter?"

She had explained how she reacted to the dappled sunlight in the Meadows, where the trees, in full leaf, were touched with gold: butter, she thought.

She looked at the skyline, at the crags and peaks of the Victorian buildings, at the spikes. "We are a spiky city," somebody had once said to her. "Our skyline says it all." And it was true, she decided: a skyline reveals a city's purpose and character. Oxford had its dreaming spires; Manhattan its glittering towers; Edinburgh its eccentric spikes. And that, perhaps, is what we are, she thought. We are not a culture of smooth curves; Scotland was a *vertical* place, a landscape of crags, both metaphorical and real.

She reached the Elephant House ten minutes early. She expected that Catherine Succoth would be punctual—she gave that impression—and she was right. At precisely the time she had suggested, Isabel saw the judge come into the café and look about her. She noticed how Catherine entered the room confidently, with an air of authority. It was because of her office, Isabel thought; when you are a judge people stand up when you enter the court, and you must get used to it.

"I hope I'm not late."

"Of course not. I was early. I walked across the Meadows, enjoying this . . ." Isabel gestured towards the window and the light outside.

Catherine sat down, smoothing her black skirt as she did so. She was, thought Isabel, the image of the sombre professional woman. She would have to be, Isabel supposed, at least while in chambers; on the bench Scottish judges wore red, providing a splash of colour. Would red suit Catherine Succoth? It would, she reckoned, although it was bound not to suit many with different colouring.

The café was busy, but Isabel had found a table near the window where they were sufficiently far away from others to be able to talk in privacy. Their nearest neighbour, a bearded man of scholarly appearance, was preoccupied with sorting out an unruly sheaf of notes. The Elephant House was more or less opposite the National Library of Scotland and served the scholars who populated its reading rooms. This man was one, Isabel thought, and she wondered what lonely furrow of scholarship he ploughed. History, perhaps. Something obscure: the history of trade between Scotland and the Netherlands in the sixteenth century. The notes were about merchants' records. Quantities of dried fish and wool transported from Fife. Salt. Lime. Wood for Dutch shipbuilders. Nails.

Catherine noticed Isabel's glance. "He's an historian," she whispered. "I have one of his books. I've never read it."

Isabel smiled. "I guessed he was."

"Trade routes," said Catherine. "Interesting . . . if you're interested in that sort of thing."

Isabel wondered how Catherine knew what she had only guessed. She would not tell Grace, because Grace would immediately say that it did not surprise her in the least. She would explain it in terms of telepathy, or something like that, whereas, as Isabel knew, it was merely sheer coincidence. It was quite within the bounds of possibility that there should be an economic historian sitting in the Elephant House and that a philosopher should come in and speculate, correctly, as to what the historian's calling was.

Then Catherine said, "Actually, no. I'm wrong. I'm mixing him up. He's somebody else altogether. He looks like the person I was thinking about, but he isn't."

Isabel nodded. "Oh well . . ."

Catherine took a spectacle case out of her pocket and laid it on the table, then put it back. Isabel noticed this. She's nervous, she thought.

"I'll come straight to the point. I want to apologise to you."

Isabel frowned. "I'm sure you've got nothing to apologise for. I—"

Catherine interrupted her. "I do," she said simply. "I have to apologise for not telling you the truth."

Isabel said nothing.

"When you came to see me the other day," Catherine continued, "you had the good grace to confess to me that you had not told me the real reason for your visit. I had reached that conclusion anyway, but it was good of you to tell me."

"I felt bad," said Isabel. "I don't like deception."

Catherine seemed to weigh this. "Who does?" she said after a while. "I have to listen to deception all the time. When I sit on the bench at a criminal trial, I have to listen to lie after lie. The only consolation, I suppose, is that one develops the ability to tell the difference between truth and lies. They sound quite different, you know."

"You develop antennae?"

"That's one way of putting it. Or you could say you develop a nose. Same thing."

Catherine looked away. She cannot meet my eye, Isabel thought.

"You came to me to tender your apology, and all the time I was standing there thinking, *I'm misleading you*. And yet I said nothing. I failed to tell you that the affair that Clara had with Rory Cameron was nothing. She went out with him briefly, I think, but she never really loved him. I don't even know whether she slept with him. Possibly. Possibly not."

"But she did sleep with somebody?"

Isabel's question was blunt. The judge turned to face her. Now she held her gaze; Isabel saw that her hazel eyes were full of regret. *This woman is consumed by sadness*, she said to herself. Oh, Catherine, I understand.

Isabel answered her own question. "Alastair Rankeillor," she said quietly.

The judge froze. "How did you know?"

Isabel could not answer, she was not sure how she knew. But if she tried to work it out, she imagined that it would be clear enough. She knew that Catherine had been in love with Alastair. She knew that there had to be some reason for her to conceal the facts. And for a woman like this to be concerned with Jane's quest—the quest of somebody she had not even met—it had to be a powerful reason.

"I should have told you," Catherine went on. "I should have said something, but . . ." She hesitated.

"But you didn't want to say anything that could implicate Alastair?"

"If implicate is the word. Are you implicated in the existence of your child? I was concerned to protect him from an awkward disclosure. I imagine that not everybody wants to hear about long-lost children. Certainly, I don't think that Alastair is the type to welcome such news."

Isabel agreed. "Perhaps not. But then . . . then there's the child to think about, isn't there? In this case not a child, but a woman in search of her father."

Catherine sighed. "I know, I know. It's just that . . ." She stopped.

Isabel waited.

"It's just that I love him, Dr. Dalhousie. I have loved Alastair Rankeillor from the moment I first met him all those years ago in a student flat in Buccleuch Place. I loved him with a yearning that I can't even begin to find the words to express. It was like a pain. When he left me I felt so raw and empty I thought there was no point in continuing with anything. Outwardly, I recovered, but not inwardly, not deep down. I thought about nobody else, nobody, and even now I think about him every day, every single day." She fixed Isabel with her gaze. "Isn't that really rather pathetic? To live one's life fixated on another person who's gone off, left you; who's out of reach? Isn't that a complete waste of a life?"

Such questions are often rhetorical, but Isabel felt that Catherine expected an answer.

"You're asking me what I think of that?"

Catherine nodded.

"I don't think it at all pathetic," said Isabel gently. "I think that there are many of us who go through a very similar experience, who lead our lives in the shadow of that which we have lost. It may be a place, it may be a person. But the effect is the same."

Catherine was listening to Isabel as if she wanted to believe what she was hearing. The confident judge was gone; the vulnerable, heart-injured woman had taken her place.

"We've all lost something," Isabel said. "Of course we have.

That's because our first glimpse of love is usually unrequited, or doesn't last very long. And then we think we've had our chance and we're never going to get the same chance again."

"I've never believed that," said Catherine. "I've never thought that you fall in love only once."

"Neither have I," said Isabel. "But what I do believe is that many of us have, usually when we are quite young, a passion, a falling in love—call it what you will—that is of very great intensity. And for some of it, it becomes the measure against which we judge everything that happens to us after."

"That's me," said Catherine.

She spoke quietly and deliberately, and Isabel knew that this was a moment of confession. Had she ever said this to anybody else, she wondered? She thought not. The judge was strong; she had to be. She had to be decisive, organised, determined, because that was what was expected of her in her position. And no doubt she was all of that; but she was also a woman who had loved a man, hopelessly, and who loved him still.

"And me too," whispered Isabel.

She had said it. John Liamor. She had loved him so intensely, although he had never loved her in return. She had thought of him obsessively, while she must have occupied only a small part of his thoughts; and it had been so difficult for her to forget him, although he must have found it easy.

Catherine clearly expected her to say more.

"I loved an Irishman. He was called John Liamor. I know that this sounds predictable, ordinary, but he was a very good-looking man. I know that has nothing to do with it—or should have nothing to do with it. There are plenty of good-looking men, and one might well say, so what? But his looks were part of his charm and I thought I had never met anybody quite so exceptional. I felt that I had come into the company of somebody who was imbued with . . . some sort of power that I couldn't quite describe. I expected other people to feel it. I thought that they too must be in awe of this man, must sense what I sensed. I wanted to share my discovery. I wanted to say: *Look at this marvellous man, just look at him.*

"And of course that is a real sign of being in love, isn't it? You want to share your discovery with others. You want to share your delight. It's exactly what we want to do when we perceive any other sort of beauty, whether it's a shell we pick up on a beach or a sunset or anything, really: we want to say *look at this.*" She stopped. "I shouldn't be talking to you about all that."

Catherine shook her head. "No, you're wrong. Of course you should be. I told you about . . . Alastair." She had hesitated before she mentioned his name. Isabel thought, it's as painful as it ever was.

"I've put John Liamor out of my mind," said Isabel. "I try not to think of him, and it works, you know. You can tell yourself not to think of things. You can tell yourself all sorts of things and end up doing as you are bidden. It's like going on a diet, or giving up some bad habit. You can do it if you tell yourself to."

"And if you want to listen to yourself," added Catherine.

"Exactly. And I'm not sure whether most of us have sufficient credibility with ourselves to do that."

"To listen to ourselves?"

"Yes."

Isabel imagined saying to herself, "Oh, it's only you going on again about that! Please! Do you think I'm going to listen to *me*?"

Catherine glanced at her watch. "I mustn't stay too long. I have some people coming to see me in chambers."

Isabel nodded. "Of course. And I suppose I should get on with what I'm meant to be doing."

The judge had returned. "So there we have it. Alastair is probably the man whom Jane is looking for. I should not have sought to protect him. I did. I'm sorry. And I'm sorry for misleading you." She paused. "And myself—as I have just done."

Isabel looked at her enquiringly.

"Yes," said Catherine. "If I'm to be honest with myself, my real reason for lying to you—and I'm afraid I did lie—was probably my resentment, my hurt I suppose, that Alastair should have had a child with another woman." She stared forlornly at Isabel. "With another woman." She repeated the words, full of bleakness.

"I know," whispered Isabel. "I know what you feel."

For a short time neither spoke. Then Catherine appeared to pull herself together. "Well, that's it," she said. "Once again, I'm very sorry."

Isabel thought out loud. "The problem is that Rory Cameron believes it's him and is, apparently, really pleased. He's spending time with Jane Cooper. He seems to be seizing what he has been given. So what do we do now?"

She wanted to say, you're the judge, you sort this out. But she simply looked at Catherine, who said, "That's all my fault. I shall go and speak to her. I'll explain why I lied and . . . well, I hope that she understands. And then I shall go to him—to Rory Cameron—and tell him too. Don't worry. I'll do all that for you."

Isabel shook her head. "No," she said. "Don't."

She did not want Catherine to suffer any more. To be in

love with a man for years and years, at a distance, to be haunted by him, was punishment enough for whatever small failings she might have, for any deceptions such as the one she had practised on Isabel. More than enough. The judge might sentence others, but was herself under a sentence of unhappiness from which there appeared to be no release, no early parole, and Isabel had no desire to add to that weight.

CHAPTER SIXTEEN

ISABEL WENT to Cat's delicatessen the following day to buy a jar of stuffed olives. The olives were not for her, although she liked them a great deal; they were for Charlie, whose precocious palate demanded them in the same breath as it called for sardine sandwiches—the sardines being mashed and applied finger-thick to buttered bread; for boiled-egg soldiers—the still-runny yoke spooned onto strips of thick white bread; or for bowls of rice pudding with deep wells of red jam deposited in the middle. It was all nursery food—the food envisaged by Lin Yutang when he made his famous remark about patriotism being nothing more than the love of such dishes—and yet it sat alongside this curious taste for olives, for gherkins, and for Italian sausage heavily flavoured with garlic.

Isabel wondered what they thought of this at Charlie's nursery school, where she suspected garlic was hardly encouraged. Charlie's tastes, she felt, were not their concern, and if they disapproved of the contents of his tiffin box, then that was unfortunate, but not something for her to worry about. Some of the children at the nursery school brought chocolate and potato crisps for their lunch; let them look to those diets, with their preservatives and bad fats, before they commented on the olives and garlic of others . . .

She entered the delicatessen, expecting to find Cat or Sinclair, but found neither. A young woman, somewhere in her early twenties, her dark hair swept back in a chignon, was standing behind the counter, ladling hummus from a large jar into the small tubs in which Cat sold it. She looked up as Isabel came in and greeted her with a smile.

"You're . . . her cousin, aren't you?"

There was a jauntiness in the young woman's manner that appealed to Isabel. And then there was the accent, which was not Scottish, but from somewhere in Northern Ireland and not unlike Georgina Cameron's; the English that Shakespeare would have spoken, preserved by centuries of relative linguistic isolation.

"I'm Trish," the young woman continued, finishing with the hummus jar. "I've just started. All this food! I'm going to put on weight, so I am."

Isabel smiled at the "so I am." It was a turn of phrase that was characteristic of that part of Ireland, and she liked it. It was a little bulwark, she felt, against the bland homogenised speech that was spreading so quickly, destroying personal, quirky, local expressions, a linguistic herbicide.

"Is Cat—"

"She's out. But she'll be back soon. Can I get you something meantime? A cup of coffee maybe? I haven't used that machine over there yet and I can't wait."

"It can be cantankerous," said Isabel. "It shoots out jets of steam if it doesn't like you."

Trish laughed. "It'll like me."

And it would, thought Isabel, because you are perfectly likeable.

Isabel said that she would be happy for Trish to try out the machine and make a cup of coffee for her. But where was Sinclair? Was he late—again?

"No, he's gone," said Trish, wiping her hands on her apron. "Cat got rid of him yesterday."

Isabel was intrigued. Sinclair had not lasted long, and while that would have been the case had she—Isabel—been in charge, it was still somewhat surprising, given Cat's proclivities.

Trish's tone became confidential. "I think something happened."

"Oh yes?"

"Yes. I don't know, mind you—not for certain—but I think he might have made a move against her, know what I mean? Something like that."

Isabel was silent. Or could it have been the other way round, she asked herself. No, she thought. I will not allow for that. I will not.

Trish began to ladle coffee into the machine. "I hope I'm doing this right," she said. "Yes, that boy did something or other, judging from what Cat said to me. You can't work with somebody if he's going to bring sex into things, can you? Cat wouldn't have liked that, would she?"

Trish had more to say on the subject. "I had that problem two jobs ago when I worked down in George Street. There was this fellow—he was seriously seedy—who thought that he was God's gift to women. He was sick-making. And he kept coming up to the assistants and putting his hand on their shoulders and whispering advice into their ears. It was horrible. And he smiled like this, showing all his teeth, and he needed to get to a dentist, so he did.

"There was this girl who worked beside me. She was from one of those places down on the coast—my geography's not much good but it was near Musselburgh, I think, and she had this tattoo on the back of her neck. I won't tell you what it was and it was always covered by her hair so I suppose that was all right. But anyway, she was tough and this creepy man comes up to her and whispers something into her ear and so she just lifts her hair—like this—and he sees the tattoo and he looks really surprised. And then, and I'm not making this up, she gets this small, hand-held vacuum cleaner—we used it to get dust off the windowsills; the boss was really fussy about that—and she switches it on and pushes it up against his nose and his nose got stuck in it, so it did. It was terrific craic. You should have seen him. You can't be a big lover-boy, can you, when your nose has been stuck in a vacuum cleaner? No, you can't."

Isabel chuckled at the thought, then returned to the issue of Sinclair. The fact that Cat had got rid of him was greatly to her credit. If she had been as incorrigible as Isabel had feared, then she would have welcomed the advance rather than re-jected it. Perhaps she was learning, after all; perhaps this was a sign of change. And as for Sinclair, he would not be much missed in the delicatessen: selling cheese and stuff, as he had put it, was clearly beneath him; and Trish was far better with customers, she imagined. Sinclair was not interested, and peo-ple did not respond well to that. There was nothing worse, she said to herself, than being served by somebody who clearly would have much preferred to be off modelling somewhere . . .

She smiled. There should be badges for people to wear: *I'm really a model*, or, *I don't really have to do this job*. She could wear that one when she worked in the delicatessen, or perhaps one that said, *Philosopher*. Or would that be pretentious? Very, she decided. A badge that said *Temporary* would be quite enough. But then she reproached herself. There was nothing wrong with selling cheese and stuff, and she would do it with pride.

Once her coffee was made, Isabel took it to one of the tables, leaving Trish to deal with a customer who had just come in. He was given the same cheerful welcome that Isabel had received, and a conversation was struck up. The customer had been in Fermanagh the year before, on holiday, and, recognising Trish's accent, asked her whether she knew the place. She did, and had cousins there, and one of these cousins had a dairy farm and had . . .

Isabel stopped listening. Trish was a vast improvement on Sinclair, but might be exhausting in the long run.

Isabel picked up the newspaper and perused the front page. There had been a political betrayal—a falling-out of allies—and insults were being exchanged. One side was calling the other hard-hearted and the other was replying that their erstwhile allies were disloyal. Representatives of both were pictured shaking hands and smiling: the picture had been taken in happier days.

Then there was a report on a war in a country in Africa, with a picture of a boy soldier, gun in hand, a ridiculously large military cap on his head. The cap had fallen forward to obscure the boy's face. He could never have seen well enough to shoot anybody with that cap obscuring his vision, but anybody else, Isabel thought, would surely be able to see him well enough to shoot him—which may well have happened by now. This little boy, who should have been playing with a toy car, or learning how to read, would have become a tiny corpse tossed into a common grave with other tiny victims. Was there a mother somewhere keening for him, as mothers have done for their sons since war was first invented? Or a father?

"Horrible."

She looked up. It was Jane.

"That photograph," Jane said, pointing to the paper. "I saw it too. Isn't it horrible?"

Isabel nodded. Now her thoughts turned from the sad subject of boy soldiers to the present moment, and what she should say to Jane. It would be easy to say nothing, but could she do that? No. She was in exactly the same position as the walker in the hills who sees another making his way towards a precipice of which he is unaware. A failure to warn in such circumstances was the moral equivalent of a deliberate invitation to walk that way—Isabel was convinced of that. And yet, did a failure to put money in the charity box amount to killing the person who would otherwise have starved to death in some distant famine? She had never been convinced of that, even if she felt uneasy about it.

That involved complicated discussions of causation, of the distinction between acts of commission and omission: the sort of issues that were bread and butter to the editor of the *Review of Applied Ethics* but were much harder to deal with when they became real, and had to be confronted while seated drinking coffee in her niece's delicatessen in Edinburgh . . .

"I'm so grateful to you," Jane said as she sat down at Isabel's table.

Isabel tried to smile.

"Yes," Jane went on. "I was out at Rory and Georgina's and we went over to New Lanark together. I'd always wanted to see it, you know. The whole idea of setting up an ideal, enlightened community is such an attractive one. And to think that they did that when everywhere else the conditions of working people were so bleak."

"Yes," said Isabel flatly. She would have to say something soon. The longer she left it, the greater the pain. "Light and air. Robert Owen believed in that, didn't he?"

"Yes, he did. And education."

Isabel was still thinking. Alastair Rankeillor did not sound like good father material, but would Jane want to contact him? What would be the point, other than confirming her identity—and that was the aim of Jane's quest in the first place.

"Then we went to the Falls of Clyde," said Jane. "I'd seen photographs—"

"Jane."

"Yes?"

Jane's expression was one of contentment. *She's happy,* thought Isabel, *and I'm about to shatter her happiness.*

Isabel drew breath. Her resolve to tell Jane was on the point of deserting her, but she had taken her decision and she must persist. "I've been giving some thought to your situation."

There was a very slight movement about Jane's lips. An innocent twitch? A flinch? "My situation?"

"Yes. You must have been thinking about it yourself, I suppose. And there must be a question mark . . ."

Jane looked away. "There are often question marks over what we do." She paused. "And sometimes it's best to ignore them, don't you agree?"

Isabel waited until the other woman looked back at her

again. She was not sure she was reading this remark correctly. Did Jane not want to know the truth? She swallowed. She could ask her directly. "Do you want to be completely sure?"

"About who my father is?"

Isabel nodded. "Yes, about that."

Jane frowned. "I know that Rory isn't my father," she said quietly. "I know. You don't have to tell me."

Isabel had not expected this. She had imagined that Jane might have been hoping that Rory *was* her father, but an optimistic belief was different from knowledge of falsity.

"How do you know?" she asked. "When I spoke to you about it before, you said you didn't want a DNA test. So how do you know?"

Jane hesitated before she answered, then said, "Georgina spoke to me."

"And?"

"And she told me that it could not have been Rory. They had tried to have children, you see, and they had consulted a specialist. He's infertile, apparently. And could never have been a father at any point."

"So he knows too? Then why is he going along with it? Why hasn't he told you?"

"Because he doesn't know."

It did not make sense.

"I can see that you're puzzled," Jane continued. "But there's an explanation. He doesn't know because she didn't tell him. He was away at the time that the results of tests came in. He was in the army, remember, and he was on a posting abroad. She went for the consultation and it was explained to her that while she appeared to be fine, he was the problem."

Jane went on to tell Isabel about how Georgina had decided to say that the problem was hers, rather than his.

"She felt that he was vulnerable. She felt that he had had too many blows to his pride anyway—he had been passed over for promotion—and so she decided to protect him from the psychological burden of the knowledge of his infertility."

"So she told him it was her?"

Jane nodded.

Isabel reflected on what she had been told. A deception was being practised by two people, and she, an outsider, had come to know about it—except that she was not an outsider: she had brought about the meeting of Jane and Rory, and was therefore implicated in the outcome.

She asked Jane whether she thought it right that Rory should be deceived.

"It's what he wants," she said. "He's already said to me that having a daughter is what he wants above all else."

"Except it's not true."

"Does it matter?" asked Jane.

"It's the difference between what is and what isn't," Isabel said. "He's giving you his love—or I assume that's what he's giving you—because he thinks you're his daughter."

Jane was defiant. "And what's wrong with that? The important thing is the love itself, the happiness. Surely where it comes from doesn't matter in the slightest." She paused, searching Isabel's expression for signs of agreement. "Suppose I have a painting that I think is the real thing, but isn't. I think it's a Picasso, but it's not. If I never find out that it's a forgery, then I'll always have the pleasure of thinking I have something special. What's wrong with that?"

Isabel shook her head vehemently. They were back in the philosophy classroom, students debating with a tutor.

"But that's not what this is about at all. In that example, you're not looking at it from the point of view of somebody who *knows* the truth. If you shift the emphasis, and look at it from the point of view of somebody who knows what the painting really is, you'll get a different answer. That person *has* to say something."

Jane would not concede the point. "Would you? Let's say you know my painting's a forgery—would you feel you had to tell me? And if so, why? Why do you have to destroy an illusion if the illusion gives joy?"

Isabel was puzzled. "But why are *you* allowing Rory to go on believing this? Do you want somebody who isn't your father to think he's your father? And what about Georgina? Why does she want him to think something that isn't so?".

"Because she loves him," said Jane. "And because she wants him to be happy. This seems to have made a big difference to him. And as far as I'm concerned, does it matter all that much?" She paused. "As for me—well, it's all rather complicated. I had invested so much emotionally in this search, but oddly enough as we went further into it the identity of my father suddenly became of less interest than I had imagined. Do you know who he is?"

"I think it might be a man called Alastair Rankeillor. He's a lawyer who lives abroad now."

She considered this for several moments. "I see. Well, at least that gives me a name."

"Which will hardly be enough, surely?"

Jane looked up sharply. "You think so? You know what

became much more important? I had not expected this, but it was my mother. What I really wanted was to find out a bit more about her, about her world. And I've done that. I thought I was searching for my father, but it was actually for my mother, about whom I already knew a certain amount. Strange, isn't it? And then I came across a man who had been her boyfriend and who, as far as I can make out, actually did love her. And that was more important than anything else. I found that he wanted to be my father and I responded."

Jane searched Isabel's face for a sign that she understood.

"I can see that," said Isabel quietly. "Yes, I can see that."

"And remember something, Isabel," Jane continued. "I was adopted. All those years ago, two people came along and pretended to be my parents so that I had a family. In a way, this is an adoption in reverse. If I can bring happiness to a man who has been unhappy for a large part of his life, isn't that worthwhile?"

Yes, thought Isabel, it is. And yet, and yet . . .

"It's messy," she said.

Jane did not argue. "Like life . . . This lawyer—"

"Alastair Rankeillor."

Jane repeated the name, as if trying it for size. "Alastair Rankeillor. Do you think I should make contact with him? I still feel a certain curiosity, I suppose."

"That's up to you," said Isabel. "If you don't, the question is always going to be there. And he won't be around for ever."

"Do you know anything about him? Do you think I'll like him?"

"I can't tell."

"Are you sure?"

Isabel sighed. "You may not like him. I'm not sure whether he sounds like the sort of man who would necessarily welcome such an approach."

Jane weighed this. "Some things are best left undisturbed."

Isabel agreed. "Many things are best left undisturbed, if you ask me."

She was about to say something else, but she now saw that Cat had returned and was standing at the counter, looking in her direction.

"Can we talk later?" she said to Jane.

"Yes. But please, Isabel, you won't spoil this, will you?"

"No, I won't spoil it."

"You give me your word?"

"Yes. I shall say nothing. I shall do nothing."

Jane reached out and took her hand briefly. "I'm very grateful."

I have done the wrong thing, Isabel thought. *I have done the wrong thing for the right reason. Again.*

AS FAR AS Cat was concerned, too, Isabel had done entirely the wrong thing in speaking to the Environmental Health department. As Jane got up to go, Cat made her way towards Isabel's table.

"Thanks a lot," she hissed. "Thanks for informing on me."

Isabel tried to hold her niece's venomous gaze. "Informing?"

"You know what I'm talking about. You informed on me to the Environmental Health people. They threatened to close me down." She stared at Isabel, her expression full of resentment. "Do you know that? They threatened to close me down, all because of you."

"Not because of me," said Isabel. "Because of the mush-rooms." She paused. "Well, actually, the mushrooms were inno-cent. It was because of the person who sold you the mushrooms."

This did not mollify Cat. "Don't play the philosopher with me! You betrayed me. Handed me in."

Isabel kept her temper, but she felt the back of her neck becoming warmer. "Look, I understand how you must feel. I'm sorry, I really am. The last thing I want is for you to get into dif-ficulties with these people. But look at it from my point of view, just for a moment. Did you expect me to lie when they asked me where they came from? What could I say?"

Their raised voices were now audible at the counter. Trish looked across the shop with interest.

"You don't hand in members of your family," Cat retorted. "No decent person does that."

"Of course nobody wants to do that. But the question remains: can one lie? And there may be some circumstances when you simply have to say something. If you call that handing somebody in, well, I suppose that's what it is."

This reply silenced Cat for a few moments. She stood quite still, holding Isabel's gaze. Then she continued, "I can't believe you just said that."

"But I did," said Isabel calmly. She was winning the encounter, but taking no pleasure in it. "Yes, we must be loyal to our family, but that loyalty has its limits. Surely you see that, Cat? Surely you see that there will be times when one has to do something that a member of one's family may not like?"

Cat half turned, but then, as if visited by an afterthought, she turned back and addressed Isabel. "Fine, just fine. So how would you react if I told you something . . . something about Jamie? How would you feel about that?"

She turned on her heel and went into her office, slamming the door behind her.

LATER THAT DAY, when Isabel was working in her study, Trish came to the house. Jamie answered the door, and Isabel heard the two of them talking briefly in the hall before he showed her in.

"So this is where you work," said Trish brightly. "Cool."

"I'm not sure if I'd describe it as cool," said Isabel. "But then I have to work here."

Trish looked at the shelves. "All those books," she muttered. "It'd give me a headache. Do you get headaches?"

"Occasionally," replied Isabel. "But more from people than from books."

Trish laughed. "That's why I came to see you," she said. "I hope you don't mind."

"Not at all."

Trish sat down uninvited. "That business this morning—"

"I'm sorry that you had to witness it," said Isabel. "Cat and I have what can openly be described as a tempestuous relationship. She'll get over it."

Trish nodded. "Yeah, I'm sure she will. But she hits below the belt, doesn't she?"

"Sometimes," said Isabel. She was not sure where this conversation was going and was being guarded.

"I heard every word she said, you know. She's got a tongue on her, so she has."

"She isn't stuck for words," agreed Isabel.

Trish gazed out of the window. "Rhodies," she said, pointing to the rhododendrons. "I had an uncle who grew those for garden centres. He even invented one—mixed the pollen, I think, and made one called 'Yeats.' He was always going on about Yeats—you know, that Irish poet. Dead now. Most poets are dead, aren't they?"

"It happens to poets," said Isabel. "And to others too."

"Anyway," Trish continued, "I heard what she said about your fellow. So I asked her later. I said: what had she meant by it, and she was blank. I asked her again, and then she said that it was nothing. She had been angry and had said the first thing that came into her mind."

Isabel felt the release of a knot that had been within her since that morning's encounter. She had barely comprehended Cat's throwaway remark about Jamie, but it had planted a seed of doubt. What could Cat possibly tell her about Jamie? Of course it had been nothing; of course. But what exactly had she meant?

"I felt that I had to come and tell you this," said Trish. "I didn't like the thought of you thinking about it. Brooding, know what I mean?"

Isabel was grateful. "That was really kind of you."

"No," said Trish. "Anybody would have done it."

Isabel looked at her with affection. The good often do not recognise their own goodness, she thought; and as for Cat, Isabel would never say that anybody was completely impossible, but there were some people, at least, who might merit that description—if it were ever to be resorted to, which she would not, or at least not yet.

A FORTNIGHT LATER, on a Saturday on which Scotland was blessed by unbroken light and warmth, a July day of high, empty skies and languid air, Isabel and Jamie were at last married. They had chosen to be married in private, or rather in circumstances in which anybody who cared to witness the ceremony could do so if they happened to be there, but to which no guests were invited other than Charlie and Grace. This was not through want of friends who might wish to join them, but because they felt that this long-awaited ceremony was something personal, the sealing of a bond about which they had never spoken very much to others, and which they wished to enshrine in vows that were as private as they were public. Charlie was there because this was, in a way, all about him; and Grace was there because somebody would have to sit with Charlie while his parents stood before the minister and exchanged vows. And Grace was family too; for all her little ways, she was as close to the three of them as anybody could be.

Isabel had been in touch with a professor of theology, Iain Torrance, who, in spite of being the president of the Union Theological Seminary at Princeton, still kept a house in Scotland and who revealed that he would be in Edinburgh at the time. Iain, as a moral philosopher, had advised her on papers for the *Review*. He had agreed to perform the ceremony.

They chose the Canongate Kirk, and at three o'clock on a Saturday afternoon they arrived in a simple taxi and entered the church. Apart from the fact that Jamie was wearing his kilt, no passersby would have imagined that this couple were concerned with anything else but the most quotidian of business.

Nobody saw the glances they gave one another as they stood before the white-gabled church with its simple, dignified Church of Scotland aesthetic. Nobody saw Isabel pause for a moment to survey the churchyard in which lay the poet Robert Fergusson and the philosopher and economist Adam Smith. They were both figures with whom she felt a special affinity, as a Scot and as a philosopher. If there were no guests at the wedding, those two were there, mute presences, friendly witnesses to a short and moving ceremony.

Jamie had arranged with the Canongate's director of music for the organ to be played. There was no choir—just the simple, unadorned notes of the organ. "Bach," he whispered to Isabel as they went in.

They met Iain at the back of the church and he led them to the altar. Witnesses were needed, and a couple of visitors were invited in from the churchyard. One was a woman who explained that she visited the churchyard every Saturday afternoon in the summer just to sit near Fergusson and look at the sky above the Carlton Hill. "It's such a privilege to be your witness," she said to Isabel. "Thank you."

Isabel had taken her hand and squeezed it. "I am the one who should thank you," she said, and thought: We should not be too surprised by the kindness of strangers, as it is always there.

A few other visitors to the church drifted up towards the front. They were welcomed with smiles from Jamie, who gestured to the empty pews, mouthing, "There's plenty of room." Charlie, wearing his small Macpherson kilt, seemed happy enough to sit calmly with Grace in the front pew, wondering, perhaps, what his mother and father were doing standing before a man in black and white robes who was saying something to them that he could not understand. And he did not disturb proceedings except once, very briefly, when he shouted out "Olive!"—a request that could not be met in the church, but brought forth from Grace's pocket a soft toffee that was popped into his mouth to be solemnly chewed during the remainder of the ceremony.

Iain performed the service and blessed their union. "Now you're married," he said at the end and shook hands with them both. Isabel looked at Jamie and thought, *Nothing so beautiful, so magnificent, will ever happen to me again.* And then she thought, *There are many who wish for this, and never find it. May they do so; may they do so.*

They signed the register. The woman who acted as witness, the admirer of the poet Fergusson, appended a signature so tiny as to be virtually indecipherable.

"I've always had very small handwriting," she said. "But I still mean what I write."

The other witness was a man who had been killing time before a journey and had wandered down from Waverley Station. He looked about the church as the ink dried on the page of the register.

"You know something?" he said to Jamie. "I've never believed in God, but I do believe in his love."

Isabel heard this and glanced at the man, who smiled at her briefly and then turned away, looking vaguely sheepish.

Afterwards, while Grace and Charlie travelled back to the house by taxi, Isabel and Jamie walked home, making a long detour to follow the path that skirted the Salisbury Crags. They held hands on the walk, buffeted by the strong breeze that had sprung up while they were in the church. Isabel's hair blew into her face, her eyes.

Jamie said to her, "I used to come here as a boy. I could run up Arthur's Seat the easy way—round the back. I ran all the way."

She pictured him in his kilt, a boy with bright eyes. And now here he was, a married man, a father.

They did not go out that night. Charlie sensed that something special had happened, but was tired and dropped off even before Jamie finished reading him his story. The tigers had not yet turned to butter, but the book was closed and the small lock of hair smoothed back across the forehead so gently by his father's hand, his loving hand.

Isabel made dinner and they ate it together, in virtual silence. What was there to say? It seemed to them both that conversation could spoil the moment, as it sometimes does when everything has been said, even if few words have been used. After dinner, Jamie played the piano for a while, and Isabel sat and listened. Then, on impulse, they put on music and danced.

"It's odd, dancing by ourselves," muttered Jamie. "Odd, but very nice."

"Yes," said Isabel.

"Let's stay up until half past nine," said Jamie.

"Yes," said Isabel. "Let's."

She held him to her as they danced. Over his shoulder she watched the minute hand of the clock creep slowly round the dial to the half hour. So slowly.

THE ISABEL DALHOUSIE NOVELS

> "The literary equivalent of herbal tea and a cozy fire. . . .
> McCall Smith's Scotland [is] well worth future visits."
> —*The New York Times*

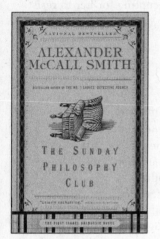

The Sunday Philosophy Club

Isabel Dalhousie is fond of problems, and sometimes she becomes interested in problems that are, quite frankly, none of her business—including some that are best left to the police. Filled with endearingly thorny characters and a Scottish atmosphere as thick as a highland mist, *The Sunday Philosophy Club* is an irresistible pleasure.

Volume 1

Friends, Lovers, Chocolate

While taking care of her niece Cat's deli, Isabel meets a heart transplant patient who has had some strange experiences in the wake of his surgery. Against the advice of her housekeeper, Isabel is intent on investigating. Matters are further complicated when Cat returns from vacation with a new boyfriend, and Isabel's fondness for him lands her in another muddle.

Volume 2

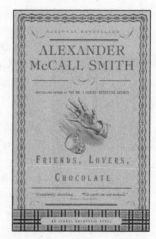

The Right Attitude to Rain

When Isabel's cousin from Dallas arrives in Edinburgh, she introduces Isabel to a bigwig Texan whose young fiancée may just be after his money. Then there's her niece, Cat, who's busy falling for a man whom Isabel suspects of being an incorrigible mama's boy. Isabel is advised to stay out of it all, but the philosophical issues of these matters of the heart prove too tempting for her to resist.

Volume 3

The Careful Use of Compliments

There's a new little Dalhousie on the scene, and while the arrival of Isabel's son presents her with the myriad wonders of life, it doesn't diminish her curiosity about other things. While attending an art auction, she discovers a mystery revealed in one of the paintings, launching her into yet another intriguing investigation.

Volume 4

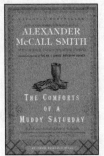

The Comforts of a Muddy Saturday

A doctor's career has been ruined by allegations of medical fraud and Isabel cannot ignore what may be a miscarriage of justice. Meanwhile, there is her baby, Charlie, who needs looking after; her niece, Cat, who needs someone to mind her deli; and a mysterious composer who has latched on to Jamie, making Isabel decidedly uncomfortable.

Volume 5

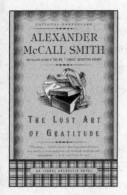

The Lost Art of Gratitude

When Minty Auchterlonie takes Isabel into her confidence about the complicated troubles at the investment bank she heads, Isabel finds herself doubting Minty.

Volume 6

The Charming Quirks of Others

Old friends of Isabel's ask for her help in a rather tricky situation: A successor is being sought for the headmaster position at their alma mater and an anonymous letter has alleged that one of the candidates has a very serious skeleton in their closet.

Volume 7

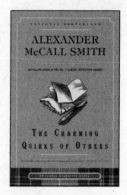

The Forgotten Affairs of Youth

A visiting Australian philosopher asks for Isabel's help to find her biological father. Isabel cannot help but oblige, even though she has concerns of her own. Her young son, Charlie, is now walking and talking, and her housekeeper, Grace, regularly attends a spiritualist who has taken to providing advice. And could it finally be time for Jamie and Isabel to get married?

Volume 8

THE 44 SCOTLAND STREET SERIES

**"Will make you feel as though you live in Edinburgh. . . .
Long live the folks on Scotland Street."**

—*The Times-Picayune* (New Orleans)

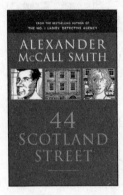

44 SCOTLAND STREET

All of Alexander McCall Smith's trademark warmth and wit come into play in this novel chronicling the lives of the residents of a converted Georgian town house in Edinburgh. Complete with colorful characters, love triangles, and even a mysterious art caper, this is an unforgettable portrait of Edinburgh society.

Volume 1

ESPRESSO TALES

The eccentric residents of 44 Scotland Street are back. From the talented six-year-old Bertie, who is forced to arrive in pink overalls for his first day of class, to the self-absorbed Bruce, who contemplates a change of career in between admiring glances in the mirror, there is much in store as fall settles on Edinburgh.

Volume 2

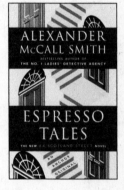

LOVE OVER SCOTLAND

From conducting perilous anthropological studies of pirate households to being inadvertently left behind on a school trip to Paris, the wonderful misadventures of the residents of 44 Scotland Street will charm and delight.

Volume 3

THE WORLD ACCORDING TO BERTIE

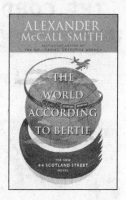

Pat is forced to deal with the reappearance of Bruce, which has her heart skipping—and not in the most pleasant way. Angus Lordie's dog, Cyril, has been taken away by the authorities, accused of being a serial biter, and Bertie, the beleaguered Italian-speaking prodigy and saxophonist, now has a little brother, Ulysses, who he hopes will distract his mother, Irene.

Volume 4

THE UNBEARABLE LIGHTNESS OF SCONES

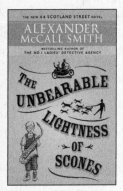

The Unbearable Lightness of Scones finds Bertie still troubled by his rather overbearing mother, Irene, but seeking his escape in the cub scouts. Matthew is rising to the challenge of married life, while Domenica epitomizes the loneliness of the long-distance intellectual, and Cyril succumbs to the kind of romantic temptation that no dog can resist, creating a small problem, or rather six of them, for his friend and owner, Angus Lordie.

Volume 5

THE IMPORTANCE OF BEING SEVEN

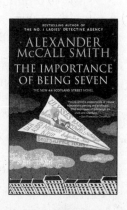

Bertie is—finally!—about to turn seven. But one afternoon he mislays his meddling mother, Irene, and learns a valuable lesson. Angus and Domenica contemplate whether to give in to romance on holiday in Italy, and even usually down-to-earth Big Lou is overheard discussing cosmetic surgery.

Volume 6

THE CORDUROY MANSIONS SERIES

"A new cast of characters to love."
—*Entertainment Weekly*

CORDUROY MANSIONS

In London's hip Pimlico neighborhood, Corduroy Mansions, a block of crumbling brickwork and dormer windows is home to a delightfully eccentric cast of residents including, but not limited to: a wine merchant who desperately hopes his son will move out; a boutique caterer who has designs on the oenophile down the hall; a snarky member of Parliament; and Freddie de la Hay, a vegetarian Pimlico terrier.

Volume 1

THE DOG WHO CAME IN FROM THE COLD

Freddie de la Hay has been recruited by MI6 to infiltrate a Russian spy ring. A pair of New Age operators wants to use Terence Moongrove's estate as a center for cosmological studies. Literary agent Barbara Ragg represents a man who hangs out with the Abominable Snowman, and the rest of the denizens of the housing block have issues of their own.

Volume 2

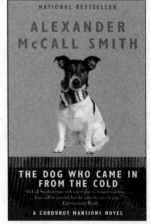

A CONSPIRACY OF FRIENDS

There's never a dull moment for the residents of Corduroy Mansions: Berthea Snark is still at work on her scathing biography of her own son; literary agents Rupert Porter and Barbara Ragg are still battling each other; fine-arts graduate Caroline Jarvis is busy blurring the line between friendship and romance; and William French is still worrying that his son, Eddie, may never leave home. But uppermost on everyone's mind is Freddie de la Hay—William's faithful terrier (and without a doubt the only dog clever enough to have been recruited by MI6)—who has disappeared while on a mystery tour around the Suffolk countryside.

Volume 3

THE PORTUGUESE IRREGULAR VERBS SERIES

"Deftly rendered . . . [with] endearingly eccentric characters."
—*Chicago Sun-Times*

Welcome to the insane and rarified world of Professor Dr Moritz-Maria von Igelfeld of the Institute of Romance Philology. Von Igelfeld is engaged in a never-ending quest to win the respect he feels certain he is due—a quest that has a way of going hilariously astray.

Portuguese Irregular Verbs

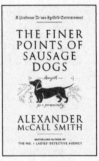

The Finer Points of Sausage Dogs

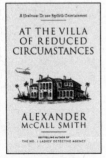

At the Villa of Reduced Circumstances

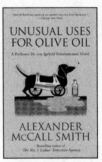

Unusual Uses for Olive Oil
Coming in December 2012

THE NO. 1 LADIES' DETECTIVE AGENCY SERIES

Read them all....
"There is no end to the pleasure."
—*The New York Times Book Review*

The No. 1 Ladies' Detective Agency—Volume 1

The Great Cake Mystery

For Children

Tears of the Giraffe—Volume 2

Morality for Beautiful Girls—Volume 3

The Kalahari Typing School for Men—Volume 4

The Full Cupboard of Life—Volume 5

Available in paperback, hardcover, and eBook editions.

In the Company of Cheerful Ladies —Volume 6

Blue Shoes and Happiness —Volume 7

The Good Husband of Zebra Drive —Volume 8

The Miracle at Speedy Motors—Volume 9

Tea Time for the Traditionally Built —Volume 10

The Double Comfort Safari Club —Volume 11

The Saturday Big Tent Wedding Party —Volume 12

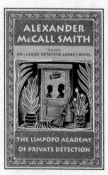

The Limpopo Academy of Private Detection—Volume 13

Available in paperback, hardcover, and eBook editions.

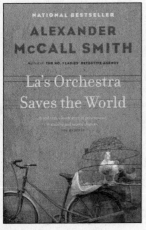